The Dark Shall Rise

The Dark Shall Rise
The Asgarnian Articles
Book 1
Calye Cochran
Westbow Press, IN

Copyright © 2012 Calye Cochran

All rights reserved. No part of this book may be used or reproduced by any means, graphic, electronic, or mechanical, including photocopying, recording, taping or by any information storage retrieval system without the written permission of the publisher except in the case of brief quotations embodied in critical articles and reviews.

ISBN: 978-1-4497-7673-2 (e)
ISBN: 978-1-4497-7674-9 (sc)
ISBN: 978-1-4497-7675-6 (hc)

Library of Congress Control Number: 2012922037

WestBow Press books may be ordered through booksellers or by contacting:

WestBow Press
A Division of Thomas Nelson
1663 Liberty Drive
Bloomington, IN 47403
www.westbowpress.com
1-(866) 928-1240

Because of the dynamic nature of the Internet, any web addresses or links contained in this book may have changed since publication and may no longer be valid. The views expressed in this work are solely those of the author and do not necessarily reflect the views of the publisher, and the publisher hereby disclaims any responsibility for them.

Any people depicted in stock imagery provided by Thinkstock are models, and such images are being used for illustrative purposes only.

Certain stock imagery © Thinkstock.

Printed in the United States of America

WestBow Press rev. date: 12/27/2012

For my friends and family who have been my support and encouragement.

> Praise be unto the Highest Power
> the rock of warriors
> who strengthens the body for war
> and the mind for battle.
> —Ψrivent 18:12

Names

Anya— \'Än-yə\
Galatrans—\Ga-'lə-trens\
Galeãns—\Gə-'lā-ens\
Galetreã—\Gal-ə-'trā-ə\
Galiphems—\Ga-'lə-fems\
Gryafans—\'Grī-ə-fens\
Jasira—\Jə-'zī-rə\
Liyah Encarcerá—\'Lī-ə\ \'In-cär-se-rə\
Navaira—\Nə-'ve-rə\
Osaun—\'Ō-sän\
Riela—\'Rī-e-lə\
Rihannai—\'Rī-he-nī\
Ryvan—\'Rī-ven\
Shanillé—\Shə-'nē-lā\
Tychel—\Tī-'chel\
Vera—\'Vē-rə\

Spells

Darkellã—\'Där-ke-lə\ (Darkness)
Savéncy—\Sä-'ven-sē\ (Repair)
Shanellé—\'Shə-ne-lə\ (Expel)
Shanéva—\Shə-'nē-və\ (Electrify)
Shetrãq—\She-'trak\ (Stun)
Vashevné—\Və-'shev-nā\ (Shatter)
Veriáhn—\Ve-'rī-en\ (Break)

Places

Asgarnia—\Az-'gär-nē-ə\
Ayaye—\Ā-'ā-ē\
Beura—\'Byúr-ə\
Corytz—\Kór-'itz\
Draconiã—\'Dra-cō-nē-ə\
Dreán—\'Drā-än\
Faeciã—\Fā-'ē-shə\
Galeã—\Gə-'lā-ə\
Geriã—\Jə-'rī-ə\
Impenatiã—\Im-pe-'nā-shə\
Mount Reolné—\Rā-'ōl-nā\
Osheyk Mountains—\'O-shāk\
Pricein River—\'Prī-sīn\
Shroeketia—\Shrō-'kā-shə\
Théa—\'Thā-ə\
Zaira Forest—\'Zā-rə\

Creatures

Djinn—\'Jēn\ (Genie of old)
Firock—\'Fiī-räk\
Minotaur—\Mi-'nə-tór\
Qaira—\'Kā-rə\
Sirens—\'Sī-rens\
Surtran—\'Sir-tren\
Vortzan—\'Vórt-zen\
Zevra—\'Zev-rə\

Vortzan Speech

Buértaken Sevuél—\Byúr-'tā-kehn\ \Se-'vyū-el\ (Leave the boy)
Shélteveré cashellã—\'Shel-tə-vēr\ \Cə-she-'lə\ (Move out your ranks)

Book Titles

Ꜫourteuricans—\Kór-tyúr-i-kəns\
δhumtan—\Shūm-tän\
Ψrivent—\Trī-vent\

Prologue

A young child huddled behind the rocks, peering through the falling rain. Her blonde hair hung limp at her shoulders, and her deep brown eyes glistened in the darkness as she gazed out into the icy black night. It was not just the storm that had her on edge, although the lightning flashed and the thunder rolled as the sheets of rain sliced through the sky to the earth. No, it was not just the storm. It was much more than that. It was the darkness and all that lurked within.

As the girl hid desperately, she finally faced the reality of all that happened. Twenty-four hours had turned her life upside down.

****

The evening had begun, and the sun shone brightly on her face as she reclined on the rich green grass within the palace walls. As far as she knew, the child stood alone. However, her caretaker, Anya, stood back, just out of sight. The child was reading out of the book Derious had given her for her last birthday. Reading its words saddened her, reminding her of him. She closed the leather-bound book and shut her eyes, taking in all the smells of life with a deep, cleansing breath. When she opened them, she saw that dark clouds had appeared in the west, which was a sure sign of rain.

Out of the corner of her eye, the child sensed movement. In that instant, she caught a glimpse of Anya, and a young man rushed out of the palace into the courtyard. He was in such a hurry that he stumbled as he raced down the stairs.

He hurried over to Anya, and a grave expression crossed over her face. She called out for the palace guards, who ran instantly toward the troubled guardian at the slightest sound of her voice.

Suddenly, the sky grew dark, and the girl heard the young man say in a quiet defeated voice, "We are too late. *She* is here."

"No, it cannot be!" Anya proclaimed. "Protect her!"

The child jumped to her feet, and light traces of green still lingered on her blue dress from the grass, soiling the soft perfection. The guards rushed toward the young eight-year-old.

Out of nowhere, a flash of purple lightning struck down toward the earth. The guards fell on the damp ground mid-stride, and the child's eyes grew wide in awe and fear. She slowly began backing away from the figure that had appeared directly in front of her.

The shadow slowly turned to face the child. Their eyes met, causing an icy chill to run through the child's veins. The shade laughed deeply—a cold, dark laugh. Before the girl could clearly make out the features of the figure, Anya swept in on a white steed. She scooped the child onto the beast without stopping.

The Dark Mistress laughed again at Anya's boldness and shouted, "Anya! Surrender the girl!"

The lightning flashed down again. A pitch black horse with blazing red eyes reared its head on the charred earth. The Dark One leaped upon the beast and stormed off after them.

The horses raced outside of the palace boundaries, through Théa and the village. The Dark One rapidly gained on them with every ticking second.

When they neared the crags, the black horse caught up and rode in alongside the white one. "Anya! Surrender the child to me, and you shall escape with your life."

"Never, Navaira!" Anya cried back through the sheets of rain, slapping the horse's flank. The white horse whinnied in surprise, then, gained momentum and sped away.

"If that's the way you want it then, prepare yourself! But don't say I didn't offer you a way out!" Navaira smiled. "Veriáhn!" She cast the spell, and purple light exploded from her palm.

The light struck the white horse, and it crashed to the earth headfirst, kicking up mud and water. The child was launched into the darkness from atop her mount, and Anya was now pinned beneath the dead horse. The child ran to her, for she had to know if her friend was all right.

"Child, listen to me," Anya wheezed. "Run; hide in the crags. You must escape her." Anya dropped the girl's hand and shoved her gently. "Keep hidden, child. I'm sorry I have failed you." After whispering these final words, she was gone.

The girl cast one last look at her friend, and then she took her advice and ran as fast as she could. She ran despite her unfamiliar surroundings, and the darkness began enclosing around her. Her sapphire heart-shaped amulet slapped against her chest as she ran, cold metal searing her flesh.

The necklace was a gift from her mother. Her sister had received one, too, but after what happened to her sister.... Her mother had only said that there was power beyond what they could imagine contained in the small heart amulets. The child knew there was something even more important about this necklace. She could feel it deep down in her soul. What she didn't know was that it held the key to it all.

She reached the crags and dove behind the nearest boulder out of sight. She hid in the darkness and waited. Waited for the dark to rise.

****

The child watched, still hidden, as Navaira galloped up to the crags and drop off her horse, smiling through the rain. Her skin glistened from the water slowly running off her to the ground.

The Mistress of the Darkness had pulled her red flaming hair back into a ponytail. She appeared to be only about sixteen years of age—eight years older then the child. Her eyes were the color of lilacs—light purple. She was wearing a black midriff with sleeves that hung loosely over the shoulders and black pants that a djinn would wear. Her radiant and fierce beauty reminded the child of a desert princess.

Navaira glanced around, and she laughed another cold-blooded laugh from deep within her throat. It was almost as if she knew where the girl was hidden.

"Young one, your attempt at hiding is futile. Come out now, and I will not harm you. All I wish is to speak with you."

When the young one did not reply, Navaira's anger flared. She began to recite a prophecy:

> "The mark of Navaira's start
> Appears in a child's fiery heart.
> Once awake, shall be Navaira's demise,
> Unless preventing the child's rise.
>
> On the eve of her eighth,
> Shall end the Asgarnian race.
> Then Navaira shall reign,
> Until she shall rise again!"

"If you choose not to come out of hiding, I will make it to where you will have no chance to ever rise!" she cried angrily into the black sky.

Then she stopped, grew quiet, and lost all traces of anger. She turned her head slowly and began to stride to the spot where the young one hid. "Come out now, child. I've sensed you. Power like yours is easily detected. Hiding is futile."

The young one stepped out cautiously, for she had no other option. Navaira smiled again. The young child's muscles tensed, and Navaira began walking toward her, smiling. "Child, what were you thinking, hiding from the great Navaira?"

She was walking ever closer. The rain never let up, never ceasing in the rising darkness.

The closer Navaira drew to the girl, the colder the air around them grew. She was just a few feet away, and it became bone chilling. Her eyes looked ice cold as they locked onto the child's own.

Out of the darkness a young voice cried, "Shanellé!"

The pair snapped their heads in the direction of the voice to see a stream of pure golden light shooting out of the forest surrounding the crags. Navaira reacted and shouted out a spell of her own, but she was aiming at the girl.

Purple light streamed out of her palm just as the golden light sliced through the darkness and struck Navaira from behind. She fell forward on her face.

Purple light struck the girl, and she flew backward onto the earth as well, sending a shock through her. She cried out in pain, and electricity illuminated the air.

Navaira, however, rose to her feet, laughing. The young voice, now startled, cried out, "Liyah! No! Shanéva!" Gold light diffused through the night once more.

As the light struck her, Navaira cried out in pain. This time, it hit her harder.

"Fine!" Navaira cried, and she mounted her horse. She rode off into the night. "She is yours for now!" The young one lost consciousness then. All went dark.

****

Part I
How It Started

Return, Highest Power!
Gaze from your domain!
Watch over your blessed warrior,
the servant you yourself have raised.
—Ψrivent 24:18

Chapter 1

Thud. The arrow pierced the target.

"About two inches off," Melanie stated, after bending down to examine the target more carefully.

"Yeah. I don't know why I'm off so much today," Liyah said. "I'm always on target—dead center."

"Yeah, yeah, yeah!" Melanie groaned. "Can we go eat yet? I'm starving, Liyah!"

"But I haven't even practiced with my blades yet!" Liyah sighed.

"Swords later, food now. We haven't eaten for hours."

"Honestly, Mel, you're a bottomless pit," Liyah smiled. "You win this time." She strapped her crossbow to her back where it belonged. Melanie wasn't carrying any of her weapons, but Liyah wished she would. Melanie said that Liyah was paranoid. Liyah didn't think so.

Liyah was seventeen, and her birthday was rapidly approaching. Her long blonde hair framed delicately around her face. Her brown eyes shone with laughter. Her brown and black outfit was made of leather and metal. The top midriff had leather straps encircling her arms, acting as sleeves. There were numerous leather straps running down each arm, a metal hook connecting each of them. Liyah's skirt was pleated leather hanging freely over a metal armor base. She was a good five inches taller than Melanie, and she was very dark from spending all of her time training in the harsh sun. She carried her crossbow on her back with arrows, double swords crossed her back, and a small knife was strapped at her waist. She believed training was the only way for her to relax. Also, Liyah had a tattoo under her skin of a half moon with flames around the outside. It looked as if it was missing more than the other half. Secretly, Liyah felt the same way.

Melanie was sixteen and would be turning seventeen in a few months. She had short blonde hair cut jaggedly, setting off her delicate jaw line. She had gray-green eyes that held a contagious smile. She wore an outfit identical to Liyah's, as was the old Faecian style worn in their village. Both girls wore three inch black heels, and neither girl's armor was battle scarred, for they had seen little action outside the training grounds. Melanie trained occasionally, but she lost patience with Liyah for the excessive amount of time she spent out in the training field. Melanie wore a small knife at her waist. Also, she wore double swords on her back when she felt like it. And she didn't find a satisfactory fit with crossbows like Liyah did. So she left her weapons at that. Melanie also had a tattoo under the skin on her arm, in the same place as Liyah, but of a shooting star. Neither girl knew how the pictures had gotten there. They tried their best to keep them hidden. People in Shroeketia frowned upon the strange ink under their skin.

The girls lived in the village tribe of Faeciã. It was a small village in the Osheyk Mountains. Neither girl had parents that they knew of. They knew not where they came from. So, they lived in a house of their own, working to develop a life geared toward the future.

However, Liyah had one other precious possession that she had carried with her as long as she remembered. It was a leather-bound book full of words of wisdom and sayings about life and a being known as the Highest Power. She could not remember where it had come from, but when she closed her eyes and smelled the pages it brought her a deep-rooted sadness she couldn't explain.

"I hope they'll still let us eat," Melanie thought out loud, bringing Liyah out of her vain attempt to reach her lost memories.

"Aw, you know Osaun will let *us* eat anytime!" Liyah laughed as she adjusted her leather vambraces. "I'm putting silver studs in these tonight."

"Good, you do that," Melanie murmured in an indifferent tone. "Wonder what there's going to be to eat."

"Mel! Chill out! We'll eat soon enough. I just don't really want to go back into town with everyone nagging at me," Liyah mused.

"Oh, they're just mad because you don't take to the village lifestyles like the rest of the people. You haven't chased after the warriors to get married to move away."

"Maybe, but I just haven't met anyone that I care to waste time on or at least no one up to my standards."

"Take your time. This weekend's party at Corresponding Point will be great. You might meet someone there."

"I don't know. We'll see. I prefer keeping to myself though. You do know that's not the only reason that the elders are angry with us, right?"

"What do you mean?" Melanie asked.

"It's also because we are she-warriors. Not to mention that the party at Corresponding Point is mainly for warriors. You and I both know this village isn't exactly a warrior tribe." Liyah's mood changed instantly when she thought a bit. "I'm ready to compete in the training match this weekend!"

"You are so crazy, but I'll be your own personal cheerleader. Go team!" Melanie smiled.

"Why don't you just compete?" Liyah asked.

"Me? Puh-lease! I don't want to put you to shame on the grounds," Melanie joked. She took off running toward the village.

"Hey!" Liyah yelled.

She started chasing after her friend, and they sped toward the village.

There was definitely something special about these two girls. Melanie didn't realize she was different, but something about both of them stirred Liyah's mind with questions. But once again Liyah pushed these nagging thoughts aside.

The pair raced on.

"What about Veronica?" Tyrese asked.

Ryvan shook his head.

"Jaqueline?"

Again Ryvan shook his head, his agitation growing.

"Tyrese! Stop trying to set me up. I want to train."

"That's all you ever do, Ryvan," Tyrese pointed out. "You need a break."

"No, you just think I do. I just want to be prepared for this weekend," Ryvan stated as he shot an arrow from his crossbow. He hit his target, and a deer fell about thirty yards away.

"I don't know how you do that, man," Tyrese smiled.

Ryvan shrugged. "Help me get this back to camp. Well, it's just how I release all tension and anger. If I didn't train excessively, then I'm afraid you might become my target," he laughed.

Ryvan was the taller of the two with dark brown hair. He had dark blue eyes that shone with intensity in his training. He was decked out in leather and metal armor covering his torso as well as his legs. The only scars on his armor were three slashes on the chest plate. They were set a few inches apart—the marks of a bear on the rampage. Ryvan was different than most people. The closest person to him was Tyrese. But, Tyrese had a problem with wanting Ryvan to be with some girl. Ryvan had thoughts of only training. *Training* was Ryvan's life. Nothing more. To Ryvan, none of that mattered. He felt as though there was something more out there for him. Yet, he knew not what. He knew he would understand sooner or later. It was approaching. That was another reason for his excessive training. He wanted to be ready. He was seventeen years of age. He would turn eighteen in a month.

Tyrese was tall as well. He was about an inch shorter than Ryvan. He had light brown hair that was cropped as short as Ryvan's. Tyrese was sixteen and would turn seventeen shortly after Ryvan added a year. He dressed the same as his companion, but he didn't have any scars on his chest plate. However, he had two holes in his armor over his ankle where a rattlesnake had struck at him. Luckily it didn't puncture all the way through though. His eyes were the deepest shade of emerald green that reflected the innermost part of him.

The two carried the deer into the village. It was just a doe, but it was food for them and their neighbors.

"It's your night to cook," Ryvan stated. He was secretly relieved to be the one to clean the meat instead of cooking it.

They were nearing the village. Their muscles flexed as they carried the young female deer. Ryvan glanced up and saw Tyrese's tattoo. He had a comet set aflame positioned on his bicep. It seemed to be moving as his arm strained from the weight.

Ryvan had a tattoo of his own on his bicep as well. Only his was different. It was a picture of a fiery sun. Neither boy knew how the tattoos got there, and it was uncommon for Dreonians to have tattoos. The boys were not native to the Osheyk Mountains, but for as long as they could remember, they had lived in Dreán.

On noting these tattoos, Ryvan was cast into deep thoughts. He didn't know about Tyrese, but Ryvan wanted to know why *they* were marked. No one else had these, or at least no one he had ever seen. It was almost like they were set apart.

Ryvan felt there was more to it than that, though.

****

"Good job on cooking tonight, Ty," Ryvan complimented.

"Thanks, I see you didn't lose any fingers pulling out the arrow blade," Tyrese joked.

"Yeah, not yet anyway."

The two boys sat around a campfire. They had just eaten venison stew, courtesy of Tyrese. Tyrese was an excellent cook. The boys' neighbors complimented him as they left. The boys enjoyed sharing with, and helping, their Dreonian neighbors. Food was hard to come by, but Ryvan had a knack for finding the right game.

"It was kind of you boys to invite us to eat with you again. Before you two leave in the morning for Corresponding

Point, be sure and come by and get some deer jerky for your trip!" the boys' neighbor, Osami smiled. "It's the least I can do."

Tyrese smiled as he replied, "Yes, ma'am. We'll be sure and do that."

With that, Osami turned and started toward her hut. Tyrese and Ryvan began cleaning up the dishes and dousing the fire. They needed a good night's sleep for their trek to the Warrior Party in Corresponding Point. What they thought was just a party was the event that would start it all.

"Rise and shine, sleepy head!" Liyah smiled. "We need to get going!"

Liyah was literally shaking Melanie awake. After a few seconds, she finally stopped and smiled as the hint of an idea sparkled in her eyes.

"Is that a warrior out there?" Liyah exclaimed.

Melanie awoke with a start and fell out of her bed, snatching at her blades and staring desperately out the window. "Hey! There's no warrior!" Melanie tossed a handful of hay at Liyah.

"Ow. *That* hurt. Come on. Let's get a move on!" Liyah laughed. She then left Melanie on the floor, glaring after her long after she had departed.

Finally, she jumped up and chased after Liyah.

****

After both girls had cleaned up, they came back to their hut from the Pricein River. They walked in their small shack and threw on their armor for the journey.

"I'm going to have to put my weapons on for the whole trip, aren't I?" Melanie complained.

"Yeah, if you want to come with me you do," Liyah stated without smiling. She pulled on her black heels.

"Aww, man!"

Liyah turned from her and grabbed her small knife, flicked it open and closed, then placed it in its place at her waist. Melanie, in the meantime, was pulling on her black heels. Liyah grabbed a larger knife and placed it in the sheath on her ankle just above her heels.

"Why are you bringing that? You *never* bring it. Unless—" Melanie pondered.

"No, don't worry. I just feel that it could be of some use to us," Liyah finished for her, calming any anxieties before they could properly begin.

Melanie shrugged and tied her sheaths onto her back, just as Liyah was doing. They put their cross-blades into the proper position, and Liyah strapped her crossbow to her back as Melanie put her knives on. Once they finished the ritual, Liyah turned to leave their living quarters.

"Get your provisions and meet me outside," Liyah called over her shoulder as she turned to walk out, securing her hoop earrings.

Melanie ran to get the items she thought she would need.

A few minutes later she came outside. "Ready to go if you are!" she smiled as she watched Liyah load her horse, Mystique.

"Alright, I've already saddled your horse. All you need to do is load it."

"Thanks!" Melanie squealed. She ran off to load her own horse.

Melanie's horse was a shimmering white mare named Marentex. She loaded her blankets, tent, extra under clothing, and cooking material, mounted her horse, and came around in time to see Liyah climb atop Mystique.

There was only one horse that could compare to Marentex, and that was Mystique. It shimmered at all times. Mystique and Marentex were two of the most exquisite creatures in the territory. The two girls had never seen any other horses like them. But they didn't know where the horses had come from, and they had been with them as long as they could remember.

"Good to go?" Liyah asked.

It was still dark outside, and the light of the waning moon lit the plains before them, casting dancing shadows around every corner. The girls were really excited to be getting on the road, so they did not mind the early start. Every evening along the way to Corresponding Point there was a party in each of the towns. It was for the warriors and she-warriors. Every year they met new people that made the trip worthwhile. The girls were anxious to reach their destination.

"Yep, shall we?" Melanie asked.

"We shall!" The girls began riding off toward their first stop, Beura, which lay to the west.

"Great! Now we have something to eat on our way to Beura," Tyrese smiled.

"That was kind of Osami," Ryvan stated as he took a chunk out of some dried deer jerky. Ryvan sat atop his bay stallion, Verexn, and Tyrese sat upon his mount, another bay stallion, Vatran. Both horses were loaded with supplies for the trip. As the two young men began to head northwest the sun was just beginning to peek over the horizon.

Ryvan and Tyrese were both dressed in their battle gear. Ryvan wore cross-blades and a crossbow on his back with a number of daggers strapped to him.

Tyrese wore the cross-blades, but he didn't carry a crossbow. He didn't like the distance required to use one, for he preferred the close range battle.

"I wonder how I'll do this year in the tournament," Ryvan mused.

"I don't know, man. I'm sure you'll do great though. You always do. What I wonder is how many she-warriors are coming this year."

"She-warriors are becoming scarce, Ty," Ryvan began.

"Scarce, yes, but not *completely* gone," Tyrese laughed.

Ryvan couldn't help but laugh at his friend. Today was going to be an interesting day. He could feel it.

They were the only travelers out for miles. The sun came up to reveal beautiful mountain ranges and lush grassy valleys. The trip to Corresponding Point was a fairly long one, and they would have to travel through several different towns. It would take a total of four days to reach their final destination.

"I'm ready for tonight," Tyrese said.

"For what?"

"The party at Beura! Where have you been?"

"There is more to life than that," Ryvan smiled.

"And there's more to life than training," Tyrese teased.

"This is taking too long. Let's pick up the pace," Ryvan grinned as he made his horse leap toward the west and race on into the sunrise.

Tyrese smiled after his friend for a moment then raced off after him.

The pair was flying toward the village of Beura closer to the sky than to the earth. However, they would be forced down sooner than they imagined.

Chapter 2

The two girls rode side by side. They were the only warriors going to Corresponding Point from Faeciã. In fact, they were the *only* warriors from Faeciã. In the elders' eyes, they were a disgrace to the entire village tribe. Warriors were frowned upon in their village. Faeciã was one of two villages in the Osheyk Mountains that didn't have a party for traveling warriors and she-warriors. The other town was called Dreán. In fact, warriors avoided both towns as much as possible.

They were about halfway to Beura. The sun was directly above them in the middle of the sky. Liyah and Melanie were making pretty good time, and they would arrive in Beura by nightfall. After a while, a couple more travelers appeared a short distance behind the girls, but they had no desire in meeting up with them.

The travelers had made Liyah uncomfortable at first. They had been approaching them at a high speed. It had reminded her of something, but she was at a loss in remembering. However, after watching the travelers for some time, the travelers slowed as Liyah and Melanie steadily moved away.

"Did you see those people back there?" Melanie asked curiously. Melanie kept turning around in her saddle to watch them.

"Yeah, they kind of make me nervous," Liyah replied.

"You're just on edge because you are nervous about the tournament!"

"Maybe." Liyah doubted it.

"Where do you think they're from?" Melanie wondered aloud.

"I imagine they are coming up from Dreán," Liyah replied.

"Dreán? No one *ever* comes from Dreán!"

"No one *ever* comes from Faeciã either."

"Good point," Melanie smiled.

Liyah smiled and laughed with Melanie, but she still felt uneasy. She reached up and felt one of her cross-blades, just to reassure herself that it would be there just in case she needed it. To be extra safe, she glanced over at Melanie to see if her blades were in place. Liyah wasn't sure why the strangers made her so uneasy, but they did.

It was peculiar that someone would be coming up from Dreán. Those people hardly ever ventured a few feet out of their own village, let alone to a town miles away. Rumor had it that they were entering into a shortage of food. That was a simple problem to solve in Liyah's eyes. If they would just go a short distance outside of their village where the deer lived in hiding, then they would find game. However, most Dreonians were weak. At least Liyah thought so. However, these two strangers were different. Liyah just knew they were, even from such a distance. It made her uneasy.

"You're awfully quiet over there," Melanie smiled sweetly.

"Yeah, I mean, no, I'm fine," Liyah spit out in a kind of frenzy.

"Are you sure about that?" she queried. It was obvious that she was concerned.

"It's all good," Liyah replied.

"You weren't acting like that a while ago. Is something bothering you, Liyah?"

"I'm fine."

"Does it have something to do with the riders back there? You didn't seem troubled until they became visible to us."

Their horses went around a large curve on the mountainside. So far all that had met their eyes was dry grass and trees, while more mountains rose hazy in the distance. All through the morning they had been approaching the more mountainous region of their land. They came around the curve and were fairly surprised by the drastic change in scenery. At least Melanie was.

Liyah had been through this same area last year on her way to Corresponding Point, so she had been anticipating it. Melanie had been too young to accompany her, and therefore, she had not been allowed to come. The village elders were strict with their old customs. Liyah had gone alone. It was not a smart thing to do, but Liyah knew she could handle it. She did, too. She made it in one piece and had a blast on the way. The only thing that could make it better was Melanie making the trip at her side. But she was now, and both girls knew it was going to be a great week.

The air was humid, making it difficult for the girls to catch their breath in the changing altitude. The landscape was lush and green, covering the mountainside in twisting, turning pathways. The girls would be able to enjoy this view the rest of the way to Beura.

A rush of bird song flew from the trees, and there were several waterfalls flowing from high up in the rocks. Flowers grew along the shore of the crystal blue lake. Their scent lifted on the breeze with a gentle spray of water. The sight caused Melanie's breath to catch in her throat. When the girls finally recovered from their awe, they were surprised to see that their horses had stopped moving. They had gradually come to a halt while the girls sat in wonder.

"This is beautiful!" Melanie gasped.

"Yeah, it's one of the most beautiful spots on our journey," Liyah explained to her friend. "Come on, let's get going again. There is a spot just a ways up the path that is great for stopping. We can eat there."

"Awesome! I'm starving," Melanie giggled as her stomach rumbled.

"I am as well," Liyah stated.

The girls began, making their way through the final part of their trip to Beura.

"When we are on our journey home, I'll take you swimming in the pool beneath the waterfall," Liyah told her friend.

"Sounds like a plan to me," Melanie smiled.

But even as Liyah spoke, she wondered if it were the truth. Perhaps they would not come back at all.

"I win!" Ryvan smiled as they stopped at a large boulder.

"Rematch. You cheat!" Tyrese cried.

Ryvan was smiling. His windblown hair hung down in his red face from the biting wind. He looked ahead suddenly and spotted two unknown riders. The smile vanished from his face.

"Dude? You ok?" Tyrese asked.

Ryvan pointed and said, "Riders."

"So what?"

Ryvan reached up for his crossbow.

"No! Ryvan, I'm sure they are just going to Beura. Like us," Tyrese made a move to stop his friend from doing anything irrational.

Ryvan paused. "Maybe, but no one came from Dreán before or after us, and the closest town is Faeciã."

"Well, then they are probably from Faeciã," Tyrese stated, thinking that Ryvan had lost his mind.

"No one comes from Faeciã. They despise warriors. The elders there are full on peace and harmony. This age is not known for that though. There would not be anyone coming from Faeciã unless they were full of guts that the people there run so short of."

"Well, then, maybe they are coming from somewhere farther north," Tyrese stated carefully. He was beginning to see Ryvan's point. It bothered him.

"You know as well as I, there are no settlements up farther north," Ryvan said.

"Well, who are they?"

"I don't know, but I think we should keep an eye on them carefully and stay on *our* path, keeping our distance."

"They *could* be from Faeciã, couldn't they?"

"I suppose, but it's not likely," Ryvan replied.

"It's not exactly likely that someone would come from Dreán either, but…," Tyrese countered. "Chances are that they are just going to Beura like us. I don't feel we have the need to worry."

"Right, now let's move."

****

The two rode alongside one other at a moderate pace. They both tried to keep an eye on the strange pair in front of them. Although around mid-day, they disappeared behind a large mountain.

"Looks like they are in the rainy region now," Tyrese stated.

"Yeah, we should be there after a while. Then we can stop and eat, but I don't want to lose them," Ryvan replied.

"Why?" Tyrese asked bewildered.

"Curiosity has the best of me."

They both laughed. The majority of their tension had gone, and they were more relaxed. The two strangers were about ten minutes ahead of them. If they *were* from Faeciã, then they would have left at the exact time or close to when the two boys had. That was a little odd. They had been riding since before sunrise.

Tyrese grabbed a piece of deer jerky and tore off a chunk with his teeth. Then he tossed it to Ryvan who did the same thing.

"Man, I can't believe it's been a whole year since we've been up to Corresponding Point," Tyrese laughed.

"Me either. Something is telling me that this year is going to be different, somehow," Ryvan replied.

"What do you mean?" Tyrese asked around a huge chunk of deer jerky.

"I don't really know. Something epic?"

"Sweet, I could do for a bit of change."

Ryvan didn't say anything else. He just focused on the road ahead. They were only a short distance from the mountain curve that once around it, revealed beautiful mountainside.

The boys reached the curve, and instantly grew tense once again. The strangers could have set up a trap for them somewhere ahead. Then again, maybe not, but the boys wanted to be on the safe side.

They came around the corner to see the breathtaking scenery. The strangers were still riding up ahead of them on the trail. The young men were closer to them than they had been before. The two riders must have stopped.

They looked closer and could tell that they were girls around their age.

"She-warriors?!" they both cried in unison.

"That's what had us on edge?" Tyrese exclaimed in exasperation. "She-warriors?"

"Chill, we should still be careful. She-warriors are not to be trusted. They are as capable of anything a regular warrior is capable of," Ryvan replied seriously.

"I'm sure. What do you mean by that?"

"Just that. Do not trust them. They are deadly."

"And you know this how?"

"I…I…don't know," Ryvan stated, frowning deeply at the snippets of a hazy memory, playing in his mind.

Tyrese looked at him stupidly. "Huh?"

"I don't know, I just remember something."

"Ok, whatever," Tyrese stated. "Sometimes you are really weird."

Ryvan laughed, "Thanks."

"Anytime."

The strangers went out of sight once again. They were a little creepy, and both carried cross-blades. One carried a crossbow as well. This intrigued Ryvan, and he was sure now that they were going to Beura.

"Good," Ryvan thought to himself. Then he openly stated, "They *are* going to Beura."

"Yep, I figured they were."

"Whatever."

"Curiosity killed the cat, you know?"

"Shut up."

Tyrese laughed at this. He laughed so hard that he almost fell off of his horse. And this made Ryvan laugh. They sat there enjoying their simple lives for a long time. However, there wasn't really anything too funny about what they were doing. The laughter bubbled up from their happiness.

"I'm ready to get to the party!" Tyrese smiled. He was red from laughing so hard.

"Why are you so anxious?"

"Because I want—"

"Don't say it! I know what you were going to say. Something about the girls."

"You can't blame me!"

"No, I can't. Just don't trust the she-warriors," Ryvan warned.

"You can't tell me that all she-warriors are bad news."

"No, not all of them, but *most* of them are."

"Man, you don't even know why you are saying that," Tyrese scoffed.

"Yes, I do. I don't want you to wind up dead somewhere. Just think of it this way, she-warriors are like regular girls except ten times as sensitive, *and* they have weapons!"

"Whatever. You know you can't say you aren't interested."

"Yes, I can."

Tyrese just stared.

"But I can't mean it."

This brought another round of laughter from the boys. This time Tyrese fell off his horse into the spongy grass below.

"Wow! It's beautiful here," Melanie declared.

"Yes, it really is. I love it," Liyah smiled.

"You just smiled."

"And your point is?"

"You are losing some of your edge."

"We should be guarded, though. They are getting closer," Liyah pointed out.

"Oh well. They are just guys. We can take care of them, no problem."

"Good point," Liyah laughed.

"I think we deserve a little break. Like, say, for food," Melanie exclaimed.

"Me, too. It's funny how we are always hungry, but we never gain weight," Liyah mused.

"Ha! Never? It looked like you have gained around fifteen pounds. You're getting kind of chubby there," Melanie joked.

"Fifteen, is that it? That's a relief, for a while there I thought I was going to wind up looking like you," Liyah countered and raced off.

"Hey!" Melanie raced off after her.

****

The girls reached the spot Liyah had spoken of around three in the afternoon. The girls hadn't eaten in a long time, so, they flopped down on a patch of lush green grass after tying their horses by the river where they grazed happily.

The girls sat, smiling in the sunshine. They took their food and began to eat some bread and dried jerky that Melanie had made. Liyah had shot the deer herself.

It wasn't much, but the girls had wanted to travel light. It was enough, however, to fill them up until they reached Beura. While they were eating, the girls kept a close eye on the strangers. They didn't want them to get too close.

Melanie was curious. Liyah however didn't really care. She would take more interest later on in the tournament. She knew it, too.

"I want to eat fast enough to leave before they get up here," Liyah stated.

"But," Melanie began.

"No. Fast," Liyah interrupted.

"Aw, Liyah! Can't we just scare them a little or something?" Melanie pleaded.

"Not this time. I don't think we can."

"What do you mean?"

"I don't know really. I just have this feeling that we would not be too lucky intimidating them."

"Why?"

"Because, they remind me, I mean, they are like us," Liyah spit out.

"Creepy."

"Yeah, tell me about it," Liyah stated.

The two sat for a moment more, soaking up the sun. Then, when the strangers got close enough, the girls untied their horses. They mounted and prepared to leave. They emerged on the trail directly facing the strangers. None of the four spoke. Instead, they all sat in the middle of the trail staring into the eyes of the strangers. They couldn't break away, and the strangers stopped in their tracks. Suddenly, Mystique and Marentex, the girls' horses, whinnied in anxious fear.

Mystique reared up, forcing Liyah to grasp tightly to her mane just to stay on. This broke the spell, and Melanie made Marentex turn around on the trail. She gave her a kick and sent her blazing on up the mountain.

Mystique landed, and Liyah glanced at them one last time. Then, she turned and raced off.

The boys remained on the trail, staring long after the girls were gone. Tyrese decided to break the silence. He shook his head. "That was weird."

"Tell me about it," Ryvan stated.

"That was really weird."

"Yeah."

"I mean, that was really, really weird!"

"Tyrese! Shut up."

They just looked at each other. Then, Tyrese moved over to where the girls had crossed onto the trail before they bolted.

He looked down and saw something shining on the earth. It was a ruby red heart shaped necklace. He picked it up. "Hey, Ryvan, check it out."

"What?" Ryvan asked as he rode up. Tyrese wasn't on his horse anymore. Ryvan jumped down, leveling with Tyrese.

"Look at this," he said as he handed the glistening trinket over to Ryvan.

"Interesting."

"It's hers."

"Which 'her'? There were two 'hers'," Ryvan asked.

"The one that left first, hers."

"How do you know?"

"Because, I don't know. Oh no."

"What?" Ryvan asked looking around quickly while taking a defensive stance.

"I'm starting to sound like you."

Ryvan punched him on the arm. "Don't do that."

Tyrese started laughing again. Ryvan took his horse to the stream, letting it drink in the cool water. Tyrese stopped laughing and stared at the amulet. He rotated it over in his hand before he finally pocketed it. Tyrese led his horse over to the stream where Ryvan had placed his.

"I have a feeling we will see them again," Ryvan foreshadowed.

"You think so?"

"Yeah, did you see how they were dressed?" Ryvan asked. "They are definitely she-warriors going to the games."

"Yeah, the one whose horse reared, she carried a lot of weapons. Wouldn't want to run into her after dark."

"She did, didn't she?" Ryvan recalled.

"Kind of weird for a chick to do that."

"Yeah, it does seem odd," Ryan smiled.

"What are you smiling about?" Tyrese asked.

"I don't really know. I just feel like smiling."
"You are so strange," Tyrese laughed.
"Maybe."

****

The boys mounted their horses after eating a quick meal. They made sure to give the girls plenty of space. Apparently, they had frightened them, but the girls had alarmed the guys as well. The horses had sensed it, causing them to start.

If the girls wanted that necklace back though, they would have to find them again. Tyrese sensed something special within the ruby necklace like a sense of power.

They set out on the trail again as rain began to drizzle down. Ryvan liked rain, and he had known it was coming because of the scent in the air. Ryvan sensed something else approaching with the oncoming drizzle. It would be upon them soon.

Something about the girl who ran first sparked something in Tyrese's mind. He was not about to tell Ryvan though, because he knew what he was going to say. He didn't trust them. That was fine. Tyrese, however, was curious about them. Secretly, he figured Ryvan was intrigued as well, but with the other girl, the one with the crossbow. She had stared directly at Ryvan, and Ryvan at her. There was a connection there. Tyrese had never seen that response in Ryvan before. Ryvan was different, and when something like that was seen in Ryvan, it was epic. But the warrior wasn't about to admit it.

Chapter 3

"What was that about?" Melanie asked.

"Not a clue. You tell me," Liyah stated.

The girls were breathing hard and shaky. It wouldn't be too long before they arrived in Beura, for they had to make it to the top of the mountain. Beura waited just around a couple of rises.

It had begun to rain, and the girls were thoroughly enjoying it. When they started up the steepest part of the mountain, the girls started laughing.

"Did you see their faces?" Melanie laughed.

"I'm sure *we* looked the same way," Liyah laughed back.

"Still, that was weird," Melanie stated, becoming serious.

"Yeah, it really was. It was like there was a connection there."

"Really? You've never said that about any of the guys you've ever met before."

"Haven't met him, now, have I?" Liyah asked slyly.

"I suppose not. That one guy was awfully interesting, though."

"Which one?"

"The one that wasn't staring at you," Melanie laughed. "I mean he was, too, but...."

"Yeah, yeah, yeah, whatever."

"Whatever yourself," Melanie grinned. "Oh no!" she suddenly cried.

"What's wrong?" Liyah asked as she drew her sword.

"My necklace is gone!"

"What? You don't mean your ruby amulet?"

"Yes!" Melanie wailed.

"Don't worry," Liyah said calmly.

"What? What do you mean don't worry?!" Melanie exclaimed.

"Don't worry. We'll see them again. They will have your necklace," Liyah stated calmly.

"Have you totally gone off your rocker?"

"No," came the simple reply.

"Is this one of those things you just know?" Melanie asked, calming down a little bit.

"Yup." Liyah rode off.

"Ok," Melanie said. She had grown to know Liyah so well that she recognized Liyah knew a lot of things. Sometimes they were things you didn't think should be known. She learned to trust her. Melanie considered calling it a keen intuition, and she just tried to relax and go with it. She put faith in her friend.

****

The girls finished their long trek up the steep mountainside. Beura was merely a five minute ride from where they were, and they still had around an hour until the party began.

The girls rode on in silence. They were both thinking of what had happened up on the trail, and the thoughts of the young men took hold over their minds.

Their heads were full as they approached Beura, and they had to work to force the thoughts to the very backs of their minds.

"Are you nervous yet?" Liyah asked.

"Yeah, a little bit," Melanie confessed.

"Don't worry. You are going to have a great time."

"I hope so. Where are all the she-warriors?" Melanie asked.

"That's all," Liyah stated sadly. "Of course, there will be more in Corresponding Point. Not very many more though, I'm afraid."

"That's sad."

From where they were, the girls could see most of Beura up close. There were around twenty warriors setting up camp. Also, on one side of all the camps, a smaller grouping of she-warriors set up their own camps. The sun was beginning to set, so torches were lit. Every few feet places were set up for warriors to feed, water, and tie up their horses. In the center of the whole village, a ring of torches stood on a blank area of land. Around it were decorations, chairs, and a table with refreshments.

"Welcome to Beura!" a short bald man ran up to them and cried.

"Thank you, sir," Liyah replied.

"I hope you will enjoy tonight's festivities," he smiled. He seemed to be fairly afraid of them. That was alright though. Liyah was used to it.

"Thanks, good to be here again," Liyah smiled back.

"Great to have you! She-warrior camp is over on the south end of the village."

"Thank you again!"

The girls rode off. Liyah watched from the corner of her eye as the little man took out a handkerchief and dabbed at his forehead. Everyone tried to stay on the good side of she-warriors since rumor had it that a woman was the cause for the destruction of the mother land. It amused the girls.

Liyah smiled at Melanie to reassure her. "The girls are nice. Don't worry. However, don't make eye contact with the warriors."

They rode past all of the warriors, and they all watched absently as the pair passed. The girls kept their gaze fixed forward.

"Hey, girls!" a brunette she-warrior smiled and waved them over.

The girls tied up their horses and grabbed their stuff.

"How are you, Liyah?" the brunette exclaimed as she, to Melanie's horror, hugged Liyah. No one *ever* hugged Liyah. Ever.

"I'm doing pretty well, Shanillé," Liyah stated. "I have someone I want you all to meet!" She had raised her voice to where they all could hear. "This is Melanie, my best friend and brand new official she-warrior."

There were four other she-warriors including Shanillé. They all jumped up and welcomed Melanie to the group while

Liyah set up camp. She did this quickly as Melanie learned everyone's names.

Shanillé was a short and slightly chubby brunette with laughing green eyes. She wore a single long sword at her waist. She had a friendly face and a smile that was contagious.

Another was Vera. She had jet black hair running a short distance past her shoulders. She was around an inch shorter than Liyah with harsh emerald green eyes. Her features were sharp, and she carried herself with a haughty air of intimidation. She also wore a single sword, but she carried many smaller throwing knives just like Liyah.

The other two were twins that were difficult to tell apart. Each had black hair that stopped at her shoulders, and their eyes were hazel with gray flecks. They were tall and slim with wild quirks and mannerism that kept the entertainment up in the group. Their names were Christina and Siscilia, and each wore regular swords at their waists. They were all from Beura.

By the time Melanie had gotten all the names straight, Liyah had everything set up, and she came out of their tent and stood up.

"Liyah, I see you still wear all of those weapons!" Christina grinned.

"She is the only she-warrior to ever wear that many," Siscilia whispered to Melanie.

"And when it comes to battle with them, she is the most accurate," Vera said with a hint of jealousy. "I see you are rubbing off on your friend there."

Everyone laughed.

"No one uses cross-blades except for—well you know," Shanillé stated.

"Guys, we went over this last year," Liyah hissed, cutting them off.

"Chill, Liyah," Shanillé said, and Liyah smoldered off to the side with her arms crossed over her chest.

"Except for what?" Melanie asked.

"Except for Asgarnians," Vera smiled sickly.

"Huh?" Melanie was confused. "What's that?"

"Don't get started guys. I mean it!" Liyah barked.

Christina leaned in and whispered, "I'll tell you later."

Everyone grew quiet and looked at Liyah who was obviously irritated.

"Welcome to Beura!" a short fat man cried as he ran toward them. "We are happy to have you!"

The boys smiled down from their mounts. "Thank you, sir," Tyrese stated as they began to ride forward into the camp.

"One moment, boys!" the man squealed.

The boys stopped where they were and briefly turned to look back. "A word of caution, the she-warriors we have this year are different. I was overwhelmed by an odd feeling when the final two rode up here a few moments ago."

"Really?" Ryvan asked curiously. "Which ones?"

"Oh! These two wore cross-blades. Very odd, mind you," he stated.

"Yes, the legend is known to us," Tyrese smiled as both boys turned on their horses to where the man could see their own cross-blades.

"Oh my! No offense!" the man squealed.

"None taken, my good man. All is well. Thank you for the just warning," Ryvan laughed.

The pair rode into camp. "Sounds like our little friends from the mountain path have arrived," Ryvan stated smugly. "I knew we would meet them again soon."

Tyrese nodded in amusement. He was secretly scanning the camp for them. Finally, he saw it—she-warriors.

There were two of them walking together, but they were not the ones he was looking for. These two had medium length black hair, and they were twins.

He looked in the direction they were headed, and he saw what he was looking for—the she-warrior camp. There appeared to be four gathered around a fire, and the boys' "friends" were there.

"Ryvan...," Tyrese began.

"I know. I've seen them," Ryvan stated as he dismounted from his horse. He tied the creature up and took care of him.

The two quickly set up camp where they could easily view the she-warrior camp without getting too close, for they wanted to know more.

All at once, several warriors came up to their camp and started talking to the boys. It was almost like a family reunion, and it seemed that everyone knew Ryvan and Tyrese. They all sat around the fire Ryvan had just made and began catching up. They met up with some of their old friends. They were friends with many people, but they had met around three warriors from Beura that were their very close friends. The warriors were named Bryen, Shace, and Creshvan. They were from Beura and had met Ryvan and Tyrese last year.

Bryen was a tall blond with laughing blue eyes. He was around Tyrese's height. He had a smile that spread like wildfire. He was around eighteen years old and had a look that screamed mischief maker. He carried himself in a cocky manner with a crossbow strapped to his back with a long sword at his side.

Shace was around an inch shorter than Ryvan, and he had black hair and grey eyes. His eyes contained golden specks, making them look like eagle eyes. He had sharp features that seemed intimidating, but he was very welcoming and kind. He carried the same weapons as Bryen and was nineteen.

Creshvan was the same height as Ryvan. He had brown hair and hazel eyes and was known as the joker of the group. He was only seventeen and had come last year even though he was underage. He finally had gotten caught over in Corresponding Point, but they had let him stay since it was so late in the games. He carried a large bow on his back.

They sat around the campfire laughing and joking. Ryvan and Tyrese kept glancing over at the camp where the girls were. Ryvan was intrigued. He had never felt the way he did when she had looked at him. Something had triggered a distant memory that he could not quite grasp.

Creshvan caught Tyrese and Ryvan staring and said, "Hey, they'll be there later. It's time to get this party started."

Everyone jumped to their feet and made their way over to the village center. The music had started, and people venturing toward the party arena. Ryvan glanced over once more before he left and noticed every single she-warrior was gone.

Melanie was staring out at the river. The sun was sinking down, and she was admiring its golden and rose hues as they danced across the skyline.

"Whatcha lookin' at there, buddy?" Liyah asked. She flopped down next to Melanie, causing a cloud of dirt to gather up around them.

"Not a lot," she replied, waving a hand in front of her face and coughing. "I'm just checking out the area."

"It's beautiful.; isn't it?"

"Yeah, gorgeous."

"Hey!" Shanillé shouted to them. "Do you guys see that group over there?" They won't stop looking this way!"

Everyone turned to see what group, and everyone, except Liyah and Melanie, was surprised when they saw who it was. Each she-warrior started laughing except for the girls who just sat staring at each other.

"Told you that you would see him again," Liyah said smugly.

"At least I'll get my necklace back."

"Yeah, way to look on the bright side," Liyah laughed.

They stood up and walked toward camp. They didn't let the warrior pair notice they had been caught staring. They carefully kept from looking in their direction. "Looks like the party is starting," Vera stated.

"Well, what are we waiting for? Let's go," Siscilia grinned.

Everyone except for Liyah rose and began moving toward the party. Melanie turned to see Liyah still sitting around the campfire. She ran back. "What are you doing?"

"Not a thing," Liyah laughed.

"Well, I'm *not* going to let them ruin my party."

"Good point. We are here to have fun."

"That's the spirit!"

"Shall we?" Liyah asked, holding out her arm.

"We shall," Melanie linked arms with her, and they headed off toward the party.

****

A few minutes later, the she-warriors stood together by the music speakers. There were about four groups of guys standing around with about five warriors in each group. The girls' "friends" had been among the last to arrive.

Melanie seemed fairly disappointed. "This is it?" she asked sadly.

This brought a round of laughter from all the she-warriors. All the guys turned to look. Vera stared them all back into their circles.

"No!" Shanillé laughed. "This is only the reintroduction party. The other towns have the real parties."

"Oh," Melanie smiled.

The music grew louder as a powerful song came on over the speakers, inspiring everyone to relax and enjoy themselves.

Just then, Liyah jabbed Melanie in the arm with her elbow.

"Hey! What was—"

Liyah interrupted, "Our friends are here."

Melanie looked up to see them. The one that intrigued her was starting in their direction. Liyah turned on her heel and ventured off to see Vera and Shanillé. Melanie stood there with the twins. They sat there and talked for awhile when Christina said, "Looks like we got ourselves a visitor."

Melanie turned to look. There, coming out of the crowd in her direction was her "friend" from the mountains.

Ryvan, Tyrese, Bryen, Shace, and Creshvan were standing in their own little group on the outer edge of the torch circle. The music was fairly loud. It was a beautiful night, and the stars were shining brightly in the rich black night.

"I'm ready to get to Ayaye," Shace stated.

"Why?" Bryen asked as he took orders for what the other four wanted from the refreshment table.

"So we can get to the real party," he laughed.

"Hey, Shace, come with me to get everything," Bryen stated.

The pair went off toward the table, pausing to say hello to the she-warriors. Two of them looked like they were ready to attack them for just speaking. One eased up a bit when she saw they weren't a threat. This was the she-warrior whose horse had reared. Ryvan recognized her instantly. The other had reached to her side for her weapon. This one had black hair. The first, the blonde with the cross-blades, had steadied her while a brunette laughed. The brunette returned the hello while the blonde nodded stiffly.

"Did you just see that?" Creshvan asked.

"They did that on purpose," Tyrese laughed.

"Bright fellas, let me tell ya," Ryvan smiled.

"Yeah," Creshvan nodded, "Idiots! I'm gonna go help."

"Well, now we know where our friends are," Ryvan stated.

"Yeah," Tyrese replied.

"I better go keep them out of trouble," Ryvan smiled as he ran off after Creshvan.

Tyrese was left all alone, and he placed his hand in his pocket, pulling out the girl's necklace. He decided to take the opportunity to return it. The girl was standing with the black haired twins. It looked like they were having a good time, and he began venturing toward them.

All at once, the music was cut. The short fat man stood on the stage in front of everyone and shouted, "May I have your attention, please?" Everyone grew quiet. "First off, the elders of Beura would like to welcome you all to the annual festivities of the Warrior Chain!"

The crowd erupted in cheers. "All right, all right! Well this year we have a very nice turnout. In all we have a total of seventeen warriors and six she-warriors!" Everyone clapped. "When we call your tribe, please raise your hand. From Beura, we have fifteen warriors." The Beura boys climbed up on crates andcheered loudly. Tyrese saw Creshvan, Shace, and Bryen attempt to climb the side of one of the huts, resulting in Creshvan on the ground in a heap. This made Tyrese smile.

"Also, we have four she-warriors from Beura." The twin girls raised their hands along with the brunette who had laughed when the one with black hair drew her sword. She had raised her hand as well. The crowd erupted in cheers once more. All of the Beuran warriors were familiar with the she-warriors. More than likely they trained together to an extent.

"We have a surprise this year," the fat man shouted. "Two young warriors from Dreán have joined us again!"

Tyrese raised his hand and saw Ryvan raise his as well. Everyone cheered for them politely except for the two girls.

"Also, we have our favorite she-warrior from Faeciã again this year! But, now she has brought a friend with her."

Everyone cheered as the two girls raised their hands. It looked like they *were* from Faeciã after all.

"Well, this certainly is a good number and welcome to those from farther away, Faeciãns and Dreonians alike! Enjoy yourselves tonight, and we wish you all luck as you finish off the week!" The fat man finished and jumped down from the stage.

The music started up again, and Tyrese started making his way toward the younger Faeciãn girl.

Chapter 4

After the host finished speaking and the music had started up again, Melanie looked to see if the boy from Dreán was still coming her way. He was. She wasn't sure if that was a good or a bad thing, but she wanted her necklace back.

Melanie wheeled around to see the twins had vanished. She looked around to see if Liyah was near, and she didn't see her anywhere. She turned back to see that she was face to face with the boy.

"Hey," he said, acting as if he had no recollection of the event on the mountain trail.

"Uh, hello," Melanie mumbled as she leaned back.

"Name's Tyrese. What's yours?" he smiled.

"Uh...uhm...Melanie," she stuttered.

"Melanie," he repeated more to himself. "That's a nice name."

"Thank you," she drifted off. Melanie was still looking around for Liyah to come to her rescue.

"Yeah, I think I have something that belongs to you," Tyrese smiled as he held out her ruby heart amulet.

"Oh! Thanks!" Melanie exclaimed. "But how did you know it was mine?"

"Lucky guess," he replied. Melanie had dropped her guard a little. She was no longer looking for Liyah.

Melanie reached out to grab the amulet out of his hand, but Tyrese pulled back. "Here, let me," he smiled.

"Uh, ok," she replied. Melanie turned around and lifted up her hair.

Tyrese fastened the trinket around her neck, carefully allowing it to fall into place. Melanie turned around and glanced down to once again see it sparkling.

"There you go," Tyrese smiled.

"Thanks," Melanie looked up at him and smiled. "This necklace means a lot to me. I don't know how I can ever repay you."

"How about gracing me with your presence tomorrow night in Ayaye?" he asked.

Melanie was taken aback. "Maybe."

At that point Liyah raced up. She grabbed Melanie by the shoulder and whipped her around. "What do you think you are doing?" She was clearly angry.

Melanie saw the other Dreonian boy grab a hold of Tyrese. He began yelling at Tyrese just as Liyah was yelling at Melanie.

"What did I tell you?" he was angry, too.

Liyah and the other boy stopped yelling long enough to glare at each other. Then Liyah grabbed Melanie by the arm and pulled her away.

Tyrese, meanwhile, was being pulled in the other direction. Melanie knew he didn't like it. He made the other one get off him, and they stood there yelling in the middle of the dance floor.

"Well, what were you thinking?" Liyah asked angrily as the pair stopped shortly after they came out of the torch ring.

"Nothing! I was just getting my necklace back," Melanie countered.

"I don't care! You trusted him and turned your back. Have you learned nothing from me?"

"No! He isn't like that. I can tell."

"You are so naïve. You just met him, and you are defending him? Don't feed me that."

Liyah softened a little, seeing Melanie's downcast expression. She began to walk away. She said quietly over her shoulder, "Just be careful, Melanie. Remember my words. About everything."

She started walking off. Melanie shouted after her, "Liyah!" It momentarily stopped her, but she didn't turn back around. Her cross-blades glistened from the torchlight. "Just give them a chance. You never give anyone a chance!"

Liyah didn't speak or turn around. However, she did look to her right. Melanie could see the side of her face. The torch flames illuminated it and cast dancing shadows across it.

She stayed that way for a moment frozen in place, letting her thoughts play in her mind. Then she just turned and walked away, back to the party, holding her tongue.

"Well? What did I tell you?" Ryvan shouted angrily. They were in the dead center of the torches, and warriors were beginning to stare.

"Well?" he shouted again when Tyrese didn't answer.

"Man! I didn't do anything!" Tyrese shouted back finally.

"Oh, yeah?"

"Yeah! I was just returning her necklace."

"You didn't have to put it on her though."

"Whatever!" Tyrese began walking off.

"Hey! I'm still talking to you," Ryvan yelled after him. Tyrese kept walking.

Ryvan raced after him. When he got to him, Tyrese was outside the circle, heading toward camp.

"What do you want me to say? That I'm sorry? That I won't do it again?"

"Well," Ryvan began.

"No!" Tyrese interrupted. "I won't apologize for anything. I did nothing wrong. I just returned the girl's necklace. Nothing more."

"I heard you. What is the deal with meeting her tomorrow night in Ayaye?"

"That? Uh, I just…was—"

"Yeah, that's what I thought," Ryvan began walking away. He was heading back toward the party. The music lazily drifted toward them as the night grew darker.

"Ryvan!" he shouted. Ryvan stopped, but he didn't turn around. "Don't do this."

He began walking again. "Ryvan!" He stopped again. His shoulders heaved as he let out a sigh. "Just give them a chance."

Tyrese could tell Ryvan wanted to say something by the way his jaw clenched, but he contained himself and went on. Tyrese was left standing there in the darkness.

****

"Hey, Tyrese! What happened to Ryvan? He's really irritated," Bryen asked as Tyrese ran up.

"It's something I did," Tyrese mumbled.

"Good going," Creshvan said under his breath.

Shace elbowed him.

"Well, where did he go?" Tyrese asked.

"Went back to camp. I'd leave him alone though. He seems to need a break," Shace stated.

Tyrese didn't say anything else. He went to go get some punch. Tyrese looked around. Melanie was in a group of she-warriors. The warrior with the long black hair was on edge more than usual. If anyone came near Melanie, the girl would rip out her sword and drive them back. It seemed a little dramatic, and Tyrese assumed Melanie's companion had asked the dark-haired she-warrior to keep Melanie safe. The other Faeciãn girl was not there anymore. In fact, he didn't see her at all. She must have gone back to camp. He hoped Ryvan wouldn't meet her. That would be bad.

Melanie looked up at him suddenly. She smiled sheepishly. He smiled back. The black haired she-warrior drew her sword and turned around. This brought out the others' attention. He turned and raised a hand as a peace offering then went back to his own kind.

****

Ryvan sat playing with one of his knives. He twirled it back and forth between his fingers and flipped it up in the air and caught it again with ease.

He was sitting alone at camp by the fire. His only companions were the horses. The fires at each campsite were still burning. He glanced up to see the she-warrior from Faeciã in her own camp. She was all bundled up in a dark gray blanket. She apparently hadn't seen him yet. He didn't care one way or another. She liked him about as much as he liked her.

He put his knife away. He didn't want the she-warrior to feel threatened. A strange thought occurred to him. Ryvan wondered whether or not she was competing in the tournament. She still intrigued him. Just then, the she-warrior snapped her gaze up to meet his. They stared at each other for a minute, the same way they had in the mountains. The she-warrior rose.

"Uh oh," Ryvan thought. She began coming toward him still bundled in her blanket.

She finally reached his campsite, smiling a bit of a half smile. "Uhm, hey," she said.

"Hey," he replied slowly. They both sat there awkwardly for a moment. Then, Ryvan said, "About tonight," he stopped. "I apologize for acting the way I did. It was unnecessary."

"That's fine," she replied. They were each still bitter toward the other. "I should apologize as well."

"That's fine," Ryvan stated.

She shot him a wary look.

He ignored it and asked, "So you have a name?"

"I never speak my name to strangers," she replied.

"What if I were to tell you my name first? Would I be strange then?" he asked.

"Maybe, I don't know you yet, so, I could not tell you," came her terse reply.

"Ok, then. Ryvan is my name. I don't suppose I could hear your name now?" he asked again.

"You are very persistent, and you sure do ask a lot of questions."

"You don't seem to answer very many of them."

They sat there silently. The night was growing colder, and the party was ending.

"So," Ryvan began.

"I better get going," she stated. When she turned to leave, a leather-bound book dropped from her blankets, stirring up a puff of dust.

Ryvan reached out to pick it up, and Liyah flinched forward. When he lifted the book, a strange sensation shocked his mind, and he nearly dropped it. Liyah quickly reached out and took the book from him. She quickly began walking away from him.

The warrior watched her leave with a sad, unsettled feeling. Suddenly, as if she forgot something, she ceased abruptly. The girl turned and smiled, "Liyah."

She grinned and walked off into the inky blackness to rekindle her campfire.

It seemed *familiar* somehow.

Melanie woke to the noises of horses and people. She shoved her pillow over her head. When she finally decided she could hide no longer, she looked around the tent she shared with Liyah. She noticed she was alone and got up to venture outside. People were already loading their horses for the trip to Ayaye.

Melanie brushed her hair and cleaned up a little bit. When she came back from the river where she had brushed her teeth, she saw that her horse had been loaded and was ready to go.

All of the other she-warriors were loading their own horses. When Melanie had come in last night, Liyah hadn't been too happy with her. She had gone outside the tent and hadn't come back as far as Melanie knew. She had probably slept outside.

Now Liyah was beside Mystique, loading her own stuff. She already had her weapons in place. She glanced up and smiled when she saw Melanie coming. "Morning!"

"Morning," Melanie yawned. "When are we leaving?"

"As soon as everyone eats breakfast," she replied.

"Oh."

"Get your cross-blades on," Liyah said as she tested her stirrup.

Melanie turned around and went back into the tent. She figured it was no time to test Liyah. So, she obediently grabbed her weapons and went back outside to put them on. She glanced over to the other campsite. Tyrese and his friends weren't around. She figured they went out to eat because all of their supplies were already loaded. She began taking down the tent.

****

"Melanie!" Liyah called. "Let's go eat!"

"Alright! Hang on," she called back. She finished loading their tent on Mystique's back. Then, she took off running toward Liyah.

"Where is everyone?" Melanie asked.

"They are already eating," she replied. She was walking fast. Her strides were so long that Melanie had to jog to keep up. They reached the same torch circle the small party was held in the night before. Thinking about it, Melanie had to admit that she was fairly disappointed in the party. She reasoned that when more people were at the later parties, she would be able to enjoy it better.

The warriors were in a long line in the circle. The she-warriors were at the back of the line. At the front were some older ladies from Beura serving everyone some sort of bread covered in white gravy.

"So, Mel, what did you think of the party?" Liyah asked while the line slowly moved up.

"It was alright," Melanie smiled.

"What did you do after I left?"

"Nothing really. We just stood around and talked."

"We?" Liyah asked. She raised an eyebrow at Melanie.

"Me, Christina, Siscilia, Vera, and Shanillé," she answered, her cheeks reddening.

"I see," Liyah replied.

"What did you do after you left?" Melanie asked.

Liyah grew quiet. "I went back to camp and waited."

"Oh," Melanie said. It was finally their turn in line. "That's it?"

"Well, no," she replied. "I have a story to tell you when we set out for Ayaye."

"Umm, ok then," Melanie replied as she got her food.

Liyah received hers, and the girls moved over, standing off to the side with the other she-warriors. They grabbed a seat and began to eat. Liyah was suddenly overcome with the eerie feeling that she was being watched. She glanced up and saw Ryvan looking in her direction.

He smiled at her sheepishly like he was caught doing something wrong. Quickly Ryvan looked back down at his food. Liyah snickered. As far as they were concerned, they still didn't trust each other. They were both going to have to watch their friends with a cautious and wary eye. They were far too different in each other's minds.

Ryvan threw away his plate. Tyrese followed. He hadn't left Ryvan alone since first light. Ryvan was in a much better mood after having a good night's sleep, and he was no longer angry with his close friend either. Tyrese didn't speak. He just followed Ryvan like a loyal puppy. This was a weakness in Ryvan's eyes.

"We will have to meet up with you guys later," Creshvan called. "We are going to load our horses."

"All right," Ryvan called. "Talk to you later."

"See ya," Tyrese called.

The pair started walking toward their horses which they had left standing in the midst of their old campsite.

"What did you do after I left the party?" Ryvan asked.

"Nothing really," Tyrese replied. "Creshvan pulled a prank on that really high-strung she-warrior."

"Oh really?" Ryvan asked. "Like what kind of prank?"

"He came up to the girls and was conversing with them while Shace and Bryen filled up a balloon with water. They climbed onto the roof of one of the houses, and the balloon just happened to fall on her."

"Are you serious?" Ryvan laughed.

"It was hilarious. You should have seen it!" Tyrese grinned. His eyes shone with boyish mischief.

"I'm surprised she didn't kill them."

"She was restrained by the other she-warriors; otherwise, I think she would have."

"What else?"

"Nothing really. They got busted. It turns out that the she-warrior was Shace's sister. The little fat man made them stand on the stage the rest of the time so he could keep an eye on them. I went and stood with them. There was nothing better to do."

"Oh, I see," Ryvan replied.

By now they had reached their horses. They seemed to be anxious to get out of the area.

"What did you do?" Tyrese asked.

"Well, I'll just say I can't be too angry with you anymore."

"Why not? I mean that's a good thing, but why?"

"Because, the other Faeciãn she-warrior came to our camp to talk with me."

Tyrese stopped. "Are you serious?"

"Yep."

"What did you talk about?"

"Nothing really. We apologized to each other and exchanged names," Ryvan replied.

"Really?" Tyrese was clearly surprised. "She seemed a little overprotective, like you. I mean—"

"Shut up," Ryvan interrupted his rambling.

"What's her name?"

"Liyah," Ryvan smiled.

"What are you smiling about?"

"Not a thing. What was the other one's name?"

"Melanie," Tyrese smiled.

"You smiled, too," Ryvan teased.

"So?" Tyrese laughed.

"I'm telling you, bud, don't get too caught up. These two could be a real problem for us."

Tyrese just smiled and shook his head. They mounted and were off to Ayaye with the rest.

Chapter 5

The girls quickly fell into the group of people going to Ayaye. Most of the warriors that joined them last night were underage, so, they couldn't proceed to the next towns. The party began heading southwest, because they were following the Pricein River until they reached a safe crossing point.

Their she-warrior friends rode ahead of them, but Liyah and Melanie held back a bit so Liyah could tell her story. The girls rode side by side at the very back of the group.

"Ok, so spill. What did you do last night?" Melanie begged.

Liyah looked around then said, "I decided to take your advice. I went over to the camp where the Dreonian warrior sat."

"Are you serious?" Melanie asked.

"Yeah, I apologized to your friend's friend. What was his name?"

"Tyrese, and you apologized? You? Apologized?" A look of shock crossed over Melanie's face.

"Well, whatever. But I stayed and talked for a while," she continued.

"How long?" Melanie asked in awe.

"Not very long. Just long enough to exchange names and apologies."

"He apologized, too?" Melanie asked.

Liyah nodded, and Melanie's jaw dropped. When she regained control over the lower half of her face, she asked, "So, what was his name?"

"His name? It was Ryvan," she replied.

"That's cute," Melanie smiled.

"What?" Liyah questioned.

"Ryvan and Liyah. So cute," Melanie smirked.

Liyah frowned. "Not cool."

Melanie took off toward the group of she-warriors. Liyah shook her head and followed.

****

The girls raced up to the small group of she-warriors. They all greeted them with a round of hellos.

"Where have you two been?" Shanillé asked.

"We got a bit of a late start," Melanie smiled.

"Have you guys been chasing after each other long?" Vera asked. "Your horses already look exhausted."

"Not too long really," Liyah smiled.

Mystique and Marentex stood out, outshining any other horse in the line of warriors. None of the other horses were even white. It was obvious that they were extravagant creatures. Shanillé rode a sorrel horse, mainly red except for a white spot where her heart was. Shanillé had named her White-heart. Vera rode on a dapple gray horse with white spots covering her flank. Her hooves looked like they had been dipped in black paint all the way up to the joint. Vera named her Veronica. Christina and Siscilia rode on identical horses. They were both paint mares. They each had a hawk's feather tied securely to their manes. Their names were Chris and Sis. Sis was Christina's horse. Chris was Siscilia's horse. Liyah shook her head in mock disapproval as they told Melanie about their horses and their choice of names. The girls rode along, talking about various things, enjoying each other's company.

"Liyah," Vera began, "do you know what happened to me last night?"

Liyah looked at her for a moment then asked, "No, Vera, I have no idea. What happened?"

Shanillé let out a giggle. Vera shot her a dirty look, and she instantly stopped smiling. "My idiot brother and his friends dropped a water balloon on my head."

Liyah suppressed a laugh. "Really? I'm sorry, Vera," she smiled. "Who is your brother anyway?"

"Shace!" Vera yelled with her hand circling her mouth to magnify her voice. A boy with dark hair like his sister's turned around. His eyes looked like an eagle's.

"What?" he yelled back angrily.

"Nothing!" she yelled. To the girls she said, "That's Shace."

Everyone looked at Shace as he grumbled and turned back around. Everyone laughed. Liyah stopped when she saw that Tyrese and Ryvan were on each side of Shace.

Along the Pricein River, rapids were slowing down. That meant that the troupe was nearing the crossing point. They would pass through this river twice. Once to Ayaye, the second time to Corytz. The river had a strange circular path that wove through the mountains, creating the need to double back.

The troupe drastically decreased since departing from Beura. The boys were all together. There were two other warriors ahead of them. They were older and knew exactly where they were going. All of the she-warriors continued. They were riding back behind them.

The guys rode along enjoying everything around them. Bryen started laughing out of nowhere.

"What's your deal?" Tyrese asked.

"Nothing really. I'm just thinking about last night's little prank we pulled," he laughed.

"That was great. I always love ticking my little sister off. She really deserves it sometimes," Shace grinned recalling the event.

They were talking and laughing about it when they were interrupted by a loud sound: "Shace!" a voice cried.

Shace stopped laughing and rolled his eyes. A disgusted look crept up onto his face as he slowly turned on his horse to face the she-warriors.

"What?" he yelled back angrily.

"Nothing!" the girl shouted. She and her friends started giggling. Shace turned back around.

"Man, *that's* your sister?" Tyrese asked.

"Yeah," Shace shot. "Her name's Vera. Don't get any ideas. She *is* my sister."

"Naw…no worries," Tyrese smiled.

"He has his heart set on someone else already," Creshvan smiled.

"Already, Tyrese? We've just started this year. Yeah, it's what's-her-name from Faeciã! We've all seen the way you look at her," Bryen laughed.

"Melanie," Ryvan stated without any change in facial expression. If you didn't know any better, you would have never guessed he had even opened his mouth to speak.

Tyrese looked straight ahead with a smile faintly creeping across his lips.

"Yeah, that's it," Creshvan grinned.

"As long as it isn't my sister, I'm good with it," Shace beamed.

The girls let out a roar of laughter that made them all turn around to see what the commotion was about. As far as they could tell, there was nothing to laugh at, so the boys turned around again. The girls were laughing and smiling about who-knew-what. The way they were behaving, the boys would have never guessed that those she-warriors were some of the most powerfully dangerous warriors on their earth.

****

The rapids gradually decreased as the group rode along the river. The she-warriors had just stopped laughing.

"The first crossing point lies just ahead," Ryvan stated.

"Alright, Ayaye, here we come," Tyrese smiled.

"Ayaye is, after all, where the real party starts," Creshvan grinned.

"Yeah, here we have the first dance, right?" Bryen asked.

"Uh, yeah," Shace replied. He was looking for the crossing point which was a few feet ahead. All the warriors had stopped to wait for the she-warriors.

When the she-warriors caught up, everyone began to partner up in groups of two. They would cross together. Ryvan and Tyrese partnered up while Bryen and Creshvan became partners. Shace teamed up with his sister, and the twins partnered. Ryvan and Tyrese noticed the Faeciân girls partnering up, while the brunette partnered up with a warrior who looked like her younger brother.

They prepared to cross the river.

Melanie looked ahead. The group was about to cross, and the first horse began to step into the water. There seemed to be something wrong because the rapids were increasing. It would be very tricky crossing through, because the horses began acting skittish. The river was about twenty yards across. The first group was halfway across, and they were having to work hard against the current. The water rose up to the bottom of the horses' saddles, but they successfully made it across while the other group was halfway. Vera and Shace entered, and then, the last group of warriors. After them, Shanillé and her brother began to venture across.

The rapids were accelerating at an alarming rate. The twins then began.

"Nervous?" Liyah asked.

"Yeah," Melanie replied.

"Don't be," Liyah continued. "Just stick close to me. You'll be fine." However, Liyah looked slightly concerned.

Tyrese and Ryvan began to enter. Tyrese looked back and caught Melanie's eye. He smiled, winked, and stepped down into the raging river.

Melanie and Liyah were the last pair to cross. Melanie's heart began to pound in her chest. She was scared.

"Is it always like this?" Melanie asked.

"No," Liyah trailed off.

The boys had made it halfway against the violent rapids. Liyah took the lead. Melanie's horse stepped down into the water. She steered it toward the shore.

The pair continued as it became harder and harder to stay erect. There was a definite strain on the horses, and their muscles began to work hard while the water continued to rise. It was covering their lower legs now. The water was icy and threatening. They reached the halfway mark.

Tyrese and Ryvan moved up onto the bank. Water dripped from their horses as they lingered on the river's edge to watch and make sure the pair made it across safely.

Then, all at once, the rapids picked up to a dangerous pace. Liyah's horse began to panic, sliding on the rocks at the bottom and began not only to fight the rapids but Liyah as well. Her horse plunged under, and she went with it. Melanie's heart flipped in her chest. She saw Ryvan flinch, and panic began to creep into his eyes. Air bubbles surged up and were quickly swept downstream.

A moment later, Liyah came up sputtering. She jerked the reigns up, and the horse shot up as well. Melanie began to relax, but then her horse became frightened and began to behave like Liyah's. Liyah was steering her horse toward shore, for she had drifted further downstream, but then she saw Melanie.

Melanie struggled to keep above water. Liyah stopped. She looked ashore at Tyrese and Ryvan, then jerked Mystique back toward Melanie, but the rapids kept her from reaching her companion.

Melanie continued to battle the raging waters. She sunk under and then came up sputtering. This went on and on. Liyah tried to reach her, but in one single instant Melanie went under. The only thing that came up was air bubbles. Then nothing.

Liyah looked up at them almost expecting them to do just what they were about to. Liyah turned her horse and fought to reach Melanie. She tried, but Melanie went under.

Everyone stopped. Liyah then fought even harder to reach her. Tyrese charged into the river after the she-warrior.

Melanie stayed underwater. Ryvan watched Tyrese enter and shot in after him. The three fought to reach Melanie. Each slid underwater dangerously every few minutes. All were soaking wet, and gripped with fear.

Liyah reached the segment of the river where Melanie had been when she slid under. They, Tyrese and Ryvan, suddenly appeared by her side. Liyah and Ryvan charged downstream to serve as a blockade while Tyrese dove down into the water, searching. His horse reared in the water and began drifting quickly downstream to where Liyah and Ryvan waited. Ryvan reached out and grasped his reins before he was lost.

Everyone waited anxiously. They waited. Waited, and nothing. Fear crept into both rescuers' faces. They couldn't do anything. If they moved, Tyrese, if he came up, would drift downstream. They had to keep the barrier. They could only continue to fight the current.

Tyrese's horse began whinnying and tossing his head. Ryvan watched the spot with anxious eyes and Liyah began to shake. After a full minute that dragged on for an eternity, they realized that they had lost. The likelihood of Tyrese, Melanie, and Marentex drifting past them unseen was extremely high. Everyone, all at once, hung their heads in despair for the lost. Their worst fears seemed to have been realized.

Liyah looked into Ryvan's eyes. Ryvan gazed back and placed a hand on Liyah's shoulder as they tried to cope with the pain. There was nothing anyone could do at this point.

But then, out of nowhere, Tyrese, Melanie, and her horse all shot up out of the depths, coughing and sputtering for air.

They smiled at each other, then, the pair remounted their horses. All of them, side by side, battled to the edge of the bank, helping each other when the horses slid under.

****

Part II
The Competitions

The depths of a warrior's soul is deep, dark torment,
but an understanding heart draws out the poison.
—ðhumtan 16:8

Chapter 6

As the four approached Ayaye, everyone stared as they passed. Melanie, Tyrese, Liyah, and Ryvan were all drenched. Ever since they made it across the river, they all rode together in their own protective pack, speaking very little. They made an interesting sight.

"Welcome to Ayaye!" a voice called from beside them.

They all turned to see the welcoming committee and were slightly surprised to see a small she-warrior with blonde hair and gray-blue eyes that shone with greeting. She carried a bow on her back and a long sword at her waist.

"Warrior camps are to the right. She-warrior camp is to the left. Enjoy yourselves!"

Liyah noticed there were only two more she-warriors. There were also about seven more warriors. The she-warriors were helping the Beuran girls set up their camp next to theirs. It was late afternoon, so, they would have time to dry off and clean up a bit before the party began.

"Wow," the girl said.

This brought Liyah back. "What?"

"Oh! I'm sorry! I've just never seen anyone actually carry cross-blades. Let alone *four* people. Together."

They smiled. Ryvan just looked at her.

"Oh, it's alright," Liyah smiled. "We get that a lot. See ya!"

They began to ride forward through the gate. They slightly paused, exchanged glances, and in Melanie and Tyrese's case, smiles. Liyah and Ryvan nodded respectfully at each other without smiling. Then, they all headed off in opposite directions to find their friends.

****

"Hello, ladies!" one of the Ayayian she-warriors said as the drenched girls rode up. "We hear you have had a bit of a near death experience."

"Yeah," Liyah said very slowly and with an agitated frown.

"Sorry, but your friends here already told us all about it," the other smiled more warmly.

Melanie just sat there. She began to shake.

"Whoah! Sorry. Sorry!" the first one cried.

Liyah jumped off her horse and helped Melanie dismount. She took Melanie's cross-blades from her, and then drew out a blanket and wrapped it around Melanie's shoulders, forcing her to sit.

Liyah unloaded everything, then went away to take care of the horses. She didn't say a word.

"Liyah! Please come back. Don't be angry," one of the Ayayian girls called.

Liyah continued on.

****

When Liyah returned, there was food waiting on her. The aroma still hung heavily in the air, making Liyah realize how hungry she actually was. The food was still sitting in the pan, keeping it warm. Everyone else had eaten already.

"Left you some food," an Ayayian she-warrior smiled.

"Thanks," she sat down and began to eat. She looked around vaguely and saw her belongings laid out to dry.

"We brought you a spare tent and a pair of sleeping bags," the other smiled.

"Thanks."

Melanie was asleep inside one of the tents. Her eyes opened when she heard Liyah's voice.

"Look who's awake," Shanillé grinned.

Melanie smiled. They had both dried off and been warmed by the late afternoon sun. The small she-warrior that greeted them ran up happily.

"Hey, what's going on?" she asked.

"Hey, Alana! Not much. You finished greeting?" one girl asked.

"Yeah, I am," the girl replied. "Oh! I'm sorry. I didn't remember," She was speaking to Liyah and Melanie now. "I'm Alana."

"Liyah. Pleased to meet you. That's Melanie."

"Hey!" Melanie smiled tiredly as she stretched.

"Well, I'll introduce myself, too," one of the girls said. She had layered black hair that framed her face. It ran a few inches past shoulder length. She had brown eyes. "My name's Maiyah."

"I'm Maicah," the other smiled. She had blonde hair that spiraled down over her shoulders. Her eyes shimmered blue.

"Pleased to meet you," Liyah said around a mouthful of food with a hint of bitterness.

"Something wrong with her?" Vera asked the other sarcastically.

Liyah just looked down. She didn't feel like putting up with people anymore.

"Dry yet?" Ryvan asked Tyrese.

"Yeah," Tyrese laughed. "Finally. What about you?"

The boys had just finished eating and were waiting for the party to start.

"Yeah, however, I didn't get as wet as you did," Ryvan laughed.

"Big hero boys. What's happening?" Bryen asked as he walked up.

"Hey! Where have you been?" Tyrese asked.

"Just spreading the word," he replied briskly.

"You didn't," Ryvan muttered.

"Of course not?" Bryen murmured sheepishly.

"Great. Now everyone is going to know," Tyrese said sarcastically.

"What's wrong with that?" Creshvan asked.

"Because—" Tyrese began.

"No reason," Ryvan interrupted.

"I'm sure," Shace stated suspiciously.

"I think it has something to do with the warrior girls," Bryen laughed.

Ryvan shot him a dirty look, and Bryen immediately ceased his laughter.

"That's *got* to be it," Creshvan teased.

Tyrese glared at him. They remained quiet for awhile, and then an Ayayian warrior came up to their camp. He appeared to be around seventeen. "Excuse me, but do you know where I can find some warriors by the names Ryvan and Tyrese?" His question was directed at Ryvan.

"Right there," Creshvan pointed out the boys.

"Thanks," the boy smiled. "We have heard about what happened in the river, and we were just curious about what exactly, well—what *really* happened."

"We?" Ryvan asked.

"Well, the elders sent me to find you."

"What?" Ryvan and Tyrese exclaimed at the same time.

"Elders?" Ryvan asked in pure bewilderment. "Why? What do Ayayian elders want with us?"

"No idea, but they sent me to find out the facts," the boy replied.

"Before we say anything, I think we need to know why," Ryvan replied.

"Ok," the boy stated. "Follow me."

Tyrese just looked at Ryvan. Ryvan stood. "Tyrese."

Tyrese rose and followed Ryvan and the boy toward the village center.

****

Warriors began to stare as the boys walked past them toward the elders' quarters. Elders were the founders that had gathered survivors and formed the villages after the darkness had risen. The elders seldom called for anyone or came out of their own meeting place. They were loners, carefully watching over their village and making sound decisions to keep peace and posterity in their community. It was very uncommon to summon warriors from other villages.

They continued on without speaking. Ryvan was quietly preparing for the worst. Tyrese was just confused. The boys really had no idea what the elders would want with them.

They reached the village center. The young warrior spoke to a bodyguard at the door to the meeting place. Soon, he let the boy pass through into the center. The bodyguard was a large man with huge arms. He stood about six and a half feet off the ground. He had black eyes and no hair. His body was scarred from many a fight, one of which ran from above his left ear to below the right side of his jaw.

As the boys waited, they took a good look at Ayaye. There was no grass within the village gate which was actually quite common in villages. The dance 'floor' stood only about ten feet from them. A ring of unlit torches and decorations were still being put up for the upcoming party. The huts were very sturdy and homey.

"You may enter," a voice called from within the meeting place. It was an older voice that sounded aged and raspy with many stories behind it. The boys went inside cautiously. The young warrior left quickly as they were entering.

The light wasn't as bright inside as it was outside, making it take a moment for their eyes to adjust to the darkness. When they did, the boys realized they were face to face with an even larger bodyguard than the one at the door. Behind him was another one about the same size. They each took one of the boys aside and removed all their weapons. Ryvan grew somewhat uneasy, but he knew there was little he could do in his situation.

The bodyguards released them, and they were now standing in front of a group of around seven men. They were all wearing long gray hooded cloaks. The cloaks covered the upper area of the elders' faces. The lower part was exposed. This part of their faces was covered with long graying beards. None of them spoke. It seemed as is they were staring straight into them even though their eyes were covered by their cloaks.

Finally, one spoke. It seemed he was the one with the highest position of power. The bodyguards positioned themselves on either side of him with arms crossed, staring straight ahead. The man's voice was one and the same as the voice that had called the boys within. No one stirred. The elders sat still as statues. It was almost like time had paused.

"Where are the others?" the elder's question was directed to his bodyguards.

"They are being sent for," one replied.

"Good," the elder grumbled. "Then, I'll begin with you two alone."

"Come on, Liyah. Don't be like this," Shanillé tried to make her smile as she sat away from the group.

"Don't know how long I'll put up with the insulting comments," Liyah replied. "I have anger problems, and we all know it. Someday, it will get me in too deep."

Shanillé looked down at the ground.

"It's alright. I'm not angry with you or the others," Liyah continued. "I don't know why I feel like this. No worries though, you don't have to say anything."

She just looked up toward the fire where the she-warriors were gathered. Melanie's cross-blades lay next to Liyah who had her own strapped on alongside her other weapons.

As Shanillé opened her mouth to speak, a dark-haired Ayayian warrior strode up to their camp.

"Excuse me, ladies, but I'm looking for Melanie and Liyah."

Vera stared at him darkly. "Why?" she asked angrily.

This clearly had caught him off guard. "Well, I was sent by the elders."

The group gasped. "Elders sent for *she*-warriors?" Vera muttered.

"Yes, they wish to speak with them," the boy stated.

Vera pointed lifelessly toward Liyah and Melanie's tent where Melanie was resting. Liyah watched the boy as he started toward the tent. Liyah was there in an instant, saying, "She's too tired to come. I'm Liyah. I will go."

"I was specifically informed to bring you *both* back with me."

"Right then," Liyah pondered. "I'll go get her."

Liyah entered the tent to wake Melanie who actually *had* fallen back into sleep.

****

The boy brought the girls to the village center where a large bodyguard stood in front of the door. Melanie whimpered. Liyah stood her ground face to face with the huge man with scars on his arms and face. The boy entered quickly. Liyah knew she had made him uneasy. And frankly, she didn't care. She was still testy. The bodyguard and Liyah just stood there, staring at each other for a long time. Then, a deep voice from inside stated with authority, "Enter."

The bodyguard opened the door for them.

The girls strode in. Liyah held her head confidently. Melanie followed closely. When they got inside, they were met with two more bodyguards of larger size. Liyah confronted them in the same manner.

The guys reached for Liyah to take her weapons. Liyah squirmed away. "Don't lay your disgusting hands on me. No one touches me or my weapons, and more importantly *me*."

The bodyguard was momentarily stunned. Then, he began to go after her again.

The elders watched intently. Finally, one stated, "That will not be necessary. Leave her weaponry."

Liyah pushed between the two huge men. Melanie followed, but what they saw made the girls stop short where they were. Tyrese and Ryvan were standing there, staring at them with a blank look creeping across their faces.

"Welcome, ladies," the elders said. "Now we can begin. We have been speaking with these two young men for a while now about something we will speak with you two about momentarily. As of now, we would like to congratulate you for your acts of heroism and bravery. We are all pleased to hear of the survival of one of our treasured she-warriors. There aren't many of you left anymore that we know of."

Ryvan and Tyrese shot the elder dirty looks that had a definite history.

"That you know of?" Liyah asked.

Everyone turned to look at her. "You have a bold heart. You could do well to contain some wisdom in your young over-inflated head, however."

Liyah took a step toward them, but thought better of acting on it.

"Yes, there could be more she-warriors in hiding, but we shall get into that in a moment. On behalf of the Elder Counsel of Ayaye, I would like to say an official congratulation to all of you. Your talents have been recognized, now you two boys may leave. We are finished here and thank you for your cooperation. It is much appreciated. Good-bye and enjoy yourselves at the party."

The bodyguards grabbed them and their stuff, and Tyrese and Ryvan were escorted out roughly.

"Now, we need to have a word with you girls."

Melanie glanced at Liyah who narrowed her eyes darkly, and Melanie grew concerned.

The boys were roughly escorted out of the meeting place. Their weaponry was jabbed at them as soon as they were out. They didn't like the elders. Not very many elders approved of she-warriors. So, the she-warriors had to be very careful around them. Ryvan and Tyrese were worried about the girls.

The boys re-equipped their weapons. The bodyguard at the entrance watched them the whole time. When they turned to leave, the large man called out to them. "Hey! Come here."

They didn't know exactly what to do, so they cautiously walked up to the man.

"What do you know of the taller she-warrior inside?" he queried.

"Not very much," Ryvan stated. "Why?"

"Relax. She just seemed familiar," he replied. "Get on with ya now!" his manner changed instantly.

They boys turned to leave. "One more thing, boys."

They turned back questioningly.

He smiled. "Don't worry about them. They can take care of themselves," the huge guy beamed. "They'll be fine."

Ryvan smiled back and nodded a good-bye. The strange part was that they believed him.

The young warriors ventured back to their camp. Their friends weren't there anymore. They must have gone to check out the Ayayian market before the party began. The boys would wait patiently for some sign that the girls would be alright.

Ryvan then realized something important. He was caring about a she-warrior's fate. That was bad. What was he thinking? Had he lost his mind? He couldn't continue on like this. He was heading for a mess of trouble.

The boys were so worried because of what the elders had told them.

****

"We'll begin with you two alone."

The boys remained obediently silent and listened intently to what the people had to say.

"First, I would like to know what you two boys were thinking," the head elder exploded.

"Huh?" the pair asked in unison. They were slightly confused.

"What were you thinking? You saved two she-warriors from a watery grave."

Now the boys were dumbfounded. "Excuse me, sir. What?" Tyrese asked.

"You 're quite thick, aren't you. You do not need to help she-warriors. They are the most dangerous creatures on the planet. The less, the better." The elder seemed insane.

"You mean," Ryvan began, "you *wanted* us to let them drown?"

"Precisely!" the elder said, exasperated. "Those two must be the most dangerous pair of she-warriors I have ever come in contact with in my entire life. And you two had the perfect opportunity to rid the world of them. Instead, you stepped forward to save their lives."

"Why?" Tyrese asked angrily.

"Haven't you seen them? They have all the signs, cross-blades, armor, steeds, tattoos, the air of fear and intimidation."

"You aren't thinking they are—" a bodyguard began.

The elder interrupted, "Hold your tongue! That will not be spoken in this meeting place!"

The boys were confused. They didn't know what was so wrong with cross-blades. And the girls' horses seemed natural to them. What the boys hadn't known was that the girls had tattoos as well.

"You may think there is nothing odd about them, but we have sound facts to believe that they are the key to something important. Them and two others. The two others are none other than the two of you."

"Huh?" they asked in unison again.

"We aren't concerned about you two any longer, though. Your valiant and heroic efforts today have proven that you have pure hearts. But the others."

"You think they are evil?" Tyrese asked. He was becoming irritable.

"In a matter of speaking, they could contribute to something big," the elder stated mysteriously.

"How big?" Tyrese asked sarcastically.

"Big enough to change our land as Asgarnia was changed."

Everyone in the chamber gasped out loud, everyone except Ryvan. He thought that was where these fat pompous old guys were heading.

"You mean—" Tyrese began.

"Yes," the elder cut him off. "They could contribute to allowing the Dark to rise once more."

The scout rushed in. "They are here," he stated.

"Fine," the elder stated. "Enter! Oh, and boys, not a word. Next time, take the opportunity."

They just stared at him. "Oh, and by the way, this year there are scouts from the Galeãns. They are looking for young, skilled warriors. We want you at your best. You are likely to be selected.

The she-warriors entered cockily, or at least Liyah did. Melanie trailed slowly behind looking confused. Ryvan and Tyrese assumed she was in shock from the river incident. They stopped short after getting into a scuffle with the guards after seeing the two boys.

"Welcome, ladies," the pompous jerk stated. "We may begin now."

The guys just stared at each other, wondering what they were about to begin. This would end badly.

Chapter 7

The boys had just been kicked out, and the girls faced a room full of elders alone.

"I'm sure you are wondering why we are speaking with you privately," the elder smiled.

"In a manner," Liyah replied bitterly. She was extremely cautious and vigilant.

"Well, we will make this short and sweet," the elder began. "Child, you may relax. We mean you no harm."

Liyah realized this comment had been directed at her. She didn't let up any. No way. She wasn't stupid. She understood elders despised she-warriors.

"Fine, have it your way," he stated. "We wanted to inform you there will be scouts from the Galiphems to find the best of the best she-warriors from the Osheyks."

"Why are you telling us of this?" Liyah retorted.

"We want you to have the best training. We have been watching you. You *are* the best of the best, and we want you to be prepared. More likely, you will both be chosen."

"Thanks for that," Liyah stated bitterly. She was very edgy, and Melanie didn't know why. "May we go now?"

"Yes, child. You have much to learn. Perhaps you will learn something useful to fill your head with instead of cockiness," the elder mused.

The girls turned to leave. As they were almost out the door, Liyah turned and smiled sweetly, and in her most angelic voice said, "Perhaps you will find something to drain *your* oversized head from all the hot air. It makes the room stuffy." She turned and stormed out.

Melanie's eyes became wide as she rushed after her.

One of the elders spoke to the leader, "Beg your pardon, sir. Why would we want them trained by Galiphems? Wouldn't that make them more dangerous?"

"Yes, but the Galiphem queen will know from the start that they are trouble, and they will be annihilated before they can disturb anything. If we are lucky, then the Dark shall never rise.

****

"The nerve of that guy!" Liyah exclaimed.

"Calm yourself. I wouldn't have handled it that way if I was you, but it sure was funny," Melanie grinned.

"Maybe I should have handled it like you," Liyah laughed. She stopped to mimic Melanie. She shot her eyes open and threw her hands up. "Deer in the headlights."

"Heh, heh. Shut up."

The girls were back at camp, getting ready for the party. Their friends had gone up early to scout for anything else they liked at the marketplace. The girls were almost ready when they heard the old music being played. They recognized the sounds of the string instruments lifting their music on the air.

****

The girls were pulling on their black heels when they heard a friendly voice call out to them, "Hey! Ready for the party?"

They looked up to see Ryvan and Tyrese strolling toward them. Tyrese was in front slightly. Ryvan seemed cautious and hung back a bit.

"Yeah!" Melanie grinned as she jumped up. Liyah narrowed her eyes.

"Cool, you want to join us?" Tyrese asked excitedly. His eyes shone with boyish hopefulness.

"Uh," Melanie began, then, quickly glanced back at Liyah. "Liyah?"

Liyah shrugged. "What the heck?" She jumped to her feet as Melanie and Tyrese started toward the party.

Liyah shook her head and brushed the dirt off of her leather top with a small sigh. Ryvan smiled, "Do you think it's a good idea to leave them alone together?"

"Yeah, I'm sure they will be fine," Liyah stated.

"Well, let's go to the party," Ryvan said.

Up ahead, Melanie and Tyrese were talking.

"Was it a good idea to just leave them back there?" Melanie asked.

"I think so. If there is no one else around, I imagine that they will speak unless they kill one another first. If we hear the sound of blade on blade, we are in trouble."

They both laughed as they reached the party. They quickly lost themselves in the crowd. Liyah and Ryvan wouldn't find them now.

****

"They are walking fast," Ryvan noted.

"Yeah, they are," Liyah replied.

They were getting really close to the party. Liyah was ready to get there so she could catch up with Melanie and strangle her for leaving her behind. She knew Ryvan was thinking the same thing about Tyrese.

They reached the torch circle, and the music was cut. The introduction was starting. Everyone grew quiet and watched as Alana stood up on stage in front of everyone.

"Wow, that bites," Tyrese stated.

"What does?" Ryvan laughed.

"The elders think the girls are evil," Tyrese said absently.

"They aren't," Ryvan smiled.

"How can you possibly know that?" Tyrese asked.

"I don't know. I just do."

"Whatever, man," Tyrese smiled. "Well, here's an idea."

Ryvan glanced at Tyrese. He was polishing his knife. "What?"

"Since they aren't evil, let's hang out with them tonight."

"Are you kidding me?" Ryvan asked, his eyebrow lifting on one side. "I said they weren't evil, not that we were clear to become best friends with them."

"Come on! Just for tonight!" Tyrese begged.

"Whatever. Let's find something to eat. I'm starving."
"Ok, let's go then," Tyrese smiled. "Step one, complete," he thought to himself.

****

After they grabbed something to eat, the guys returned to camp. They noticed the party was just beginning, and the girls were still at their campsite. The guys let out a sigh of relief. Well, Tyrese did. Ryvan just sighed.
"Well, shall we?" Tyrese asked.
"Whatever," Ryvan replied. The two boys began to head for the she-warrior camp. It was probably not the smartest idea after all.
"Hey! Ready for the party?" Tyrese called out merrily. They had reached the camp where the two girls were preparing for the dance.
They spoke for a moment; then they all headed off toward the center of Ayaye to have fun after a long, stressful day…or at least to try.

****

"Welcome to Ayaye!" the short she-warrior bellowed into the microphone. "Hope you are all pumped for an awesome time!"
The crowd yelled and clapped their hands to express their enthusiasm. Ryvan lightly clapped. He noticed Liyah didn't do anything but stand with her arms crossed, frowning up at the stage. He couldn't help but wonder what the elders had spoken to them about.
"Well, we hope you enjoy yourselves here tonight and have a safe trip tomorrow!"
A few people turned and looked at Ryvan and Liyah. Liyah frowned darkly, and they turned back quickly.

"Ok, then!" she continued. "This year we have seven warriors and three she-warriors continuing on. I am one of them!"

Everyone clapped politely.

"We have a good turnout this year! Oddly, we have seven warriors and four she-warriors from Beura. Also, we have two warriors from Dreán and two she-warriors from Faeciã! These are your heroes!"

Everyone clapped and yelled again. Ryvan's face flushed scarlet. He didn't want to be recognized as a hero. He didn't feel like one.

Wherever Tyrese was, Ryvan knew he felt the same way, but he wondered how Melanie was reacting. Liyah looked like she could have drawn her bow and shot the she-warrior on stage even though they appeared to be friends. She apparently didn't want anyone to talk about it.

"We will say no more! Enjoy yourselves!" the Ayayian girl stepped off the stage, walking in Liyah's direction. When she began walking past, Liyah reached out, twisted one arm around her waist, and flipped the small Ayayian girl backward into the dirt. People began moving away quickly.

Ryvan secured his weapons out of habit. Not many people wore their weapons to the parties. They sensed no threat. Everyone calmed, and the atmosphere subsided as the music began again. The pounding beat was louder than it had been before. Liyah looked up at him, half smiling. It looked like the evening wouldn't be that bad after all.

"Hey!" Liyah yelled over the music. "Follow me!"

Ryvan looked at her. She began to stride off, weaving her way through the tangled bodies of people mingling and dancing. The lanterns hung low from the trees overhead, casting ghostly shadows across faces and illuminating the dance floor. Food piled on a small table to the side of the dance floor, and Ryvan's stomach growled. When he looked back, Liyah was almost gone. He had to run to catch her. She walked incredibly fast.

Liyah led him through the pulsing crowd to the edge of the dance floor. She continued to lead him to an area where the music wasn't quite as loud.

"Hey!" Ryvan called. He had no idea as to what Liyah was doing. "Where are we going?"

"This will work," Liyah said as she stopped, turning to face him.

"Uh, ok," Ryvan mused. "What are we doing? The party is back there."

"I could tell you wanted to speak with me," Liyah stated simply. She gracefully raised an eyebrow into a sarcastically questioning face. Impatience lingered in the corners of her eyes.

"How could you possible know that?"

"I don't know. I just could tell," she smiled briefly. Then she grew serious once more.

Ryvan didn't know this girl very well. She was a complete mystery. However, the more time he spent with her, and the more he found out about her, the more his confusion grew. But, he was continuously drawn to her, and he found that there was nothing he could do.

"Do you see Liyah anywhere?" Melanie asked Tyrese as she scanned the crowd. She rose up to the tip of her toes to get a better view, and she wouldn't look at Tyrese. She felt a sort of uneasiness growing in her gut.

"Nope," Tyrese grinned. "I don't see Ryvan anywhere either."

"Oh, don't worry," Melanie stated. She was fairly distracted. "He's not in any danger. Liyah can handle almost anything."

Tyrese looked at her. He stared for a moment, and then he burst out laughing. He laughed so hard that he doubled over with his arm across his stomach and the other hand braced on his knee.

"What?" Melanie asked, annoyed. Her gaze snapped down at him for a moment. Then she began her search again.

Tyrese laughed in response. Melanie frowned and stopped looking around altogether. She crossed her arms and glared at the boy whose ribs were racked with laughter.

Finally, Tyrese drew back up to his full height. He smiled at Melanie, "It sounds like its perfect."

Melanie was confused and still annoyed. "What are you talking about?"

"I'm sorry," he laughed. "I was just thinking. Ryvan is exactly the same way. He can handle just about anything and is definitely used to being the leader. They both seem to know it, and that is why they can't figure each other out. They are too much alike. More or less, that is what bothers them about one another and why they don't see eye to eye. They don't want to face it."

Melanie turned her head to the left and contemplated. "Do you really think so?"

"I know it."

Melanie grinned as she realized he was right. She still wanted to know where Liyah was along with Ryvan.

The music paused for a minute as the songs switched. Tyrese smiled at her. Melanie forgot Liyah for a moment.

****

"What is it you wanted to ask me?" Liyah asked. She brushed a lock of her long blonde hair from her face. She was facing Ryvan now, and he could see a strange shape on her arm. He glanced at it, realizing that it was a half moon encircled in fire. His stomach twisted, and he felt his sun tattoo burn beneath his skin.

Already unsettled, Ryvan tried to focus. "Well, I don't really know how to put it," Ryvan stumbled.

"Go for it," Liyah stated calmly. "Shoot."

He remained quiet and looked away toward the party. He finally gazed back at her when he found the words to say. He suddenly lost all his words when he spotted her. The moonlight laced down on her face, drawing her, radiant, out of the darkness. All words were lost to him.

Liyah had no idea as to what possessed him to stare at her like that. She grew uncomfortable, shifted her weight, and finally said, "Hello? Care to come back and join me on Earth?"

That seemed to snap Ryvan out of his trance.

"Well?" Liyah asked. She proudly folded her arms.

"To start, I'll ask the question that has been bothering me the most," Ryvan began. Liyah raised one of her eyebrows. "Ok, the elders told us that you and your friend could contribute to allowing the dark to rise once again. As in the fall of Asgarnia. What do you know of this? Is it true?" he blurted the end without even thinking.

He knew it wasn't, and he mentally kicked himself. That was a stupid question to ask. Normally, one does not walk up to someone as mysterious as Liyah and say, "Hi! Are you evil?"

Liyah grew silent. Then the girl did something Ryvan would have never expected. She laughed loudly.

Ryvan stared, flabbergasted, as she laughed.

"Ok…ok…what? You're telling me, hold on a sec," Liyah wiped her eyes. "So, you, right here, are telling me, right now, that the elders think that we, Melanie and I, are evil?"

"Well, yeah," Ryvan said.

This brought another round of laughter from Liyah. Tears were streaming down her face now. "Are they crazy? Did you actually believe them?" she paused. He half nodded. "Are *you* crazy?" She tried to sustain her laughter a little more.

"Excuse me?" Ryvan asked.

"I'm sorry, but that's absurd!" Liyah became serious again. "In answer to your question, no, we have nothing to do with the dark side."

Ryvan looked doubtful.

"What? You don't believe me?"

"Uh—"

"You don't. Do you?" Liyah asked in shock.

"Well, I—"

"You don't! You've got to be kidding me. This is ridiculous!"

"What am I supposed to think?"

"I," Liyah trailed. "I don't have to put up with this."

"Liyah, wait!"

"I don't think so," Liyah stated coldly. She turned back toward the party. She stormed away as fast as she could, leaving Ryvan to stare after her.

He knew she wasn't evil. What was he thinking? Personally, he didn't know. Liyah stormed out to the party. She stomped directly past Melanie and Tyrese without even realizing it.

"Liyah?" Melanie asked in bewilderment. "Liyah!" Melanie stared for a moment, looked at Tyrese and stated, "I'm sorry, but I—"

"I understand," Tyrese replied almost sadly.

Melanie smiled and called after her friend once more. She ran to catch Liyah. Apparently, they were headed for camp.

"Oh boy," Tyrese sighed. "What did he do?"

Bryen raced up to Tyrese after Melanie had raced after Liyah. Bryen asked quickly, "Hey, what happened?"

"I don't know," Tyrese replied, "but I'm about to go find out for myself."

"How are you going to do that?" Bryen questioned.

"I'm going to go chat with my good friend Ryvan." Tyrese stalked off in the direction Liyah had charged away from with such bitter fury.

****

Tyrese walked until he saw Ryvan. He decided that before he spoke with him, he would calm down. That way, he wouldn't do anything irrational he would wind up regretting later.

Ryvan sat on the ground with his back to Tyrese, and for once he wasn't aware of anything. He didn't even realize Tyrese was approaching him. He sat with his face in his hands. He had seen the pained expression on Liyah's face of hurt and disgust.

Personally, he was disgusted with himself. He hadn't meant to come across the way he had.

"Ryvan," Tyrese called out.

Ryvan didn't speak or turn to face him.

"Ryvan!" Tyrese repeated.

"What?" he mumbled the answer quietly.

"What happened?" Tyrese asked in a more gentle voice. "Why was Liyah so upset?"

Ryvan looked at him and stated monotonously, "I'm a jerk. She thinks I don't believe her."

"About what?"

"About not being black hearted."

"Oh, I thought you believed her."

"I thought I did, but," Ryvan frowned.

"What?"

"I got confused. She confuses me. I look at her, and I get confused," Ryvan blurted.

Tyrese laughed.

"It's not funny!" Ryvan barked. "Now she is mad at me, but I really do believe her. I was just curious. That's all."

Tyrese sensed movement behind a building. He noticed Shace, Creshvan, and Bryen crouching in the shadows, listening intently.

"Mad is an understatement, my friend," Tyrese stated.

Ryvan shook his head. "It's more like she hates my guts."

Tyrese sat quietly, allowing Ryvan to blow off some steam. It was the only way he could because there were no training grounds in Ayaye for out-of-town use.

Finally, Tyrese began to speak. "Maybe you should apologize?"

Ryvan lifted his head from his clasped hands. He rose up off of the ground in one swift motion. Then, he stated, "What's the point? She won't listen, and when I see her next I'll try, but she *won't* listen to me."

"How do—" Tyrese began.

Ryvan interrupted, "Man, just forget it!" He stormed off toward their campsite. Ryvan's temper had been set off because of a girl. Oh, not just *any* girl…*no*…a she-warrior.

Tyrese breathed another, "Oh, boy."

He turned to his friends once Ryvan was out of earshot and smiled, "Here we go."

"What was *that* about?" Bryen asked.

"I don't think I have ever seen Ryvan behave in a manner like that before," Shace stated matter-of-factly.

Tyrese stared at the ground for a minute then glanced back up, beaming from ear to ear and said, "I know why."

"You know why Ryvan is acting like this?" Creshvan asked.

"Yup. Well, it's an assumption," Tyrese smiled as he watched the eager faces of his companions.

"Well?" Bryen asked.

"It looks like he *actually* cares about her."

They all raised their eyebrows at Tyrese's unexpected comment. A few jaws even dropped.

Chapter 8

"Liyah!" Melanie called as she pursued her friend. "Liyah!"

Liyah didn't want to stop. It was obvious, but she turned around anyway. "What?" she asked. She knew what Melanie was going to say, but she didn't want to answer that either.

"What happened?" she asked as she finally caught up with her.

"You'll never guess," Liyah began. "He thought—"

Just then, Shanillé and Alana ran up. Shanillé looked concerned. Alana seemed confused.

"Are you alright?" Shanillé asked gently.

"Yes, I'm fine," Liyah replied.

"Are you sure?" Shanillé pressed the issue.

"Yes."

"Ok, then, let's go back to the party!" Alana laughed. She was trying to cheer Liyah up. She meant well.

Melanie glanced at her stupidly.

Alana grabbed Liyah's hand and started back toward the party. Liyah stood her ground. When Alana realized that Liyah wasn't coming, she dropped her hand and asked, "What's wrong?"

"I think I'll just go back to camp," Liyah replied. Shanillé and Alana looked at her quizzically. "I'm tired. I don't feel like going back."

"Ok, suit yourself," Alana stated blandly. "Come on, Melanie, let's go."

Melanie glanced back and forth between Alana, Shanillé, and Liyah. "I think," Melanie mused, "I'll go back to camp, too."

"Fine, have it your way," Alana grumbled as she stalked off sadly because the two girls had rained on her parade.

Shanillé looked at them and then, stood in the same spot for a while, looking them over. Alana finally came back and cried, "Shanillé! Are *you* coming?"

Shanillé gazed questioningly at the pair, and they encouraged her to go back to the party. "Yeah, I guess so," she called back to her irate friend.

Shanillé left the pair to join Alana who waited impatiently. Alana's face changed to a complete look of contentment when Shanillé appeared at her side. They turned to go, leaving Liyah and Melanie standing in the middle of nowhere.

Liyah turned back toward camp and began walking in a calmer manner.

"Are you going to tell me?" Melanie asked as she fell into step.

"Yes, but not tonight. I will tell you tomorrow as we are leaving for Corytz."

Melanie stopped in her tracks. Liyah stopped, too, and asked, "What's the matter?"

"I don't want to cross the river."

Liyah realized that the thought of crossing scared Melanie into a state of immobility.

"Hey, it will be alright," Liyah comforted. "The river isn't always like that. It was unnatural that day. I can guarantee that nothing will go wrong tomorrow."

"I don't know."

"I do," Liyah stated wholeheartedly. Nothing hazardous will befall you."

****

The girls woke to the smell of food cooking. They withdrew from their tent after cleaning themselves up. When they withdrew, they saw all of the she-warriors packing up.

"Morning!" Miacah called.

"Morning," the girls said in unison.

Melanie let out a yawn, and her stomach growled. "I guess I'm hungry."

"We are, too," Siscilia grinned.

"We decided to wait for you!" Christina smiled.

"You guys didn't have to do that," Liyah stated around a yawn. She stretched, appearing like a giant.

"Yeah, we wanted to," Vera stated as she packed her items onto her horse.

They all smiled happily and joked with each other as the nine she-warriors meandered up to the village center to eat breakfast. It was their day to be first in line.

Once there, the girls charged to the front of the line aggressively. The guys patiently stepped aside. When Liyah reached the halfway point of the line, she noticed Ryvan watching her from the corner of his eye. She walked right past him without even looking up. She was determined to enjoy her breakfast.

After the girls ate, they quickly returned to their campsite to resume their packing. Once they had finished loading their horses, they still had some time before setting out to Corytz. So the girls decided to go check out the market.

After looking around for about half an hour, the girls headed back.

"It's a shame you didn't get to have a better look around Ayaye," Liyah smiled.

"Oh, well," Melanie replied. "We can always check it out on the way back."

Liyah considered that briefly and very slowly and carefully said, "Yeah."

Melanie stopped bounding along and asked, "What? Do you think we might not come back?"

"I don't know. It's just a feeling."

Melanie raised her eyebrows.

"Or, maybe it's something more." Liyah turned away and frowned darkly. It was usually wise for her to trust her instincts.

****

The she-warriors mounted their horses. They were off to a late start. Everyone else had left already. They all coaxed their horses into a trot. Liyah and Melanie lingered near the back, so they could speak of Ryvan.

"So now there is no one around," Melanie exclaimed when the other she-warriors were a good distance from them.

Liyah drew in a deep breath and told Melanie all that Ryvan had told her last night.

"Wow," Melanie replied, awestruck. "I didn't think we were evil. We aren't, are we?"

"No!" Liyah snapped.

"Well, I think you need to talk to Ryvan a little more about it before getting too angry. Not to mention, you might be throwing something important right out the window forever."

"What is that supposed to mean?" Liyah barked.

"Oh, nothing," Melanie smiled innocently as she urged her horse to up its pace.

Liyah was left staring after her, feeling annoyed, hurt, and angry. She willed her horse to move faster. It was simple. Melanie thought she was overreacting, and that he was actually *good* for her.

Liyah scoffed at this. A man was the *last* thing she needed. She was at the apex of her ability and was on top of her game. They were of no need to Liyah. At least she willed her mind into thinking so as she opened up her leather-bound book. She needed some of the peace she sometimes found in reading it.

"What's the plan?" Tyrese happily asked Ryvan as he mounted his horse.

"What plan?" Ryvan questioned.

"You know, the plan where you apologize to Liyah."

"Oh, that plan," Ryvan mumbled.

"What are you going to do?" Tyrese asked intently.

"I'm going to try to talk to her when we reach the river," Ryvan stated as he climbed into his position atop the horse.

"I see," Tyrese contemplated.

The pair of warriors followed the others onto the trail of Corytz. They were drawing closer to Corresponding Point every day.

Tyrese quietly glanced around, trying to spot the she-warriors. They were nowhere within his line of vision. The guys continued on without hesitation.

Tyrese went over Ryvan's 'plan' in his mind until he came up with a plan of his own. Ryvan wouldn't like it, and neither would Liyah, but Tyrese was certain it would work. Ryvan just needed a little help getting started.

When the group was just a few yards from the river, they heard fast-approaching hooves coming in their direction. Everyone turned to see the she-warriors racing toward them at a high speed. The she-warriors drew closer, but none of them showed signs of slowing down, let alone stopping. The warriors' horses were growing tense. The girls were not going to stop. They ripped right past the guys, making some of their horses rear and making the hair on the back of their necks stand on end. One warrior was thrown from his horse.

That wasn't the end to their daring moment. The she-warriors raced straight on toward the river's crossing point. They weren't slowing down, and it appeared that they would run directly into the river. At the very last moment, their horses slid to a halt, and the she-warriors stared expectantly back at the warriors. The leader of the whole troupe, closest to the river, sitting atop her prancing and rearing mount, with her hair flying in the wind, and eyes aflame with a cocky look in them, was Liyah, staring down into Ryvan's soul.

This made Ryvan's horse rear back again. When he calmed it, Liyah was no longer staring at him. She was talking to Shace's sister who laughed loudly, but Liyah contained herself and prepared to cross the river.

The warriors approached and jumped down from their horses to secure their belongings. Liyah was at Melanie's horse securing the load. When she left for her horse to secure her own items, further away from all of the other she-warriors, both guys made their moves.

Ryvan led his horse over to Liyah's while Tyrese led his over to Melanie's. They began to talk while Ryvan attempted to apologize—something he was *awful* at.

"Liyah," he began. She looked up from her work to see who it was, only to glance back down. "I think we need to talk."

Liyah didn't look up or reply. Silent treatment.

"Ok, I'll talk then," Ryvan stated.

Liyah acted like he wasn't there and mounted. At this point, everyone was partnering up. All of the groups were the same except for two. Apparently, Tyrese had taken matters into his own hands, because he was now partnered with Melanie.

Ryvan felt his anger sizzle inside him once again.

Liyah noticed, too, and Ryvan waited to see her reaction. She just stood there, in one spot, staring at the river. Ryvan could see the wheels turning inside her brain. Everyone had partnered except for her and Ryvan.

Ryvan rode up to her and stated, "I guess we're partners."

She glared at him, and Ryvan noticed her eyes had a red tint to them. She faced back to the river.

Two warriors from Ayaye were about to cross the river when Liyah silently rode up behind them and venomously hissed, "Move."

The warriors whipped around. Liyah looked straight and entered the river alone.

"You can't go in there alone!" one of the warriors cried.

Liyah didn't turn or stop. Her horse was completely in the water now.

The warriors began to panic, and one yelled, "Who is her crossing partner?"

Ryvan raced up to the river and splashed into it. Liyah continued to cross on her own. Ryvan ventured after her quickly. She was clearly ignoring all dangers of crossing the Pricein River alone. Even when her horse slipped she continued on as if nothing happened as water reached up to her shoulders.

After that, she made it across fairly easily, however, because the river's currents were hardly pulsing against the horse's body. Liyah steered her horse to the bank and spun around with an acrid look on her face.

Ryvan crossed and looked back to watch the others. Liyah stared silently watching. He decided it was best that he wait and let her calm down before he tried to talk to her again.

Tyrese and Melanie were the last to leave the bank. Melanie wouldn't enter the water. Tyrese willed her to follow him. They conversed for a long period of time. The ones on the other side of the river couldn't hear what was said, but eventually, Melanie entered and crossed the river to where Liyah and the other she-warriors waited. When they got there, Liyah met them and hissed, "Don't help."

They didn't speak anymore. Melanie attempted, but Liyah turned her horse away in the direction of Corytz in silence.

Melanie gazed at the two warriors and shrugged her shoulders apologetically. The two halfway smiled at her. Melanie wheeled around and followed.

Ryvan decided that this girl was extremely headstrong.

"Liyah, I'm sorry," Melanie stated.

Melanie was totally surprised by her reaction.

"It's ok," Liyah smiled sweetly. "It was just uncomfortable. That's all."

"Oh, ok," Melanie grinned. "It was Tyrese's idea anyway."

"Oh really?" Liyah asked. "Remind me to thank him later." Satisfaction surged through her voice.

Melanie mentally kicked herself.

"I know you want me to speak with Ryvan, but I couldn't bring myself to do it. It just wasn't the time. Perhaps tonight."

"Ok, I trust you," Melanie replied.

Liyah grinned at her.

Suddenly, a terrifying woman's shriek rose up from the back of the traveling party. Liyah flipped in her saddle, tearing her bow from her back. She was unprepared to see one of the warriors from Ayaye torn from his saddle and thrown to the ground. The scream everyone thought to have belonged to a woman actually belonged to a six foot long, from tail to nose, mountain lion.

Now, she pinned her prey, looming over him while he was trapped beneath her weight. Liyah released an arrow from her quiver, lodging her weapon in the beast's right front leg. When the arrow struck, the mountain lion jerked back, lifting off the warrior, releasing another wild scream into the mountain air. While she turned to fasten her lantern eyes on Liyah, the warrior scrambled out of harms reach.

However, Liyah had become the cat's target. She heard Melanie whimper beside her. Liyah locked eyes with the tawny cat's green ones. The cat had a fierce beauty and sleek walk as it began to circle Liyah and her horse. At Liyah's guidance, Mystique slowly began to circle in response.

Everyone remained still. The tension hung in the air, and the monster cat emitted a low growl, ducking her head. Liyah prepared another arrow. The she-warrior slid her left foot out of the stirrup and dug her right further down. She could feel the weight of everyone's eyes on her. She smiled slightly. With the slight show of Liyah's teeth, the cat pounced, muscles straining and claws extending, toward Liyah.

The she-warrior had anticipated the moment, and time seemed to slow. In one fluid motion, she released her arrow and leapt back from her saddle by placing all her weight on the right stirrup. This caused Mystique to rocket forward out of harm's way, and Liyah freefell back, watching as her arrow sunk into the cat's chest.

Liyah landed hard on her back. The cat landed directly on top of Liyah, and she heard several screams come from the group. A cloud of dust wrapped around the two of them, and Liyah found she could not move her arms or legs as they were pinned beneath the weight of the great cat. The she-warrior was trapped helplessly, but the teeth and claws did not tear into her flesh. After a few seconds, Liyah felt her oxygen return to her as the giant cat was pulled off of her body.

She looked up as Ryvan stood over her, offering a helping hand. She glared wildly at him and refused his offer of help. She lifted herself up, ignoring her aching limbs, and dusted herself off. The warrior seemed to sigh as he put his crossbow back in place on his back.

Liyah frowned and looked toward the massive body of the cat. Four other arrows had been lodged just behind the cat's foreleg. These arrows had killed the cat, and she owed the archer her life.

As Liyah came to this realization, Ryvan walked over toward the cat, reached down, and pulled the four arrows out of the cat's body.

****

"'Ello there! Welcome to Corytz!" a big man with a shaggy beard smiled when the girls entered Corytz. "Well, well, well, it appears we have a few more she-warriors this year. That is *just* what we need," the man breathed. "She-warrior camp will be to the right. Enjoy yourselves."

"Well, that was rude!" Shanillé exclaimed as the group moved away.

"What do you expect, Shanillé?" Liyah stated. "This is Corytz, the only village on the way to Corresponding Point that doesn't allow she-warriors from their hometown."

"Really?" Melanie asked.

"Yeah," Miacah replied. "The elders do not tolerate them."

"I have a question," Alana said.

Everyone looked at her.

"Are there elders everywhere, or are they just in the Osheyk Mountains?"

"It is said that not all villages have elders. Very few outside of the Osheyks do, like Draconiâ. Also, it is said that there were elders in one other place," Christina said.

"What place?" Melanie asked.

"Well, Asgarnia," Siscilia replied cautiously.

"Asgar—" Melanie began.

"Sh!" Vera exclaimed. "Don't let them hear!"

"Hear what?" Melanie asked.

"Sh!"

The girls finished speaking and slid out of their saddles to set up their campsite, avoiding some curious looks from the warriors they had passed on the way.

It was about five o'clock, and there was a booth set up in the village center with food on it that people could take for themselves. The girls were starving, so, after they finished setting up, they decided to go eat while several Corytzan warriors watched. They didn't want to approach she-warriors after both the river incident and the mountain lion situation, knowing one of the she-warriors was severely angry. Then the games would start after everyone had their fill, and they would be able to join in until the dance started.

The food tasted great. The girls sat at the booth and savored the sweets until they were satisfied. When they finished, they noticed all of the warriors coming their way. They decided to get out of there and check out the village while the guys ravaged the table of food.

After crossing the river, Tyrese rode up to Ryvan who stared blankly after Liyah. Tyrese knew he was preparing to explode. The warriors and she-warriors began to follow Liyah and Melanie. When most of them cleared out, Tyrese braced himself. The explosion would begin in three…two…one."

Ryvan whipped around to face him. "What did you do that for?" he snapped.

"What was what for?" Tyrese asked innocently.

"Don't play dumb, Tyrese. Why did you leave me to partner with her when you *knew* she wasn't even *speaking* to me?"

"I figured it would break the ice, man. I'm really sorry. I really didn't think she would act like *that*. Melanie didn't think so either," Tyrese explained.

"It's ok," Ryvan had calmed down a bit. "You should have seen it. Her eyes turned red!"

"Red? Ryvan, are you feeling ok?" Tyrese asked.

"I'm fine. Her eyes really were red," Ryvan stated. "It was cool and creepy at the same time."

Tyrese laughed. "After she had crossed, it looked like she was trying to prove something to you."

"What do you mean?" Ryvan asked.

"I don't really know. It seemed like she was trying to prove a point and challenge you at the same time. It was weird. You can't tell me you didn't notice," Tyrese stated.

"I know what you mean," Ryvan replied. "I noticed. I just wanted to hear your ideas."

"What was your point of view on it?"

The guys had begun moving along, but they lingered near the back to avoid being overheard. "I think the same thing you did, but the way she looked at me, it was like she was looking *into* me, not *at* me."

"Creepy," Tyrese laughed.

"It kind of was," Ryvan drifted.

"You want to know what I think?" Tyrese asked, becoming serious once more.

"I have a feeling that you are going to tell me."

"Ha, ha!" Tyrese grinned. "No, seriously, this is what I think. I think she likes you, or at least tolerates you, but she keeps willing herself not to. She is calloused and cold. That seems to be her interior and the harder part is the exterior…just like you."

"Hey!"

"Face it, man. You *are*."

That was when they heard the mountain lion scream and watched as the warrior was torn from his saddle. Ryvan tore his crossbow from his back, catching a glimpse of an arrow fly forward into the monster's front leg.

He scanned the crowd of scattering warriors, searching for the warrior who had been brave enough to interfere. Somehow, he knew it would be Liyah.

She sat atop her white horse, hair flying back from her face, tangling wildly. Her eyes were fierce, and her anger seethed. A knot of horror clutched Ryvan's stomach as the giant cat turned on Liyah. It was then that he felt an overwhelming urge to protect her at any cost.

Tyrese turned to his companion and saw Ryvan turn pale. Ryvan eyes blazed as he leaped from his saddle, rolling on the earth to keep from harming his legs. He bolted upright and charged toward the cat and Liyah as they circled one another. As the cat leaped, Ryvan began releasing arrow after arrow into the giant cat's heart even after the first had killed it.

****

Ryvan grew silent. Tyrese guessed he was consumed in his own thoughts. Liyah's rejection of his offer of help had stung him. He also could not understand the surge of protective instinct that had overtaken him. He tried to ignore it, but even suppressed, the idea ate at his soul.

The warriors and she-warriors still had about two hours to Corytz. They had run out of deer jerky on the way to Ayaye, so they naturally grew hungry. When they reached Corytz, they would be able to eat at the food booth. The only bad thing about that was they had to wait and let the ladies go first. They did every year. And if the she-warriors didn't get their way, then there would be trouble.

While Ryvan thought about whatever was going through his complex mind, Tyrese thought about what the Ayayian elders had said about scouts coming down to look for warriors. Tyrese was excited and nervous at the same time. He wondered if he really was the best of the best. Any warrior would dream about being a member of the Galeãns. They would even envy a member of the Gryafans, which was the second best group of warriors in the entire land of Shroeketia. It would be a great honor to be considered for a position in either. Not very many people made it. It was the same for she-warriors who tried to get into the Galiphems or the Galatrans. Tyrese wondered if she-warrior scouts were coming down. He imagined they were going to if warrior scouts were coming.

"Do we really act alike?" Ryvan finally asked. This jerked Tyrese out of his thoughts.

"Huh? Oh, yeah, you guys really do. I hate to break it to you," Tyrese replied.

Ryvan grew silent again and left Tyrese to think again. Ryvan thought about things, too, as they continued on their journey to Corytz. The only difference was that he thought on a different level than his companion.

Despite the circumstances, they were enjoying themselves. They loved these games in Corresponding Point. Every year they enjoyed coming. Ryvan felt a twitch of sadness inside. He suddenly felt he wouldn't see anything in the area again. It was an absurd thought, but it attempted to overtake him. It would have, but Ryvan forced it out of his mind.

****

"Welcome to Corytz!" a fat man with a beard greeted them. "Good to see you boys! It's always good to see so many young warriors and so *few* she-warriors!"

The boys glanced at one another briefly, and Tyrese stated, "Thank you, sir."

"Anytime!" he boomed. He was a friendly man, but he was a typical Corytzan. He appeared to extremely dislike she-warriors. "Warrior camp is to the left! Enjoy yourselves, boys!"

Once again, Tyrese smiled, "Thank you, sir."

The guys reached the designated area and found their friends. They set up their tents, tied their horses, and flopped down on the ground in the center of the circle of tents that belonged to their friends. The rest of the guys also sat down on the ground next to the two boys. They sat around and joked with each other while the she-warriors ate. They waited around for awhile with nothing to do.

"Those girls can really pack it away," Creshvan laughed.

The guys joined in as well. Creshvan was right. The girls just kept eating.

"I don't know about you all, but I'm going to go eat," Shace grinned as he jumped off the ground and dusted himself off.

"Are you serious?" Bryen asked.

"Yeah, I'm serious!" Shace beamed. "Who's with me? What about you, hero?"

He was talking to Ryvan who glowered at him.

"Hey, I'll go," Tyrese stated. "I'm starving."

Shace helped pull Tyrese to his feet, and the two of them began to venture to the snack booth. All the others jumped up and followed their lead. Along the way, Corytzan warriors joined them. When the she-warriors saw them coming, they scattered like frightened rabbits.

"Hey!" Creshvan grinned. "Let's feed our faces, boys."

They all dug in. They tried to hurry because they wanted to get to the games, but they were so hungry that they wound up taking their time and ate their fill. Eventually, the games started without them.

Chapter 9

The Corytzan games were not much different than Corresponding Point games. When warriors were in Corytz, the games were like a giant carnival. There were different booths with different games. The only difference was they were able to play for free. There were games where warriors could win prizes by throwing a ball through a ring or knocking over bottles. There were also different card games being played for the warriors who were willing to bet.

    The girls wandered around, watching the people set up the booths. The games would be open until the dance ended.

    Liyah ventured off to play some Corytzan warriors in some old gambling card game. The player to get the highest number without going over the limit would win. The warriors would have to bluff their best to keep the other players from figuring out what kind of hand they had. When Liyah sat down, she received some wary looks, and catcalls were heard.

    She merely smiled and said, "Deal me in, fellas."

    Eventually, she hustled the guys and took her earnings along with the warriors' pride.

    The girls then viewed the area and decided to come back later. It was always more fun when it grew dark. Corytz and Corresponding Point threw the best parties.

    The trek back to camp was uneventful. The highlight of it was watching Vera run into a Corytzan warrior when they walked past the food booth.

    She wasn't paying any attention to where she was going. When they were passing the booth, a warrior was getting up and had his back turned to where he couldn't see her coming. By the time he turned around and saw her, it was too late, and she ran right into him. Vera was knocked to the ground.

"I am so sorry!" the warrior exclaimed. He reached out a hand to help her up.

"Hey! Why don't you watch where—" Vera yelled. She suddenly changed her tone when she saw the guy that had knocked her down. He was about six feet tall. He had concerned dark brown eyes and dimples in his cheeks when he smiled. She actually took his offered hand and said, "Oh, it's alright. It was my fault anyway!"

They stood there and stared at each other for a long time. Out of nowhere, Shace ran up to Vera and stood behind her angrily.

"Oh, sorry! Is this your girlfriend?" the guy asked innocently.

"No!" Shace exclaimed. "Sister!" His words dripped with venom.

"Sorry, dude," he turned to leave and looked back at Vera again. "I hope you are alright."

Everyone stood there, stupefied. Shace grew angry and walked off after Vera punched him on the arm violently. Every one of the she-warriors burst out laughing and took off running back to camp while Vera chased them down.

Liyah briefly ran back to grab some cookies for herself and Melanie.

****

About an hour later, it began to grow dark. The torches were lit, and the music began to play. The girls were preparing to go to the Corytzan games.

The dance would begin in one hour. The girls had that much time to waste at the games. For once, Liyah didn't put on her bow or cross-blades. She even left her knives behind except for one, but it was hidden. She didn't want them to interfere with the outcome of the games.

"Are you guys ready?" Vera asked happily.

"Yeah," Liyah called over her shoulder. "Ready when you are."

"Let's go then!" Vera grinned.

"Ok," Melanie smiled back. "We're coming!"

The girls ventured toward the gaming area. The guys had left the booth and were playing several of the different games already. The girls strode into the area, and they split into different directions immediately.

Melanie and Liyah raced off to play the games they wanted to play. They wound up winning a lot of prizes off the game where Melanie had to knock bottles over using a small ball. Liyah was better with a game where she threw daggers at animal skin pouches, bursting them open, releasing bright colored liquids onto the ground. One of the prizes Melanie won was a bag of rare chocolates that the girls shared as they continued to play. Melanie frowned at the candy, trying to figure out the best way to eat it. She flicked her tongue out, licking its edge. She did not get a satisfactory taste and decided to bite into the end. Her eyes lit up as she bit down, letting the smooth richness flood over her tongue. Chocolate had become scarce in Shroeketia.

They were walking past different gaming booths to see which one they wanted to play next. Liyah noticed an old game that some warriors, Shanillé, and Alana were playing. The players were all tangled up, reaching in different places at different colored spots.

Suddenly, two of the three warriors fell and took out Shanillé. Alana and one warrior remained. A few more moves went by, and their arms and legs began to twitch.

At that moment, the loudspeaker came on, and a voice boomed, "Will all warriors and she-warriors please report to the village center?"

Alana and the warrior collapsed in a pile and laughed at each other. Liyah and Melanie giggled quietly and rushed away. Then, when Alana was out of earshot, they burst out laughing.

They reached the center as the man that "welcomed" them spoke. He listed the numbers and blah blah blah—same old same old. He finished speaking, and the music started up again. The people actually began to dance. Liyah was surprisingly having a good time, despite her earlier mood. She hadn't seen Ryvan for awhile and smiled to herself.

A slow song Liyah and Melanie didn't know came on over the sound system. Warriors began to find she-warriors to dance with. Liyah noticed Vera was dancing with the guy she had run into, and Alana was dancing with the boy from the game. Liyah shook her head.

Everyone had lost their minds.

At that moment, Liyah became aware of someone approaching. She glanced up and saw a warrior striding confidently toward Melanie and herself.

"Excuse me," he said, "but I was wondering if you would like to dance with me?"

His question was directed at Melanie. She glanced at Liyah questioningly. Liyah smiled at her and walked off to get herself some punch while the pair danced.

Most of the warriors knew who Liyah was, and they were afraid of her. Melanie, however, was new meat. Liyah had placed third last year in the Corresponding Point games. Most warriors avoided the top marksmen and combat experts. Plus, Liyah had not improved her image with the stunt at the river. She didn't care.

The two that had beaten her were twin sisters from Ayaye. They had supposedly been recruited by the Galatrans, which were the second best league of female warriors in Shroeketia, maybe even the world.

Ryvan stood toward the back of the group, observing. The boys just returned from the games. They hadn't done great. They won a few prizes, but not many.

Tyrese and Ryvan were scanning the crowd silently, watching for their targets. Then, Tyrese decided to go looking for Melanie since he couldn't see her from where he was standing.

Ryvan rolled his eyes, not just at Tyrese, but at himself as well. He realized that he had come across completely wrong. He decided that he would apologize tonight. He had to at least try.

Finally, Ryvan spotted his elusive target. She was standing alone by the punch bowl. Now was as good a time as any. Ryvan took a deep breath and began walking calmly toward Liyah.

Liyah glanced at him, then glanced away as if she hadn't seen him, and she snapped her head around again to face him. Her eyes grew large, but she just stayed where she was.

Ryvan slowed a bit and approached cautiously. "Hey!" he called over the music.

She glanced at him shortly, "Hey." She looked away.

They both grew silent. They watched the people dancing. Ryvan decided to break the solitude. "Liyah?"

She looked up at him respectfully and took a drink of her punch.

"I," Ryvan paused. "I think I owe you an apology."

Liyah looked confused. A pained expression crossed her face, and grimacing, she put down her cup. "No, well, I owe you an apology as well."

Ryvan grinned at her and said, "I really would like to talk to you more about this."

"Come on!" Liyah shouted. "Let's go somewhere we can talk."

Ryvan stood there hesitantly and realized that was why they got in a fight in the first place. Quickly, he chased after her.

The pair walked side by side without speaking. They walked to a deserted area outside the center of Corytz. A garden full of different flowers and small man-made pools sprinkled throughout greeted them. The town was much more lucrative than Dreán or Faeciã combined. Since Corytz could afford to splurge in décor, it was far more elaborate than either of their small villages.

They found themselves in a small central garden. It was quiet enough that they could speak privately, yet they could still faintly hear the music in the distance. The pair walked along a path past assorted bushes, trees, and flowers. Everything was lush and green.

It was a still night. There wasn't much of a breeze. The stars glistened in the sky above. Fireflies danced among the plants. At the end of the path, a small gazebo waited. The pair walked into it and saw a small bench where they decided was the best place to sit and discuss the matter privately.

"I really am sorry, Liyah. I went about this all wrong. I should have spoken calmly about the matter with you."

"Yes, you should have," Liyah quickly responded, "but I shouldn't have become so angry so quickly. I have a bad temper which is one of my worst characteristics."

They had to laugh at that. "So, thank you for saving me today. I owe you my life. Is it possible for us to talk civilly about our problems now?" Liyah asked, becoming a bit more serious.

"Don't mention it, Liyah. I couldn't live with myself if I hadn't rescued you. If you would like to talk now, I would as well," Ryvan replied.

"Yeah, I would," Liyah smiled. "So, tell me exactly what happened."

Ryvan told the whole story, even the part about the bodyguard. Liyah stared ahead, mystified.

"Why would they think that?" she asked, bewildered.

"I have no idea."

"Why would they want me dead?"

"No idea."

"Evil? Really? What were they thinking?"

"Once again, no idea."

Liyah seemed upset.

"They just think you two are the most dangerous 'creatures' on the planet," Ryvan stated sarcastically. "No big deal."

"Maybe," Liyah mused.

Their conversation commenced, and they spoke long into the night. Eventually, Liyah began to calm down a little, and they even laughed every now and then. Even over their laughter, they could still hear the music from the dance.

"Well, I wouldn't worry too much about any of this," Ryvan smiled.

"That sounds like the best thing for me to do."

"Don't worry about telling your friend, either. Tyrese was going to talk to her about it," Ryvan said.

"Ok then," Liyah stated.

Suddenly, the music stopped. Both of them looked toward the camp. The torch lights were going out, too.

"Wow! We talked this whole time," Liyah exclaimed.

"Yup," Ryvan smiled. "Sorry for monopolizing your time."

"We better get going back to our camps before everyone begins to worry," Liyah stated. Ryvan thought she might have seemed a bit saddened by it.

"Yeah, probably," Ryvan replied. "Let me walk you back?"

Liyah thought, then, surprisingly said with a half-smile, "Sure."

The pair stood and began to walk toward the campsite, laughing and joking the whole way.

****

"Where is Ryvan?" Bryen asked impatiently.

"He's fine, guys," Tyrese stated. He had been trying to reassure these guys for hours. They hadn't seen Ryvan since the dance had begun.

"Where did he go then?" Shace asked.

Tyrese didn't *actually* know. So, he shrugged his shoulders, but when he looked up, he saw Ryvan and Liyah walking toward the she-warrior camp.

Liyah departed from him, and he started slowly back toward his own camp. Creshvan saw, too, and laughed, "Speak of the devil!"

When Liyah returned, she noticed *all* of the she-warriors were in their tents sleeping. Melanie was even asleep. She was positive Melanie and Tyrese had the same talk that Ryvan and herself had. However, Liyah was certain theirs had been a little less hostile.

Liyah flopped down and took off her earrings, single knife, and heels. She glanced at her necklace. Briefly, she looked at Melanie who rolled over. Liyah rolled her eyes and smiled. The two had the exact same amulets, except for the color, and neither girl knew where the jewelry came from. Liyah pondered these things and then fell asleep mid-thought. Her sapphire amulet hung around her neck, seemingly radiating light through the darkness.

****

"It looks like the tide has turned!" Melanie laughed. She smacked Liyah over the head with a pillow. "Wake up."

Liyah woke up and looked around. "What's going on?"

She realized that the tent was gone along with all of her other stuff.

Melanie grinned, "We are going to get breakfast. I've already packed your stuff!"

"You? *You* packed *my* stuff for once?" Liyah teased. "I'm shocked."

Liyah hurriedly cleaned up, and the pair ventured up toward the village center for breakfast. The she-warriors were at the back of the line, but they were so late that the warriors had already been served. The girls jumped into line.

After a breakfast of pancakes, eggs, and bacon, the troupe set out lazily toward Corresponding Point. The girls lingered near the back of the group, talking about the activities from the night before. It turned out that Melanie and Tyrese *did* speak of the same things. Liyah and Melanie then talked about what they did the past night. Melanie and Tyrese had danced together while Liyah and Ryvan sat in the garden.

By the time the girls finished their little talk, they were only a few miles out of Corresponding Point. The closer they got, the more excited Melanie grew. She was anxious to see the city that every warrior and she-warrior bragged about seeing.

"Ready for this?" Liyah asked.

"Oh yeah!" Melanie laughed.

The noises from the city grew louder as they approached. When they drew closer, the immense crowds of people could be seen. They drew up to the gate and turned left.

There was no one to welcome them like in the other cities. The crowds of people were either setting up camp or sitting around their camp while the village people carried on with their lives, bartering and trading in the market place over eggs, cattle, hens, and fabrics for clothing. Precious vegetables and fruits filled some of the carts in the marketplace.

There were many warriors who were laughing and talking, creating a large buzz that filled the city. This was the largest city in all of the Osheyk Mountains. The sounds alone rocked Melanie.

A few other she-warriors were there as well. Melanie asked Liyah who they were, but Liyah didn't know most of them. They found their own friends and began constructing their campsite.

The air hung heavy with the sound of laughter and the smell of campfires being lit. Many people, as in the other towns, stared at the girls as they had passed. They figured it was mainly because of their horses and blades.

After they finished with camp, Liyah dusted off her hands and grinned, "Well, what do you think?"

"It's great!" Melanie replied. "What do we do now?"

"We kick back and relax until we absolutely *must* go to the party," Liyah said sarcastically as she stretched out along the ground.

****

The she-warriors gathered lazily around their campsite, soaking up the sun.

"I want to go check this place out," Melanie finally demanded.

Everyone turned to look at her. "Ok, I'll show you around," Liyah stated as she stood to her feet. "I think you will enjoy yourself."

"Hope so," Melanie beamed.

The girls set off after Liyah grabbed her money pouch and tied it securely around her waist. As they walked, Melanie realized that Corresponding Point was just as beautiful as the mountainous region near Beura. The view was just as spectacular, and you could smell the ocean from the east.

The girls meandered through the town. Liyah showed Melanie the training grounds and the challenge arenas. Melanie didn't think too much of them, but Liyah had expected that. The girls kept walking through the city.

They passed by a food booth full of people inside serving whatever the warriors and she-warriors wanted in return for money. Liyah purchased some of the sweeter confections, and Melanie enjoyed them with wide eyes while they kept walking.

Corresponding Point also had a place with games similar to that of Corytz, but the warriors had to pay for them. The she-warriors passed by and entered the noisy market place near the gate. They looked around at the immense sizes of Corresponding Point before beginning their walk back to the campsite.

The townspeople were putting up the decorations for the party, and a band was preparing to perform for them tonight, so they were practicing briefly as well.

The girls looked around for awhile; then they ambled down a village path toward the river. They sat down on the bank and finished washing down the sweet treats with their drinks.

Liyah asked, "So, what do you think?"

Melanie took a sip and smiled, "I think this is going to be great!"

Liyah smiled at this, "I hope you have fun."

"I hope you do, too," Melanie replied, "and thanks for showing me around."

"Oh, no problem. Anytime," Liyah laughed.

The pair quietly sat by the river watching the rippling water whirl and twirl past them. Liyah realized that her birthday was coming up in a couple days, and she hadn't even remembered.

Melanie had though, and she was secretly spreading the word. Everyone would surprise her when her birthday rolled around. Melanie smiled to herself as she imagined the look on

Liyah's face when she thought she had been totally forgotten, and was faced with a great surprise instead.

"We better get back," Liyah smiled.

"Yeah, let's go," Melanie laughed.

"Ryvan, Ryvan, Ryvan," Creshvan smiled when Ryvan approached camp. "So, her name is what?"

Ryvan looked at him stupidly.

"I think it is Liyah," Tyrese beamed.

Ryvan shot Tyrese a dirty look, silencing him up completely. Tyrese coughed and glanced down at his horse with a smile still spread across his face. Everyone grew silent, and the next time Tyrese looked up, they were nearing the gate to Corresponding Point.

"Hey, look!" Creshvan exclaimed. "Is that Liyah?"

Ryvan glared at him, too.

****

"You guys ready for the party?" Shace asked, glancing into the tent.

"Yeah, we're ready," Tyrese beamed.

A few seconds later, the two warriors stepped out from the tent. They both looked nicer than usual as if they had actually spent some time getting ready for the night's events. A tense feeling began to hang over the camp. Everyone was growing nervous. After all, the competition would begin the next morning. Even the group of five felt the nervous tinge. Tyrese, Ryvan, Creshvan, Bryen, and Shace were all competing. The she-warriors were all tensing up even more, and that was saying something.

However, the dance in Corresponding Point was always one of, if not, the best. The warriors planned on doing their own thing because it was their last chance to unwind. Now that Ryvan had apologized to the she-warrior, there was *nothing* to weigh on his mind or conscience. He was determined to relax and prepare for the challenge to come the following morning. Now that he recalled, Liyah had beaten him last year along with two other she-warriors. He frowned at the thought.

The dance had already started when they reached the village center. There were quite a few people at the dance seemingly enjoying themselves, talking and laughing in large groups. Several torches encircled the entire dance floor, casting light over the people's laughing faces and illuminating the food tables. The band played their sweet music on flutes and lyres. The sounds calmed the group and several warriors and even she-warriors were dancing together in the center of the ring of light. The guys entered the torch circle and stood near the back, scanning the crowds.

As soon as they entered, three she-warriors cantered up and asked Shace, Creshvan, and Bryen to dance before being dragged into the center of the circle.

Tyrese and Ryvan were left looking at each other. "Wow, that shows how much they liked us," Ryvan laughed.

Tyrese spotted Melanie and patted Ryvan on the shoulder, saying, "Hey, it doesn't faze me in the least!" And he left Ryvan standing alone, staring after him.

Ryvan shook his head. He looked around and saw one of Liyah's friends dancing with some of their own guys. The song switched to a slow one, and everyone kept dancing. Ryvan decided to sit down and relax.

Ryvan sat, minding his own business when he noticed someone sitting next to him. He glanced out of the corner of his eye, and then quickly did a double-take back.

He jumped back and fell out of the chair. Sitting in the chair next to him, with hand on chin, elbow on knee, and legs crossed, staring straight ahead with no emotion, was none other than the trouble causing she-warrior herself, Liyah.

"Irony," Ryvan thought to himself.

"Boo," Liyah said without even moving or shifting her gaze from the dance floor.

Ryvan looked at her.

She turned to face him, smiling. "Scared you, didn't I?" she joked.

"Sure," Ryvan stated.

"Having fun yet?"

"Just got here."

"Really?"

"Yup, what about you?"

"Uh," Liyah rolled her eyes. "I've been sitting here for awhile now. I was with Melanie, but," She gestured to the dance floor.

Ryvan laughed, "Yeah."

An awkward pause followed. They sat there listening to music as the slow song switched to another fast one.

Melanie bounded up happily. "Hey, Liyah! Hey, Ryvan!"

"Hey," they stated at the same time with very little emotion.

Melanie looked back and forth between them for a moment. Then, she laughed and said, "That was creepy. I just came over to tell you that I'm going to hang out with Tyrese for the evening."

Liyah raised her eyebrows into a questioning stare.

"Oh! Don't look at me that way," she exclaimed. "You'll be fine." She glanced at Ryvan, grinned, then looked back to Liyah and giggled. Then, she said to Ryvan, "Babysit her for me, will you?" Liyah glared after her as her cheeks tinted red. Ryvan assumed that she was contemplating how to get away with a possible murder.

Melanie ventured off into the crowd to find Tyrese. Liyah shook her head once more. Ryvan smiled at her, and she grinned. They sat there quietly until the song changed back to a slow one.

They both were thinking the same thing. All at once they both began to talk. "Do you—?" They stopped and laughed.

"What?" Ryvan asked.

"Go ahead," Liyah smiled.

They both laughed. Ryvan looked at his hands, then back up at Liyah. "Do you want to dance?"

Liyah grinned at him, "Sure."

They both stood up and started to dance. They were tense at first, and then, they both started to relax. Ryvan allowed himself to have fun, and eventually, he felt Liyah relax in his arms as well.

Tyrese and Melanie were dancing a short way off. Tyrese saw Liyah and Ryvan, and his eyes grew wide. "Hey! Look!"

Melanie stopped dancing and looked in the direction Tyrese was pointing. She smiled and looked up at Tyrese.

"It worked!" she laughed.

"I had my doubts, but—"

"It worked!"

Tyrese laughed, "I have to hand it to you; it was a good idea."

"Thanks, but Liyah knew what I was doing. I think Ryvan did, too."

"Oh, well, that's alright. They'll get us back later."

Chapter 10

"Good night," Ryvan smiled at the end of the party after he walked Liyah to her tent. "Hope you had fun."

"I did, and good night," she replied. They looked at each other, and Ryvan took a step toward her. Then Liyah turned and entered her tent, ending up face to face with Melanie.

Melanie sat there grinning. Liyah smiled back and began to take off her weapons. "Have fun?" Melanie asked.

"Yeah, I guess I did," she replied, caught herself and said, "Or, as much fun as possible."

"So, do you like Ryvan?"

Liyah did not answer. Instead, she shot Melanie a silencing look.

Melanie looked questioningly up at Liyah with innocence.

"I know what you are trying to do, and it will not work."

"Liyah," Melanie grinned. The way she said it made Liyah feel guilty.

"Ok so maybe it will work. Why did you have to go and do that for?"

"Why, whatever do you mean?" Melanie batted her eyelashes.

"That's enough! You know what I'm talking about."

"Ok, one, I didn't want you to be lonely and die alone, surrounded by your weapon collection. Two, he seems like a great guy. And three, Liyah, no matter what you say, he is perfect for you."

"Whatever," Liyah replied. "Good night."

Liyah blew out the candle, and the girls went to sleep. A big day awaited them.

****

The next morning, Melanie awoke to find that Liyah was gone. Melanie ambled out of the tent. Shanillé and Siscilia were sitting around the fire eating breakfast. When they saw her, Siscilia smiled and said, "We saved you some breakfast."

Melanie rubbed her eyes sleepily and said, "Thanks. Where is everyone?"

"Liyah, Alana, Maiyah, and Vera all went to train for the competitions. Christina and Maicah went to go get some juice," Shanillé stated.

"Are they the only ones that are competing?" Melanie asked.

"Yeah, and we watch," Christina stated as she came up merrily. Maicah and she wandered up with some orange juice.

"Where are the training areas?" Melanie asked. "Liyah showed me, but I don't know if I can find it myself or not."

"I'll show you when you finish eating," Shanillé grinned.

Melanie smiled at her and began to scarf her breakfast down.

****

A little while later, Shanillé and Melanie ventured off to find the training grounds. Warriors and a few she-warriors dotted the practicing grounds, warming up for their battles. The girls didn't linger to watch; instead, they continued on to find Liyah. At the archery grounds, they found Vera, Christina, and Maiyah.

"Have you guys seen Liyah?" Melanie asked.

Vera shot, and when she missed the bulls-eye by an inch, she grimaced. Then she said bitterly, "She's over training on the blades course."

Melanie and Shanillé glanced over and saw the area completely surrounded by warriors and she-warriors alike. The girls trotted up, pushing their way to the front of the group.

In the dead center of the course stood Liyah, completely fixated on her training. For all she knew, she was there alone without a soul for miles.

The blades course worked in an interesting way. A set of controls was programmed to start and stop the time and to make targets shoot up all along the course. The targets would shoot up in various locations, and the warrior would slice through them, delivering their lethal blows. The targets were crafted to resemble various evil creatures and were made of cloth stuffed with hay. The dummies were hooked up on a moving belt underneath the course.

When the time began, the machine would automatically start on a low level and work its way up to a higher one. It increased until the warrior shouted for them to stop. Points were awarded for number of targets, style, and accuracy.

Liyah was on a medium level, and it came easily for her. She had only one blade out which, in the real competition, would allow for additional style points. She struck every single target, dead on. As she sliced off the head of one target, she saw her friends and called, "Melanie! Shanillé! What are you guys doing here?"

"We came to see you!" Melanie called back.

"Ok, we'll talk in a minute!"

Just then, the level increased to six. In all, the machine could get up to level ten, but no one had ever made it past eight. Liyah felt the change and kicked it up a notch. She continued hitting every target with extreme accuracy.

She kept fighting, and the level increased to seven. Once more, Liyah felt the change and ripped her other sword from her back. Now, she would really amaze the others.

She continued making it look easy. Melanie watched her best friend intently. She realized that Liyah was much more than a friend to her. She was just like a sister. Melanie was amazed by how good Liyah had gotten.

Melanie looked across the course and saw Ryvan and Tyrese watching as well. She waved them over, and they came around to where Melanie and Shanillé were. They began a conversation while they watched. Tyrese finally said, "Ryvan, she—" he trailed off.

"What?" he asked, keeping his eyes on the she-warrior.

"She fights like you," Tyrese stated, thunderstruck.

Ryvan folded his arms across his chest. Liyah went up to level eight as Ryvan smiled, "So, she does." Then, he turned and walked away. Tyrese followed.

"Stop!" Liyah panted. Someone by the controls shut it down, and she replaced her cross-blades with an overhead twirl. She still made it look easy, but it had taken a toll on her.

Excitement and intimidation surged through the crowd.

"That was great, Liyah!" Melanie exclaimed.

"Thanks, bud," Liyah breathed. She was tired and sweating.

"Even better than last year," Shanillé complimented.

"Thank you!" Liyah replied.

The crowd began to dissipate, and a voice came over the loudspeaker saying, "Welcome warriors and she-warriors! We hope you enjoyed yourselves last night. Just making sure it is clear that the games will begin in exactly two hours. The question is, are you ready? That is all, and we wish you the best of luck!"

"Are you finished?" Melanie asked Liyah.

A young warrior ran up, handing Liyah her crossbow which she strapped onto her back. "Thanks!" she said to him, tousling his short brown hair. "Yeah, I'm finished for now."

"So, what are you going to do for the next two hours?" Shanillé asked.

"I'll sleep for one and relax for the other."

They laughed and headed back to camp.

When Ryvan and Tyrese left the blade training course, they ventured back to their camp to sleep for an hour, because they had just finished training on their own terms. They walked through all of the training warriors and she-warriors. Tension hung heavily in the air. Everyone was on edge because the tournament would begin in two short hours. The typical routine for Ryvan and Tyrese was to get up early, train hard when no one was awake to watch, then go back to camp and sleep in attempts to ease the tension.

Bryen, Creshvan, and Shace were gone. Bryen and Shace were probably training. Creshvan was probably off eating somewhere even though Creshvan was competing with them in the tournament as well. He rarely took anything seriously.

When they reached their campsite, Ryvan and Tyrese dropped down around their campfire. Tyrese propped his head up on a rock, and Ryvan just reclined in the dirt. They drifted off to sleep to wake up around eight and compete in the tournament. If they were lucky, they would be recruited by one of the scouts.

****

"Ryvan! Wake up," Tyrese was shaking Ryvan to wake him.

Ryvan wouldn't wake up. Tyrese was ready to quit, but it was eight-thirty, and the tournament started at nine. Creshvan was watching him, laughing.

Someone tapped Tyrese on the shoulder, and he waved them off, mumbling, "Not now, Creshvan. I have to wake him up," Tyrese stared at the ground.

Someone came and stood directly in front of him—actually, three someones. These someones wore three inch black heels. Tyrese stared up at them. There, standing in a triangle shape, stood Melanie and Shace's sister, Vera, with Liyah standing in front. All three had their hands on their hips, and Liyah and Melanie were smiling.

Two out of three, Tyrese thought.

"It looks like you need some help," Liyah grinned. She was loving this.

Tyrese shrugged. "Yeah."

Liyah held out her hand to Vera, who handed her a canteen of water. Liyah opened it and meandered over to Ryvan nonchalantly. She stood over him, looking down, and then opened the canteen to take a drink.

Tyrese was amazed. She couldn't possibly be about to do what he thought she was, but—

Sure enough, Liyah flipped the bottle upside down while her cohorts snickered. The contents of the open canteen fell out on Ryvan's face. The warrior shot up coughing and sputtering. Water ran down his face, soaking through to his under clothes.

When the contents finished pouring out, Liyah dropped the empty canteen on Ryvan's stomach, dusted her hands off and said flatly, "Glad I could be of service. Good luck, boys."

Ryvan stared at her blankly. Creshvan's mouth hung open, and Tyrese's eyes grew wide.

Liyah's accomplices followed, only after Melanie smiled at Tyrese and Vera snickered threateningly. The guys stared after them. They were clearly surprised by the girls' guts at having emptied the contents of a canteen on one of the most dangerous warriors in the middle of his rest.

Creshvan and Tyrese took one look at Ryvan, who still had a blank look on his face and took off running.

Ryvan stared after them for a moment, stood up, carefully positioned his weapons, and then took off, sprinting after them. Tyrese and Creshvan were headed toward the competing grounds. They sprinted, full speed, past the cocky she-warriors who stopped walking and glanced at each other questioningly.

They stood like that for a moment. Then out of nowhere, Ryvan ripped between them. Liyah shook her head, "Did we do that?"

****

"Welcome, everyone!" a man's amplified voice exploded over the crowd. The man stood up on a platform. "As you all know, the first event will begin in a few minutes. Your names are all posted on the board to show you when you will be competing in the blades and archery segments."

A cheer rose from the crowd.

"This year, though, we have a new competition! There are three segments now: archery, blades, and a battle tournament!"

Everyone gave a faint cheer.

"This is the process of elimination round, where you will battle each other. It will take place after lunch. For now, be prepared for the challenges at hand because, remember, every year, scouts come to watch. Good luck to all of you, and the starting warriors or she-warriors, report to the arenas!"

Everyone cheered and fought one another to check the board. Ryvan saw that he was on archery first, along with seven other warriors and Vera and Shace.

In all, there was one archery course with ten targets. A warrior or she-warrior was positioned a few yards away, and they shot three times each. Points were awarded for how close they got to the center—one for the outer ring, three for the inner ring and five for the bulls eye. There were thirty warriors and nine she-warriors competing. So, there would be four archery rotations.

Ryvan noticed that Christina and Tyrese were on the blades course first. Ryvan saw he was on the blades course in the fifth round. There would be eight rounds because there were only five areas for blade work. They parted and ventured off to their own competitions.

Liyah read her name off. She was on the second rotation of archery along with Tyrese, Creshvan, Maiyah, and Alana. Also, she was on the sixth rotation of the blades course.

She decided to go watch Vera on archery because that was where she was going to be competing next. Melanie was just going to watch Liyah the whole time. So they both went to watch Vera in the archery.

When they reached the course, they glanced around to see Vera with Shace directly beside each other. Liyah smiled at this. Brother versus sister would make a show worth seeing. Also, Liyah noticed Ryvan was in this rotation. He appeared to still be a little damp. Liyah caught herself chuckling and forced her eyes away from him.

Melanie caught Liyah smiling and quickly asked why. Liyah mentally kicked herself and then replied, "Nothing important."

"I hate it when you do that."

Liyah shrugged.

The announcer explained the rules, and the competition began. The archers let loose their first shot. The girls mainly watched Vera, Shace, and Ryvan. Vera shot a three, and Ryvan and Shace both received fives. Vera's temper flared, but she subdued it with haste.

The group tending to the course withdrew the arrows and recorded the outcomes. The archers received the command for a second shot and then the third. The competition ceased quickly.

In the end, Vera shot thirteen, Shace thirteen, and Ryvan had received a perfect fifteen. The first shooters cleared out, and the second rotation entered. Liyah stood in front of her target.

She drew her bow, awaiting the command. After the first shot was fired, and Liyah received a bulls-eye, she glanced up to see her two friends with her two acquaintances next to them, sticking around to watch.

They reloaded and drew their bows to await the second command. Liyah's arrow quivered a bit on release. She couldn't anticipate where it would land, but to her surprise it struck dead center.

People cheered off to the side while they prepared for the final shot. The warriors waited. The shout was heard, and, once more, Liyah's arrow flew awkwardly. She watched intently as the arrow stuck into the target. The arrow fell right into the center for a perfect score.

She looked up with a satisfied smile at her lips. Melanie was in the same spot she had been in, but now, Ryvan was with her.

Liyah glided towards them. "Good job!" Melanie exploded.

"Thanks," Liyah grinned. "It was a little shaky. I suppose it's nerves."

"Yes, well done, Liyah," Ryvan smiled, fairly cautiously. "And you."

Ryvan smiled and nodded a goodbye then departed.

"He couldn't believe you got a perfect score," Melanie exclaimed.

"Well, he has a run for the money, doesn't he?" Liyah grinned, replacing her crossbow.

****

When Liyah and Melanie made it over to the blades course, it was about ten-thirty in the morning. They were about to start the fourth blades rotation.

They had stopped to check out the scores since the archery portion of the competitions had just ended. Only six out of thirty-nine competitors had made a perfect archery score.

The points awarded for the blades course were a bit more complex. There were four different areas to judge. Each was recorded on a one through ten scale. Then the average was viewed as the number of overall points given. The grading categories were the following: speed, accuracy, style, and level. Liyah's goal was to reach the ninth level.

The fourth rotation began, and Liyah watched intently as the competitors fought to receive the high score. At the end, the last warrior stopped at level six. Liyah snickered.

The area was cleaned up, and scores were recorded as the fifth rotation moved on. Who happened to enter the ring directly in front of them? None other than Ryvan, and he was the only one competing that the girls recognized.

It began. Liyah watched. There was something peculiar about the way Ryvan fought, and she couldn't place it. She contemplated. Then it struck her. He fought just like her! Her jaw dropped.

"Shut your mouth, honey," Melanie stated, without even looking up at Liyah.

The level went up to six, and two competitors stopped. Ryvan was fighting two handed now. Level seven. One more dropped out. It continued.

Level eight. The other stopped, but Ryvan went on. The spectators watched, fascinated. They began to cheer him on. *Level nine.* Shortly, level *ten!*

Impossible! Liyah screamed in her mind. Ryvan kept fighting, then suddenly cried out, "Stop!"

The machine powered down, and he stepped off while they tended to the debris for the sixth rotation, which Liyah was set to compete in. The crowd exploded for Ryvan.

Liyah unhooked her crossbow and handed it over to Melanie to hold. She also handed Melanie her arrows and all her knives. She was determined to do better. She *had* to do better.

If she didn't beat Ryvan out here, then, the chances were that she wouldn't get any farther in the overall tournament.

She saw Ryvan hang around to watch her. She stepped into the ring confidently and drew one of her cross-blades. She grinned bitterly at Ryvan the instant before the competition began.

"She means business, doesn't she?" Ryvan asked Melanie who laughed merrily.

"She's just trying to intimidate you. It's strictly business with her. She does it all the time. She tries to get into your head," Melanie replied. "What else do you think she was doing practicing this morning? However, she does act somewhat different towards you."

"How so?"

"Well, for instance, the way she—oh!" Melanie drew back a bit. "I've said too much."

"No, you haven't quite said enough. Please continue."

"No, no, no!" Melanie exclaimed as she backed away shaking her hands. "I...I...have to...bye!" she mumbled as she turned and sprinted to the other end of the training grounds to watch her friend compete.

Ryvan shook his head and laughed as the machines kicked in, and Liyah began. Ryvan could tell it was extremely easy for her, however, he was not concerned. After all, he had just broken the Shroeketian record.

She reached level five, and she still seemed to be fighting *easily*. Ryvan examined her fighting style. She really did fight the way he did. She was battling much better than she had been this morning, but even then she had been doing very well. Ryvan snickered as he recalled what Melanie had said. She tried to get in people's heads. This morning she had only shown a snippet of what she was capable of. Ryvan smiled.

Level six approached while two people dropped out. Liyah still fought one handed. She would gain more style points for that particular move.

Level seven. Ryvan watched happily, knowing he had this one in the bag. He laughed to himself, and the warriors around him stared at him stupidly.

He smiled awkwardly, cleared his throat and went back to watching Liyah silently. She was on level eight, and she suddenly ripped her remaining sword out of her holder. She continued to make it seem easy, but beads of sweat were beginning to run down her face. The other two warriors had dropped out on level seven.

Nine. Ryvan began to grow nervous. Liyah slashed every target with deadly accuracy. She fought harder than Ryvan thought she could. Then the level increased to *ten*.

No way! Ryvan exploded within his mind. He anticipated the cry for the cease in fighting to come from the girl, but none came. She fought with skill he had never even *seen*. He wondered if he appeared this way when he battled.

Out of nowhere, the machine began to make strange noises. Sparks began to fly, and smoke billowed from the machine. The crowd began to mutter.

The machine suddenly made one last explosive sound as it died, and one lone target shot up behind Liyah, who without glancing in its direction, sliced the head off with her left blade. She froze with the left blade straight out and her right directly in front of her on a horizontal path. The wild look of battle still lingered in her eyes.

She stood still for a moment in that position, breathing deeply, calming herself. The crowd burst into cheers and applause. Ryvan joined in.

She regained her composure, straightened up, and then twirled her cross-blades above her head. Quickly following, she placed them in their original positions and *smiled*.

It could have been Ryvan's imagination, but he was almost sure that she was smiling at him. She waved thanks to the crowd as she stepped out of the ring. She walked past him with a sly smile.

Melanie walked up after Liyah walked away. She placed a hand upon his left shoulder and tapped her temple with the middle finger of her other and stated, "She's in your head."

She raised her eyebrows and walked away. The sad thing was she was right.

****

"Tied!" Tyrese laughed. "You and Liyah are *tied!*"

"Let me see that!" Ryvan pushed past Tyrese and examined the bulletins. "Wow," he breathed. "She's good."

"Attention all warriors and she-warriors!" the loudspeaker boomed. "Congratulations to all of you! It appears we have two people tied for first! Ryvan of Dreán and Liyah of Faeciã!" Everyone applauded politely if not somewhat bitterly. Envy filtered through them all. "Everything *can* change in the third challenge. At this time we will be serving lunch. Good luck, everyone!"

Everyone flocked toward the serving area to get their food. Ryvan and Tyrese met up with their friends, and they went over to the benches to eat. Everyone relaxed and enjoyed the company and the opportunity they were faced with. While they ate lunch, the announcer explained the rules for the third challenge.

Afterward, everyone was left with excitement and intrigue. Ryvan thought to himself, *"This* will be fun."

****

Tyrese stood, facing his opponent, a warrior from Corytz that he did not know. They shook hands and parted.

The third challenge was a tournament of battles between the warriors and she-warriors. The names were drawn randomly to determine who battled each other. The rules were simple: they would fight fair—that meant no cheap shots, no attempts to injure one another *too badly*, and they would wrestle the opponent's weapon away or pin them in order to win. When the game was over, the loser was eliminated from the tournament, while the winner moved on to play another round with a winner from another game. Only the top four would receive points: fourth would receive five points, third would receive ten, second twenty, and first would gain twenty-five points.

When it all came down to it, Tyrese won his game. Ryvan and Liyah won theirs as well. They waited while the other games went on.

After weeding out the competition, the top six were Liyah, Ryvan, Tyrese, Vera, Shace, and Bryen.

The group knew from that point on that it would not become personal and that it was just business, but they weren't completely prepared for what lay in store for them all. All three games would be played at once.

When the roster went up, a sick, sinking feeling grew within Ryvan's stomach. The roster read: Ring 1—Liyah of Faeciã versus Vera of Beura; Ring 2—Bryen of Beura versus Shace of Beura; Ring 3—Ryvan of Dreán versus Tyrese of Dreán.

Chapter 11

"Ok, ladies, we want a fair fight. Don't cut each other to ribbons. One cut on your opponent, and you will be out of the whole game," the referee stated.

Liyah and Vera shook hands. Vera's face was set in stone. This would not end well. Liyah knew this.

They stepped away. Then the whistle blew. Vera stepped toward Liyah and pulled out her long sword. Liyah withdrew both cross-blades and prepared for a barrage of attacks. She had watched Vera fight, and she knew how to defend.

As predicted, Vera lunged forward and began to slash and hack violently. Liyah managed to block the pattern.

Vera continued her attack, which Liyah could easily block because of her cross-blades. Vera was giving it all she had.

Liyah figured she would allow Vera to attack, and then, when she tired, Liyah would strike. Her thoughts were interrupted by an unexpected slash from above. Vera used both hands powerfully on the sword to bring it down. Liyah, in the last possible second, formed an X with her cross-blades, not only preventing Vera from delivering the blow, but trapping her long sword between the pair.

Vera looked concerned for a moment. Liyah spun and whipped her cross-blades around so that Vera's blade flew into the air, hitting the ground shortly after its master, for the force had knocked her to the ground.

The whistle blew. It was over. Liyah picked up Vera's blade and helped her to her feet. Liyah held the long sword out to her. She took it and ducked out of the ring as Liyah twirled her cross-blades victoriously.

****

In the end, Ryvan had beaten Tyrese by pinning him to the ground with his neck under a cross-blade X. Shace and Bryen both lost. They threw their game away by accidentally cutting each other. They didn't do it on purpose, but they were disqualified.

So, there were only two left. Liyah of Faeciã and Ryvan of Dreán. *That* would be a *real* fight to attend.

****

They shook hands. At this point, Ryvan looked at Liyah strangely. He looked deep into her eyes for a brief moment in time. Liyah couldn't place it. Before she had much time to think about it, they stepped away to begin. They both knew that it was going to be a tough fight, but they were both too proud to let that faze them.

The whistle blew. They drew their blades, and at the exact same moment, they formed an X with the blades in front of their faces and bowed.

Neither of them had ever done this before, and neither knew why they had done it. The only thing that felt different than normal was a type of memory, pulling at their minds. That held them up for a moment. Then the fight began when they both uncrossed the blades.

Liyah smiled the same smile she had when she stepped out of the blades arena. "Good luck, Ryvan," she smiled angelically.

He was clearly taken aback. Liyah's idea worked. She loved confusing her opponents, especially warriors.

"And you."

Liyah raised an eyebrow, and they began the battle, Ryvan charging with one blade. Liyah blocked with her left and struck with her right, but Ryvan blocked her as well.

For a time, they used their left blades as shields, but Liyah grew frustrated and began her attack and defense with both. She slashed out at him, but he continued to block. She brought down her blades above him, and he blocked her again. They stood face to face, matching up their strength.

"You're pretty good," Ryvan complimented.

"You aren't half bad yourself!" Liyah stated as she brought up her right leg and kicked Ryvan square in the stomach, knocking him clear of the clinch. Ryvan found himself thinking about how grateful that one of the rules was no throwing cheap shots. It could have been a lot worse.

Ryvan managed to hold onto his blades, but he landed on the ground. He quickly leapt to his feet, before Liyah could strike.

Liyah eyed him warily with one blade curving above her head and the other in front of her. She brought herself into a strong defensive position.

Ryvan stepped toward her and brought a barrage of attacks. He used Liyah's two-handed method. She saw what was coming and anticipated it.

When he brought down an overhead attack, Liyah tucked and rolled away as he cut into the air. She regained herself but was aware that she was in a bad situation. She couldn't see him in that split second.

She stood completely still, *listening*. Quickly she whipped around to block an attack, but forgot one minor detail. Ryvan kicked her in the stomach, knocking her to the ground.

Liyah scrambled to her feet. She had managed to keep her weapons. They fought equally for a time. The fight grew more violent every moment. The only sounds were metal upon metal of the blades squealing their displeasure as the pair blocked and hacked at one another.

This went on for quite some time. Liyah slung both swords down above him once more. Once blocked, Liyah realized he had trapped her. Then he shoved her away with his blades.

They ceased fighting and stared at one another, breathing heavily. They stood this way for a few minutes, catching their breath, and the crowd grew silent. Sweat and blood from small cuts mixed and fell to the dusty earth. A surreal stillness settled over the warriors and spectators as a small breeze kicked up, lifting Liyah's damp hair away from her face and tousling Ryvan's.

Then out of nowhere, they both lunged forward with all they had left in them. Their swords clinched above their heads so that they were once more face to face.

They did not speak. Ryvan and Liyah gave every ounce of energy in matching their strength. Liyah gritted her teeth and knew she couldn't last much longer. No matter how much she hated to admit it, he was superior to her in strength.

The blades protested with a tormented squeal. Every muscle in Liyah's body screamed for release from the torture. When Liyah was certain she would fall if kept in this position for too much longer, the referee sprinted up. He blew the whistle and cried in incomplete thoughts, "You two. Never in all my life. You are going to destroy one another! We have come to the simple conclusion. You both win. If you fight it out, one of you, or possibly both, could wind up seriously injured or worse. TIE!!"

Liyah and Ryvan released one another. Liyah's muscles breathed in the calm. The crowd erupted in cheers. Apparently, they had put on a good show for the crowd. It was about to get even better.

They smiled at each other. Liyah noticed Ryvan had beads of sweat running down his face. She became aware that she did, too. She wiped away the blood from a cut on her arm. Ryvan had a small nick over his left eyebrow.

Ryvan held out a hand for her to shake, but Liyah only stared at it. Then she did something she had never done before. She looked at him with a smirk and suddenly hugged him. The crowd went wild.

Melanie and Tyrese stood nearby. Their jaws dropped.

Shortly after leaving the ring and meeting back up with Tyrese, the boys started talking. "I know what you are going to say," Ryvan smiled.

Tyrese's eyes shone with mischievousness. "Really? Then answer the question."

"I don't have anything to explain. *She* hugged *me*."

"It takes two people," Tyrese began.

Ryvan interrupted, "Whatever. Amusing?"

"Oh yeah! You guys fight exactly the same. You both did great!"

"Thanks, and sorry for…well, you know."

"What?" Tyrese asked.

"Well, knocking you out of the tournament," Ryvan looked at the ground.

Tyrese busted out laughing. Ryvan was confused. "Ryvan, I don't care! Training and battle aren't everything to me."

Ryvan smiled, relieved. In that moment, someone placed a hand on both boys' shoulders. They spun around defensively to see a boy around their age. His eyes were fierce, and he had a serious look about him. His hair was light brown, and his armor was very battle-scarred. The boys would have been concerned, but a friendly smile spread across the boy's face.

"Hello, guys!" he smiled. He lowered his voice and stated, "May I speak with you in private?"

They followed the warrior out of Corresponding Point to speak without being overheard.

Ryvan and Tyrese stood expectantly. The warrior glanced around to make sure the area was secure. Then, when he seemed completely satisfied, he began, "How would you two boys like to become honorary members of the Galeãns?"

Ryvan and Tyrese stood, speechless.

"Yes, this is for real. We think you've got what it takes to become one of the few Galeãn warriors. We've been watching you for quite some time now, and we feel that you are ready."

They remained silent for a time.

The boy finally said, "You don't have to give me an answer right now. In fact, here." The boy pulled out a card. "This will tell you how to find us."

He handed the card to Tyrese. Then he turned around and left. The two boys were left staring at the single card.

****

The boys stood outside of their camp. They weren't allowed to say that they were offered a chance to join the Galeãns. It was one of the unspoken rules. True warriors did not go around bragging about how great they were. So they tried to mask their content.

The others sat around the site relaxing. Shace and Bryen were bandaging their cuts. They had slashed each other on their right forearms. Both were bandaged tightly, and the blood had just ceased flowing. The boys realized how tired and sore they were from battling. The third challenge had taken up the whole afternoon. The party would start in one hour.

Tyrese glanced over and saw the canteen that Liyah had dropped on Ryvan and laughed.

Ryvan glanced at him. "What?"

"Just remembering this morning."

"What about it?"

"How Sleeping Beauty was awakened."

"Oh, that. Why were you thinking of that?" he asked sullenly.

"I don't know. It was really funny though."

"Why?"

"Just the way she did it was…I don't know. It made *me* laugh."

"Whatever."

They grew silent. Ryvan broke the silence by saying, "If we take this opportunity, then chances are, we won't see them again. Don't get too attached."

Liyah's hair had grown damp. She was very tired. She had to admit that Ryvan was a good fighter.

Melanie caught up with Liyah. She handed her the crossbow. "You did great!" She gave Liyah a hug. "Oh, wait. You've already had a congratulatory hug!"

Liyah turned red and opened her mouth to comment, but a voice from behind made her stop.

"You fight well, Liyah."

The girls turned to face a she-warrior around twenty years old staring at them. She had wavy long brown hair that cascaded down over her shoulders elegantly.

She wore different armor. It was like Liyah and Melanie's, but the only difference was, instead of regular metal, she wore silver. Pure sterling silver.

Her eyes were severe, but she seemed kind.

"Thank you, ma'am," Liyah replied.

She glanced at Melanie and said, "You do, too."

"Uh, thanks, but when have you seen *me* fight?"

"I'm sorry. I must explain myself. Is there some place we can speak privately?"

"I suppose, well," Liyah stuttered.

"In that case, follow me."

The girls trailed after her. They wove in and out of the crowd of people enjoying the sights of Corresponding Point. Melanie was confused and whispered, "Didn't she ask *us* if there was a private place?"

Liyah shot her a silencing look.

When they were finally out of earshot, the girl turned to face them.

"How do you know I fight?" Melanie asked.

"Let me explain. My name is Rihannai. I am a Galiphem warrior."

The girls were surprised by this answer. They stood, speechless.

"The Galiphems and Galatrans have been watching you for a while, even in your home village, and we have realized that you both are worthy. You are *real* Galiphem material. We would like to give you the opportunity to become Galiphems. You don't have to answer now, but take these cards." She handed them two yellow tinted cards that felt like old parchment.

"It's blank," Liyah noted with a confused grin.

"Yes, but it will tell you all you need to know when you need to know it. When all seems lost, take a look. You will find what you are looking for. Good luck to you."

She turned and vanished into the crowd before anything could be said.

They began walking toward their campsite to get ready for the party. By now, they only had around half an hour to get ready.

"What do you think?" Liyah asked.

"I think this is great! I can't wait to tell Tyrese!" Melanie exclaimed.

"Melanie, you can't tell him. You can't tell anyone. It's in the rules," Liyah stated. Then a thought slapped her right in the face. "Melanie," she trailed off.

"What's wrong?"

"We, if we take this job, then, we'll probably never see the two warriors again."

They both grew quiet as the realization knocked the breath out of them.

They got ready for the party quietly as their friends secretly wondered what was bothering them, unaware of their heavy thoughts.

****

The girls were almost ready. They began to withdraw from their tents to head over to the party. When they were leaving, Liyah ran back to get her hoop earrings that she absentmindedly left in the tent. Lying on the earth next to them was her blank yellow card.

Liyah was faced with reality once again. This time she knew what she had to do. She had to speak with Ryvan as soon as possible. Regardless of the consequences.

****

They reached the village center late thanks to Liyah. When they *did* get there, the announcer was already speaking.

Melanie wasn't paying any attention to him though, and when he called out Liyah's name, she jumped, which startled a couple of warriors who were eyeing her warily. Liyah ventured through the parted crowd that made way for her. She climbed up on the stage at the same time Ryvan did.

It took Melanie a few minutes to realize what was going on, and she realized they were announcing the winners.

The crowd cheered loudly as the two were named the champions of the Corresponding Point Games.

They shook hands and were congratulated. Then the music started up, and the party began. Everyone rushed on stage to congratulate the pair. Liyah didn't get the opportunity to speak with Ryvan. She knew she had to soon, or it would be too late.

Melanie was thinking the same thing. She finally came to a decision that she knew Liyah wouldn't like, but she knew she had to. She went to find Tyrese.

Chapter 12

After the winners were announced, and the music started back up, Ryvan became surrounded by the congratulatory crowd. He quickly became depressed, for he wanted to speak with Liyah. She, too, must have been overpowered by the crowd because she couldn't be seen through the surge of people. He knew he shouldn't do what he was going to do, but he felt like he had to, or he would forever regret it.

The crowd pressed further upon him. He was polite to all of them, but he silently willed them all to depart from his presence. Finally, the people left him alone, but by now, Liyah was gone. He threw his hands toward the stars in exasperation.

"What next?" he shouted, causing some nearby warriors to stare.

After this scene, he departed to find the she-warrior that tormented him.

****

Tyrese scanned the huge crowd looking for Melanie. He figured Ryvan would be angry when he found out about what Tyrese was about to do, but it burdened him to think that Melanie would never know what was about to happen to him and his companion.

The sea of people all moved in time with the music, creating waves. The waves of people crashed down all about him. When the song ended, there was a brief pause as a slow song came on. The people slowed their pace, which made everything easier for him.

Then, he saw her. She stood under a spotlight. The light streamed over her extravagantly. He walked up to her, noticing that she seemed a bit upset. When she saw him, her downtrodden face lit up, making her eyes shine as they always had when she was happy.

She cried, "I've been looking all over for you! There is something I need to speak to you about."

Tyrese smiled at her, "I need to talk to you, too. It's important."

They stood silently for a moment. Tyrese held out his hand without saying a word. They walked out of the village center, hand in hand, to tell each other their forbidden secrets.

****

Ryvan rushed through the crowd. He had been looking for quite a while. He ran his hand through his hair and sighed. Just as he had given up hope, he backed into someone. That someone just so happened to be Liyah, and she just so happened to be taking a drink of punch at that time. So punch streamed down the lower part of her face.

"Liyah! I'm sorry! I didn't see you," Ryvan apologized.

Liyah ran her hand over her jaw, swiping away the punch. "No, it's alright. I'm fine," she laughed.

Ryvan smiled and said, "Hey, I've been looking for you. There's something I need to tell you."

"Me, too, but not here."

"No, not here," Ryvan agreed.

They quietly walked side by side out of the area. The things they were about to tell one another weighed heavily on their hearts and minds.

They began to talk as they walked. Ryvan began, "I don't know how to tell you this, but heck, I don't even know *why* I'm about to tell you this—"

"Ryvan! What is it?" she asked, impatiently stopping his word flow.

Ryvan stopped and looked at her. She halted as well and waited vigilantly. Ryvan told her what happened, and her jaw dropped.

She beamed, "Wow! You, too?"

"Huh?"

"Sorry, first off, congrats! Second, I was selected, too, for the Galiphems. Melanie and me!"

"Wow!" he exclaimed. "Congratulations to you, too."

"I suppose that I won't see you again though. Am I right?" Liyah asked solemnly. Her voice was quieter.

Ryvan became serious, too. "It's...not likely."

Liyah's eyes grew cloudy, not teary, but murky. "I...I'll miss you," she stated with her eyes cast down.

Ryvan replied, "I'll...miss you, too."

Liyah lifted her eyes to meet his.

"Liyah!" a voice called out. A figure approached rapidly. *Two* figures.

They distanced themselves with one last look. Liyah smiled sadly as Melanie ran up practically dragging Tyrese.

"Liyah! Guess what?"

Liyah raised an eyebrow.

"Tyrese was accepted, too!" Melanie exclaimed.

Liyah glanced at Ryvan who glanced at Tyrese who in turn glanced at Melanie.

"What?" Melanie asked.

"We have to tell her," Liyah stated.

"Now or never," Ryvan muttered.

Liyah sighed as the pair began to explain the situation thoroughly to their comrades. Nothing had changed. Not really.

Liyah awoke from her deep sleep to find Melanie gone. She got around and withdrew herself from the inside of her tent. When she saw that none of her friends were around, she decided to go get some breakfast on her own.

The day was foggy and rainy. Mist crept through the mountains so thickly that she could only see a few yards ahead. The plants and soil itself seemed to soak in the moisture and enrich themselves.

Liyah thought to herself. It was her birthday—her eighteenth to be exact. She hadn't told a soul; in fact, she wouldn't, but she was fairly surprised that Melanie hadn't remembered.

After thinking for awhile, Liyah decided to skip breakfast entirely and take a walk in the mist. She was enjoying some alone time. She hadn't been alone since before the trip to Corresponding Point. This thought led her to a strange realization. Every year on Liyah's birthday, a heavy mist would set in. Liyah loved it. The mist made a certain air of calm surround her—an inner peace, rejuvenating her. At the same time, though, she found it odd that it came in every year no matter what the weather was like the day before.

After she had a long, quiet walk, she decided to go back to camp. The fog wasn't subsiding, and Liyah was still deep in her inner realm.

When she approached the camp, she noticed numerous shapes around their fire. There were, at most, thirteen people. Liyah braced herself.

She reached the camp. Everyone whipped around to face her and yelled, "Surprise! Happy birthday, Liyah!"

"Uh, thanks," Liyah said slowly.

Melanie was standing off to the side, holding a large cake. "We had the Corresponding Point cooks make this for you."

"Thanks, guys!" Liyah exclaimed. She finally grasped the fact that they were really here to celebrate her birthday. All nine she-warriors were there, and lo and behold, Ryvan, Tyrese, and their crew were gathered around as well.

They passed out the cake and sat around the fire, enjoying themselves. Liyah knew Melanie started this whole thing. Secretly, she was grateful. At first, she felt forgotten. It was good to feel special. She took a large bite of double-chocolate cake and relaxed.

****

After everyone finished eating their cake, they all began to fade out and do their own thing. Liyah began to thank Melanie,

"Thanks for this, Melanie. I was beginning to think you had forgotten me."

"Never could," Melanie laughed.

Ryvan decided to venture up and say, "Liyah, could I speak with you?"

Liyah glanced at Melanie who shot her an approving smile. Liyah stood up, and the pair walked off into the lazy mist.

"What's wrong?" Liyah asked.

"Nothing! It's just I wanted to wish you a happy birthday."

They both laughed.

Ryvan continued, "Also, I got you this." He pulled out a black ribbon choker necklace with black beads criss-crossing, forming a pattern all around it. A small silver cross hung from the black thread.

"I...wow. Thank you, Ryvan! You didn't have to do that!"

He placed the choker around her neck. Just as he thought, it contrasted perfectly with her light hair and tanned skin.

"I love it!"

"You're welcome," he smiled.

She gave him a hug, and out of nowhere a bloodcurdling scream was heard from out of the mist in the direction of their camp.

Shock suddenly leapt into Liyah's eyes. She quickly forced the feeling aside and replaced it with a look of the fierce warrior that rested just beneath the surface. They tore away and ripped their cross-blades out. The feeling in the air rose heavily toward danger.

They raced back to the camp to see who had caused the scream. The camp was in chaos. Everyone was running in every direction. A few people had their weapons out.

Ryvan stared into the fog to see around twenty black horses with streaming black manes and pulsing muscles riding toward them. Atop these mounts were dark creatures in black armor. They were huge, and their upper bodies were massive shield-shaped walls. It was a wonder the horses even supported the weight. Their faces were covered, and they all carried crude swords and flaming torches.

Ryvan was suddenly aware of a presence to his right. "What are they?" Liyah asked.

"It...I'm not sure," Ryvan muttered with a frown.

They were approaching rapidly. They suddenly slid to a halt when they reached the village center. The largest one of all took a torch and threw it atop the nearest home. The others followed suit. Each, save three, threw their torches upon the houses. The three creatures took their remaining torches and began riding through the camps, burning every tent.

Ryvan noted that Melanie and Tyrese stood over by Liyah and Melanie's tent with drawn weapons. When the creature noticed their defiance, he stopped his horse and glanced in their direction as the creature drew his sword. Tyrese stepped forward as the monster dropped from his mount with a dull thud that made dust fly in all directions. His sword hung from one of his massive arms. The blade was crafted from the same black metal from which the armor had been forged. The blade had a slightly menacing curve to it.

The black armor the creature wore screeched and clanged as it walked. The sound echoed in their ears. Tyrese swung at the demon but was blocked. They fought. Tyrese briefly lost his ground, but that gave the creature enough time to strike.

Tyrese cried out when the blade slashed his arm. Blood flowed from the open wound. He swung the sword up at the beast's large head, making contact. He knocked the monster's helmet off to reveal a putrid face. Red glowing eyes were embedded deep into the creature's skull. Its ears curved up like an elf's, but to a more grotesque manner. The nose was slightly similar to that of a human's. However, it was pointed along the end and appeared to have been smashed back into its face. The creature's mouth opened to reveal yellowed, jagged, rotten teeth that jutted out at odd angles—each a sharp fang. Its skin was the shade of green that resembled that of a corpse long past death. A dark purple slash streaked across its neck as a sort of brand.

The creature roared in fury. The noise was a deep cry of anger. Its eyes flared with fire. Tyrese sat, kneeling upon the earth in pain. He couldn't defend himself any longer. The demon brought his weapon in both hands high above for the final strike. Tyrese looked up with everlasting defiance and braced himself.

The instant before the creature delivered the final blow, an arrow slashed through the air and landed in the demon's throat. It gurgled, gasping for air as he fell forward onto his gruesome face. The weapon was forgotten.

Tyrese looked down at the body.

Everyone turned in the direction the arrow had come from to see the archer. Liyah stood still, aiming. She brought her bow down with a stern expression.

Tyrese struggled to his feet, cradling his right arm. Liyah and Ryvan approached the creature. Liyah kicked it.

"What *is* this thing?" Liyah cried. This time it seemed that she *needed* to know.

"Vortzans," Ryvan breathed in awe.

"What's that supposed to be?" Melanie asked.

"They are ancient. Supposed to be a legend!" Tyrese exclaimed through gritted teeth.

"But not for good. They were to serve as henchmen in the Dark One's rising army," Ryvan stated grimly.

The village smoldered. The Vortzans were destroying everything and everyone in their path. Nothing remained unscathed. The smoke rose into the air as the majestic city burned, creating a beacon of despair and anguish through the mist. The four resisting militants stood ready to defend themselves. They knew, however, that it was too late for Corresponding Point. It was beyond their power to control. They were suddenly noticed.

Apparently, the other Vortzans heard the cry from their fallen companion.

They whipped their covered faces toward the four resistant warriors. The leader cried out in a dark throaty voice that rasped out roughly, "Forget the others! Get the infidels!" It sounded like he had a hard time speaking.

They redirected their attention from the burning building to the group of four.

"No way!" Tyrese blurted.

Melanie gulped as Liyah said, "Aw, heck no! I am not getting killed by one of those twisted freaks!"

"Brace yourselves," Ryvan stated seriously.

The monsters surrounded them from all angles. The four were contained in a circle of demons. They stood back to back so they could defend from all angles.

The leader stepped forward from the group. "You! Girl! Come here!"

He was referring to Liyah. "Why?" she asked spitefully.

"Just do it!" he rasped.

She had no choice and stepped forward. He removed his helmet. "Put away the weapons. We won't harm you."

"You lie. I see it in your eyes," Liyah spat.

"Calm yourself, Liyah."

"You know my name. How?"

He did not reply. He pulled her closer to him by her neck and lifted her off the ground. The others flinched. Ryvan jerked forward but was restrained. "There are some things you need not worry your pretty little head about," he replied menacingly, chuckling as Ryvan struggled. His putrid breath filtered through her lungs and stung her eyes.

He was still holding her above the earth. Her eyes narrowed in defiance and disgust as she drew back and spit square into one of his red eyes. He cried out in pain. Liyah was dropped to the ground. The beast howled louder. Liyah couldn't understand why. She stared at him. Steam rose from the eye.

Both of the monster's hands covered it. Liyah felt slight warmth on her arm where her tattoo rested.

The creatures murmured amongst themselves. "Silence!" the leader exploded. He turned back to Liyah. His face filled with rage, and blood was pouring down from the ruined eye.

He seemed at a loss for words.

Liyah rose, dusting herself off. "Keep your hands off me, and it will all be good," Liyah stated angrily as she brushed off her shoulder.

He grabbed her by the arm and pulled her close again. He whipped her around and twisted her arm behind her head as she struggled against him.

He looked at her arm and shoved her away. This made her even angrier, and she cried with rage, "I said, keep your hands off of me!"

When no one replied, only gave her odd open-mouthed looks, she backed away and looked down at her arm. The moon on her bicep glowed with a radiant white light.

"It cannot be!" he breathed. "The Dark One will wish to see her. Keep her here. Don't let her out of your sight! She'll arrive soon." He turned to nine Vortzans and continued. "As for the others, do with them what you wish. The rest of you, come with me."

Liyah was taken by two others to be tied. She watched as all but the nine Vortzans left. Liyah stopped walking. The two Vortzans turned to face her as she whipped out her cross-blade, slashing one's throat and holding the sword to the other's neck.

He stabbed his sword toward her gut, but she ripped her other blade out, stopping him just before he penetrated her stomach. In one moment, he fell over his fallen companion.

Liyah replaced her blades and drew her crossbow. She had to help her friends. Yeah, friends with an s. She shook her head at the thought.

By now, they all had their hands tied behind their backs. One threw Melanie to the ground and raised his sword. Liyah's heart flipped. She aimed and released. The arrow flew through the air to stop in the Vortzan's neck. It fell over backward with his sword still raised.

The other Vortzan charged her as she raced for her horse, and Liyah cut the rope tying her horse to the rack, racing after the horse. She managed to mount while still running. Then, she turned on the horse, releasing an arrow, and another Vortzan fell.

Five Vortzans were left. Liyah withdrew her blade as she approached her friend's horses, slashing their ropes as well. Liyah quickly rode toward her friends, cut them free, and charged the Vortzans. She rode through the small troupe, destroying two and wounding one other. Her friends reached and mounted their own horses. Tyrese seemed to be having trouble holding on, and he was very pale. Ryvan went after the remaining Vortzans while Liyah and Melanie assisted Tyrese back onto the horse.

At that moment in time, the sky grew dark, and the air grew colder. Liyah rode up to Ryvan who had the last Vortzan on his knees begging for life. It grew even colder as the wind picked up. Thunder boomed. Lightning crashed. The Vortzan muttered with a sneer, "She's here."

Liyah kicked him square on the bridge of his nose with her heel, sending the bone up into his brain, killing him instantly. He fell over backward, unconscious.

"Sorry," she stated when Ryvan gave her a surprised look.

Chapter 13

The storm approached rapidly. When the lightning struck the earth, a dark horse appeared. Atop it sat a delicate figure covered with a dark cloak covering the face, obscuring its features.

"Enough of this! It ends now!" a powerful voice demanded.

The voice struck Liyah's memory, pulling at the back of her mind. As quickly as it had come, the thought left her as the Vortzans returned out of the burning village.

"My lord," the lead Vortzan said as he kneeled. "There she is." He pointed toward Liyah.

"I know who she is, you idiot!" the Dark One snarled. It was definitely a woman. "Take them away!"

The Vortzans took the three away and left Liyah alone with the Dark One. They stood, facing one another, in the darkness.

"What? Do you expect me to fear you?" Liyah scoffed.

"I don't expect that at all from you, Liyah."

Liyah tossed her hands in the air in exasperation. "Will somebody tell me how everyone knows my name?"

"You'll learn soon enough. Tell me, do you remember anything of your past?" she asked.

"What...what do you mean?" Liyah questioned.

"Apparently not. I'll help you though, dear. Vashevné!" the mistress cried, lifting her palm. A purple blast struck Liyah in the ribs, and she flew backward off her horse, and Mystique reared and bolted. Pain surged through every joint in Liyah's body. Every nerve ending burned. Liyah groaned and somehow managed to stand.

"Ring a bell?" the Dark One cackled.

"Who are you?"

The Dark One laughed violently. She dismounted and drew a blade. Her voice dripped malice as she stepped to Liyah and hissed, "Fight."

Liyah drew both cross-blades. She felt a growing sense of hatred for this woman that she could not place. Liyah slashed toward her opponent who blocked her with ease. As soon as the blades struck one another, a stream of white and purple light issued from the joint. The purple light streamed down the cross-blades and issued into Liyah. It sent her backward onto the ground once again. Pain shocked her as it burned her veins. She looked down. Her cross-blade lay shattered on the ground. She felt rage grow in her.

"Where are they taking my friends?" Liyah demanded.

"What?" the witch asked innocently.

"You heard me," Liyah stated from her kneeling position. Her head was bowed and hair covered her face.

"They'll be executed," she laughed lightly.

Liyah lashed out with her remaining blade. Again, Liyah felt the searing pain, and her blade shattered.

She laughed again. Liyah's blades lay broken. The pain was so intense that it took her a moment to get into a kneeling position.

"You never learn, Liyah. You didn't then, and you haven't now."

"Why?" Liyah asked.

"I don't know. I'm not you," she replied, sheathing her sword.

"You turned into a real firebrand, didn't you?" she smiled. "In answer to your question, to make you suffer!"

"What have I done to you?"

"You shall learn soon enough. I've said enough already. I would much rather show you as we get to know one another again. Oh! Look at the time." she exclaimed. "Your friends should be dead by now."

Liyah frowned. A deep anger boiled within her, rising to fury.

"Be grateful, I spared you."

Liyah charged her.

"Vashevné!" the witch cursed. This time the light struck Liyah in the forehead, confusing her and making her head spin.

"Until we meet again, Liyah. Shetrãq!"

It struck her between the eyes, and things grew dark as the Mistress of the Darkness rode off to see to the execution.

Liyah was left on the ground, rain spattering over her unseeing eyes.

****

Mystique nudged Liyah's neck to wake her. Liyah lifted a hand to reassure her companion. She groaned and grabbed onto Mystique's neck. Her sapphire eyes met Liyah's brown ones.

Liyah gathered her remaining strength and stood. Her head ached. She pulled her crossbow out to see that it was cracked. It wouldn't break for a while, but eventually it would become useless.

Her cross-blades lay in ruins at her feet along with the remains of Corresponding Point. The great city was reduced to burning rubble and ash coated in blood.

Liyah felt pain all over her. She looked down to see small cuts covering her stomach and upper arms where her armor had not protected her from the shattering blades. Shards of her blades had sliced right through her, and a few fragments remained.

The city smoldered. There was no sign of human or any other form of life. Bodies littered the ground, and Liyah had to force herself to look away, dreading meeting the hollow eyes of someone she once knew. Liyah began to pull the shards out of her arms and legs instead.

It hit her. Melanie was really gone. Never again would Liyah be face to face with her closest friend who was like a sister to her. Pain stabbed at her heart.

Tyrese. He was gone as well. Once more, she was stabbed by the bitter realization.

Her she-warrior and new warrior friends were gone, too. *Grateful*...the dark witch had said she should be grateful. Liyah wished it could have been her instead.

She cursed the Dark One and mounted her horse. She began to ride through the debris. She had nowhere to turn. No provisions. Nothing. Everything was gone.

Then, the final thought hit her. It stabbed deep into her heart like a knife. *Ryvan*. He was gone as well. This topped off the pain, and it took over. A silent tear fell from her eye for her lost friends as she rode on with her head bowed.

****

So much pain stabbed at Liyah's heart. She toyed with the idea that a shard of her broken cross-blades had penetrated it instead of pain of loss. She knew they would have wanted her to carry on. She was only faced with one option—the Galiphems. She had to find them. They held the only thing left for the young, humiliated she-warrior.

She pulled out the card. It was still blank. Liyah shook her head and cast the card down onto the ground. Sitting down next to it, Liyah folded her arms around her knees. She rested her head on her arms and thought about what she had to do.

After some time, she looked up again at the card and saw it just as it began to change. Elegant blue lettering began to sweep across the surface. She snatched up the card. It read:

> Follow the River as It Runs
> To Find the Land of Golden Sun.

Liyah pocketed the clue and decided then and there, she was going to become a Galiphem.

She kicked Mystique lightly, and the horse reared, racing off toward the running river. It was Liyah's only option, beginning her journey through tears, pain, and hatred.

****

Liyah reached the river and began following it southwest and rode without stopping. She had never been to this part of the Osheyks. Very few people had. She didn't know what to expect, and she knew that unfamiliar territory could be perilous.

As night fell, Liyah dismounted to allow Mystique to drink, eat, and rest her muscles before pressing on. She didn't want to stop, but her horse needed the break.

Once Mystique was rested, Liyah mounted and continued. All through the night, she rode along the river as the moonlight made the water glisten, running through rapids.

The moonlight gave everything an eerie sheen. Every tree seemed like an enemy ready to strike. Liyah's sadness had turned to bitter rage, and she wanted revenge. However, she could clearly see that she needed more training. No matter how good she had become, it was not enough to compete with the Dark One. The Galiphems were her answer; they would help.

When the sun rose, Mystique slowed to a walk. Liyah didn't want to injure her horse. The smell of salt began to fill the air more and more as she followed the river. She assumed that she was nearing the sea that surrounded Shroeketia on all sides.

She noticed that the rapids began to steadily increase. Mystique slowed. She was getting too tired. Liyah dismounted against her better judgment to give Mystique a break. She looked around, facing the river. She had to admit that it was a breathtaking view. Liyah stood on the bank admiring it all.

Suddenly, something charged her from behind, and Liyah fell headfirst into the river. The current pulled her under as the rapids pushed her forward. She couldn't do anything. She was finally forced back above the water and gasped for air, continually sweeping downstream. It was a struggle for her to just stay above water. Liyah thrashed about, but the rapids were violent. She was taken by them as they struck her hard against a large rock. The blow injured her, and her strength drained.

Liyah turned her attention downstream, and to her horror, she saw a giant waterfall tumbling down over rocky cliffs just as she would soon do.

She tried harder to swim away from it, but her attempts were useless. Just before she was swept over, she glanced upward. Off to the side, she saw a pair of yellow eyes looking out from the bushes. When Liyah had nothing left in her, she was swept over the falls, and she fell down into the mist.

****

Liyah splashed down into the water. She sank deep under the surface. The waterfall had been a large one, and it seemed as if she had fallen forever. There was no energy left in her. She could feel no new injuries, and she decided to relax and float on her back until she reached shore.

Then she felt a strange pull against her body. She looked up. There, in front of her, generating the strange pull that was steadily increasing was a giant whirlpool.

"Oh, awesome," Liyah stated emotionlessly.

She tried to swim away once again, but it was useless. Down into the spinning funnel of doom she went. It took her under quickly, spinning downward, until she wasn't aware of anything around her—only darkness.

****

Liyah lay motionless on the sandy shore of a distant land. She washed up directly after the whirlpool spit her out into an open area. She was unconscious again.

She moaned as she woke. Liyah moved herself onto her stomach and then to her knees. She wasn't fully awake, yet. "I hate that river."

Liyah spat blood on the ground and realized that the rock she hit busted her mouth. Grimacing, she looked up to see a palace made of metal that sparkled in the sunlight like gold as if it were made of millions of shining stars against the inky black sky line. It was one of the most wondrous sights Liyah had ever seen. Her eyes dilated, and she blacked out once more only to fall heavily sideways to the earth with a dull thud.

"Where is she?!" the lead Vortzan exploded.

"If you speak of Liyah Encarcerá, then you need not know," the Dark One replied.

"Sorry, your Highness."

"Where are the others?"

The Dark One and the commanding officer were walking back toward the army to prepare to leave Corresponding Point.

"One was escorted by three main guards to be executed. I will be taking care of another one personally. The last is here with us as you know."

"What of Corresponding Point and the other village tribes?"

"Nothing is left but ash."

"Very well. We must ride before the morning light," the witch stated.

"Yes, your Highness," the lead Vortzan bowed. He turned toward his fellow mutilated monsters and cried in his the language of old, "Shélteveré cashellâ!"

The Vortzans mounted their dark horses. As the beasts carrying the monsters began to distort, the darkness enveloped them. Then they were gone. Only a few Vortzan guards remained to accompany the execution victims back to camp.

****

Part III
Becoming

Change, warrior. Do not blend with the way of this land.
Be changed with the refreshing of your soul and mind.
—Courteuricans 12:2

Chapter 14

Tyrese's arm bled badly. The Vortzans sensed his pain and seemed to grow stronger. They could not speak in his language. However, they continued speaking.

When Tyrese showed signs of confusion, the Vortzans made a despicable coughing sound. Tyrese assumed that this was their twisted form of laughter.

Before the four were separated, Melanie, Ryvan, and Tyrese had been bound. Tyrese's weapons were stripped away from him. However, they left Melanie's and Ryvan's weapons in their places. They had scoffed and snapped Tyrese's blades with such a superior power that it made the three young warriors feel inferior to their strength.

The lead Vortzan had approached the others and spoke in the unknown language. Then, nine of the largest Vortzans drew out from the crowd of the small army that had appeared with the Dark One's arrival. They divided into groups of three. Each trio brandished their weapons and took each one of the three humans in different directions. And so they were separated.

They could do nothing. Tyrese hung his head in shock as he walked. Every now and then he would stumble. He felt the blood in his face drain. Also, he knew he was losing his lifeblood from the wound on his arm. He was so weak. He soon wouldn't be able to lift his head and carry on. Then, who knew what would happen to him.

Then, Tyrese tripped and could not continue. He stopped in a curled over position, facing the earth. Just before the Vortzans began to torture him, lightning flashed down directly in front of Tyrese—purple lightning. The Dark Mistress stood about a foot in front of Tyrese.

A sick feeling snaked into Tyrese's stomach. He knew this wouldn't be good.

"What's going on?" she asked.

The Vortzans seemed to understand her but replied in their own native tongue. Apparently, she understood, for she smiled and said to Tyrese's amazement, "Assist him. He shall not be executed. He is under my protection as of now."

Tyrese's jaw dropped. She approached him, and the three Vortzans stepped back out of her way. She placed her finger delicately under his chin. A surge of cold ran through his veins like ice, making his skin crawl. She smiled, like she knew the effect and forced his eyes to meet hers. She crouched down face to face with him.

He glared at her, but she acted like she didn't notice. She never stopped smiling a dark smile that Tyrese couldn't take his eyes off of. She forced him to look at her alone. Her mouth was the only part of her face that was not hidden by the cloak, yet Tyrese felt like he was looking directly into her eyes. "You shall not be harmed. I'm watching over you now." She said to him in a voice that made Tyrese's stomach crawl yet again. She glanced at his injured arm which was hanging limp at his side. She forced him to stand up to his full height, making him wince. "We must take care of that," she spoke mildly like it was a paper cut.

She reached out tenderly and touched his arm. He winced again, but she ignored his pain and increased the pressure. She breathed a single word, "Savéncy."

Dark purple light protruded from her palm into his open wound. He cried out. White-hot pain surged through him, searing his skin like acid. Smoke even began to rise from the wound. He could feel the heat of her power running through his bloodstream. Then, as quickly as it had begun, she removed her palm, and the pain left him. He stood, flexing his arm, working it, testing it. He grew angry at the thought of evil power healing him.

She smiled, "There now, you have been healed. I can be anything you wish if you will only join me, Tyrese."

His anger burned like flames. He knew what she was trying to say. He couldn't take it anymore. Then, he spat bitterly, "I would rather die than be healed with your dark powers, witch."

Anger tweaked her nerves for a moment. Then she calmed herself and replied seriously, "You are young and foolish, but think on my proposition." Darkness began to creep around them. "You could be great, Tyrese. I know of your past."

Before Tyrese could say any more, she disappeared into the surrounding darkness. Tyrese wasn't finished, and he wanted to ask her some questions. He started to say something, but a voice came out of the darkness saying, "Vortzans, take him. Do not harm him. And as for you, Tyrese, I shall give you time. In time we shall see if you can become what it takes.

The darkness enclosed around the group, and the Vortzans drug him along. When the darkness cleared, Tyrese realized they were standing beside three of the dark horses. There was something sinister about them.

As he watched, the horses seemed to change. Eyes grew slanted, and fangs protruded. When something began taking place, darkness enclosed again. Tyrese was suddenly struck over the head by the bottom of a Vortzan blade. He collapsed. The darkness became deeper, or perhaps that was merely Tyrese's vision abandoning him.

****

When Tyrese awoke, he was lying on a patch of soft grass just outside of a Vortzan campsite. There was a myriad of them. Groups of around six of the Vortzans sat around a single fire inside of a ring of tents. It closely resembled the warrior and she-warrior campsites. Tons of fires glistened in the distance. Tyrese realized it was dark. The smell of smoke and Vortzan filled the air. It stung Tyrese's eyes and nostrils. He coughed and rapidly silenced himself, for he didn't want the Vortzans to hear him. However, he analyzed that the demons were paying him no mind.

Tyrese's head throbbed from the Vortzan blade. He rolled onto his back and looked up, expecting to see a starry sky, but what he saw made him yelp and draw back. Standing above him was the Dark Mistress. He stood.

"Welcome back," she grinned. Her face was still covered by the dark cloak. She walked around lightly. Tyrese wondered if she even touched the ground. She seemed to float just above the earth. "What's your answer, Tyrese?"

"I've told you what I think," he replied tersely.

"Don't voice your opinion so hastily," she purred, taking a step toward him.

He stepped back. "I won't change my mind."

"Oh, Tyrese! Forget her." Tyrese snapped to attention. "By now, she is gone." Tyrese glanced at her in shock. "Yes, she's been taken care of. No worries though, I am much better."

"I don't believe you."

"Oh, but it is true," she smiled, showing all of her teeth.

Tyrese's brain slowed, and he thought her canine teeth seemed too sharp.

"I would never work with you. Melanie is alive. I know it, and she will always—in life or death—be better than you. You disgust me."

This hit a raw nerve. She called for her guards, telling them, "He is of no more use to me. Prepare to execute him tomorrow at dawn. Farewell, Tyrese. It's a pity and a sin—you have no idea what you are throwing away. You could have had it all, but, sadly, you have chosen destruction, devastation, and death."

"I know what I do."

"What a waste."

She stalked off. The guards bound and gagged Tyrese with thick ropes. Then, one Vortzan took his blade and stabbed the warrior in his shoulder socket. Tyrese winced, and more lifeblood flowed. They tied him to a mighty oak tree set far from their camp for the night. Tyrese watched for any sign of hope. But none came.

Melanie fell to her knees. Her hands were tied behind her back. She could not catch herself; so she fell hard and tasted ashy dust.

The three Vortzans laughed menacingly. She pulled herself up once more as she had done many times. The demons seemed to be taunting her. They would shove her to the ground repeatedly, only for her to rise and fall over and over again, and her knees had become a bloody mess.

Then a Vortzan sliced through her ropes. Melanie rubbed her wrists where the rope had rubbed her skin raw. The Vortzans drew their dark blades with malicious grins on their hideous faces. They wanted to fight her.

Melanie drew back. She cautiously pulled out her cross-blades. She had no choice. If she didn't fight, she would have no chance of survival. They were going to kill her here. That was why they had separated her from the others.

One monster charged her. She blocked and slashed. The other two joined the battle with their comrade. The Vortzan armor was strong, and Melanie realized she wouldn't be able to do much damage unless her aim was perfectly to the throat. Three to one wasn't exactly a fair fight, and Melanie was beginning to falter. Despite this, she managed to fall an enemy.

The others attacked more viciously. She blocked them both at once, pushed them back, and turned, shifting her weight, thrusting her head down below her body near her stable leg. She swung her other foot around high above to meet the Vortzan's face. The roundhouse kick landed a blow to the helmet, knocking him into its partner. They both went down—one trapped below its disoriented companion.

"I did it!" she exclaimed. She bent down and said, "Hah! I've been trained by the best." Then, to herself, "Liyah was right."

The stunned Vortzans groaned, and Melanie ran while she still had time. She raced toward the burnt camp. She needed to reach her horse.

****

When Melanie reached camp, there were no signs of life anywhere. The fire burning in Corresponding Point continued to blaze. The two Vortzans had regained their senses and were rapidly gaining on her. One single stride of their powerful legs was equal to three of Melanie's own.

She searched frantically for Marentex. Suddenly, she caught a glimpse of pure white. She knew instantly that the radiant light issued forth from her horse. Melanie leapt upon the animal and raced away from the dark creatures, but she couldn't shake them. So she raced into the thick clouds of smoke that billowed from the town.

She finally eluded the Vortzans and slowed Marentex to a trot. She knew that the beasts would soon track her down, and that she had to get somewhere safe, but she didn't know where she could possibly go. Melanie thought about the other towns but instantly knew that they were no more.

When she thought all hope was lost, an idea blinked in Melanie's head. She reached for the card the Galiphem warrior woman had given her. It was her only option. She desired to find her lost companions, but knew that there was only a small sliver of hope. They would have wanted her to continue on.

Melanie looked at the burning meeting center as a tear silently rolled down her cheek. She could recall Liyah's words as this occurred, "She-warriors do not cry." Melanie turned her horse toward the river.

****

Melanie followed the river swiftly, pausing only to give Marentex a break. She clambered off the horse's back, sitting on the rich green grass. It was still warm from the sunlight. She stared up into the inky, black sky spotted with burning stars. Out of nowhere, a spidery crawl of lightning flashed down from the sky above Corresponding Point. It was purple.

"That's odd," Melanie said aloud to herself. She looked but could not see anything for the trees. "I suppose it's for the best."

Zing! She felt a surge of pain on her right ear. She reached up lightly and touched it. Then she drew her hand away, seeing blood. Melanie looked up. The two Vortzans she had knocked out were racing toward her on their black horses. And if that wasn't enough, they were shooting arrows at her.

She leapt onto Marentex once more, and they raced down the river bank. Arrows flew past her head, barely missing her. Each time the vortzans were getting more accurate. It wouldn't be long before the arrows found their target.

Melanie looked ahead to see a great waterfall and a dead drop off, but it was too late to stop Marentex. When the horse noticed the cliff, she tried to stop but only slid on the dry gravel and dirt, bringing up clouds of dust.

They exploded off the side of the cliff into a free fall into the devouring mist below. The Vortzans approached the edge, scoffed, and fired a few arrows down into the mist before they turned away. They knew they need not waste their time with the dead.

Ryvan stood rigid and strong despite the three Vortzans guarding him as they traipsed toward the burning village center. The mixing smell of Vortzan (a combination of every nasty rotting thing under the sun) and smoke made Ryvan nauseous.

They approached the lead Vortzan who was throwing another torch aboard the already burning meeting place of the elders. He turned to face Ryvan and scoffed.

"Oh, he's here. Buértaken Sevuél!" the beast laughed.

The three guard Vortzans departed and left Ryvan facing the evil thing alone. Ryvan was amazed at the size of the beast.

"I have orders to destroy you personally, boy," he grinned with malice. "It seems you are of no need to my queen. It will be all too easy. However, I'll give you a chance. Stand tall and fight me, boy."

Ryvan saw that it was his only choice. This would be a challenge for him. The Vortzan towered over him and was much stronger. Ryvan drew his cross-blades as the Vortzan brandished his weapon. He was teasing Ryvan.

The Vortzan lashed out at the human who dodged the blow. Ryvan flipped his blades back and forth in various attacks to tire the large creature, but he was mostly tiring himself. They went on for quite some time. Ryvan barely escaped the deadly blows from the Vortzan's sword.

"I have to say, you are better than I thought," the thing panted.

Ryvan didn't reply. Instead, he doubled his blades as one single blade and swung beneath the Vortzan's helmet. It was the shot capable of ending the demon's life but was shaken off as if he was merely a child attacking.

There was so much power in his blow that when blocked, his blades shattered into tiny fragments, knocking Ryvan to the earth, defenseless. He noted that his bow had disappeared. The thing cackled and took slow menacing steps toward Ryvan.

"Now, you shall rejoin your friend, his companion, and that *she-warrior* you have come to know so well." The way he had said the word "she-warrior" made it sound like a dirty word or some vile filthy being.

Ryvan stared blankly at him.

"That's right. They are all dead by now. The boy and girl—executed by Vortzan guards. The other, she will have been destroyed by the mighty Navaira herself. Don't mourn, you shall see them all again—very soon in fact. I'll assist you."

The Vortzan ripped the weapon down through the air toward Ryvan's head. Ryvan rolled aside safely as the blade drove into the earth.

"Why are you making this so complicated?" the Vortzan sighed.

"You killed them."

"Certainly! The two were inferior."

Ryvan tensed.

"They were of no use to us. The she-warrior, Liyah—she was something else, though. I have a question for you. Did you *really* think she cared for you as well? She is a *she-warrior*. Oh, my mistake—*was* a she-warrior. They are not capable of feeling *anything*. They are cold. She was to become the most dangerous, heartless, cruel being on the face of the earth. I bet you didn't know that. She would *never* care for you—a lowly warrior. Don't make me laugh."

It was the final tease before the monster finished it.

Ryvan grew angry.

"It seems I've hit a sore spot," it laughed. "Why *would* you even care for *her*? She was *nothing* but a ...but a proud—"

"Stop."

"Cruel—"

"Stop it!"

"Heartless—"

"I'm warning you!"

"Sorry excuse of a—"

"I said *stop*!!"

"Sub-human creature. Uncaring and unloving. *Never*, I said *never*, would she care for you."

"STOP!" Ryvan cried with so much blind fury that something strange happened. A strong force in the form of golden light blazed out of him in the surrounding directions. It struck the demon, and it issued a pained scream.

The power pulsed through the ground as an earthquake. Strength left him. The power departed as quickly as it had come, and it grew silent. He looked up to see that the Vortzan lay on his back, eyes wide, destroyed by light.

****

Night set in as Ryvan watched the Vortzan camp from a safe distance, hidden by the protective cover of trees. After he had exuded power of some sort from within, he decided on a whim to follow the dark creatures to find any small sign that might prove that even one of his friends were still alive. He knew the chances were slim, but he felt that he owed it to them. They all owed Liyah, especially Tyrese. She had saved his life.

It was very late, and some Vortzans were already turning in. Ryvan's eyes ravaged the camp. There seemed to be nothing, but he couldn't give up just yet. There had to be some sign.

Ryvan had no idea how he had gained so much power and exerted it so quickly. He didn't even realize what he had been doing. His anger had burned so strongly, and he felt his life-energy drain significantly. Ryvan was not a sorcerer. They were dark creatures which all warriors detested. He didn't know magic—unless this strange, new power was a part of his dark, unknown past.

Ryvan pulled out the calling card of the Galeãns. The moonlight shone down on it, and he could make out shimmering blue letters saying:

> The Card has Felt Your Time of Need,
> In the Time You Need be Free.
> Follow the River as It Runs,
> To Find the Land of Golden Sun.

Ryvan looked up to see that at last all of the Vortzans were sleeping inside their tents, and all the fires were extinguished. The only light came from the moon and stars in the heavens. They wrought ghostly shadows all throughout the demon camp. It was deathly quiet, and there were no signs of life. Ryvan was about to give up hope.

Suddenly he saw a faint motion of something moving on the other side of the trees. Verexn, Ryvan's bay horse, grew unsettled. A few Vortzan guards gathered around one single tree. They laughed and seemed to be enjoying themselves thoroughly. After a time, the creatures left, seeking rest before setting out in the morning.

Allowing the guards time to fall into a deep sleep, Ryvan guided Verexn over to the tree where the guards had gathered only a moment before, to see for himself what was so funny. As Ryvan drew closer, the silhouette of a person grew visible. Ryvan approached with caution, and the bay seemed to calm. The person hung his head, defeated. Then he raised his head, hearing the sound of gravel crunching underfoot. He looked almost like—

"Tyrese?" Ryvan whispered to the figure.

Ryvan leapt off the horse and ripped out one of his knives that hadn't been broken in his fight. He took the cloth out of Tyrese's mouth and worked furiously on the ropes. Halfway through, Ryvan saw movement out of the corner of his eye. He froze. Out of the trees, a figure appeared. Tyrese's horse wandered out of the forest.

They sighed their relief, and Tyrese said, "Now we can get out of here faster."

"Yeah, when I get you free, we'll start on the plan."

"What plan?"

"The plan I'm about to tell you."

"Oh, that plan."

"Well, my friend, how many people have saved your backside today?" Ryvan taunted.

"Shut up."

As Ryvan finished cutting Tyrese out, the sun began to creep up over the mountains just enough to shine a touch of light through the morning valley. Ryvan and Tyrese discussed a plan.

While they were speaking, a Vortzan stumbled out of his tent. Instantly, he spotted the two light horses and their riders. It only took him a moment to raise the alarm cry to awaken the whole camp of demons. To top it all off, the boys were unarmed.

"Awaken…awaken, Liyah Encarcerá…awaken!" a soothing voice murmured from far off. It drew Liyah back from her distant place.

Liyah was aware that she was lying on a soft bed. She was warm and dry again, but she wasn't in her armor. She wore something light, but comfortable.

Liyah opened her eyes. The owner of the voice came into focus. "Welcome, Liyah Encarcerá," the voice said. The person was a she-warrior of sorts. She wore an all white cloth material in place of armor. The top piece was a midriff that draped across her left arm and cut in underneath her right arm.

The warrior wore a short skirt about the length of Liyah's armored one. It was frayed at the bottom and cut into jagged strips. Her straight, golden-brown hair reached down past her shoulders. Her eyes were a deep brown, and her face was covered by freckles from spending time in the sun. She carried no weapons.

Liyah looked around, and saw that she was in a small, bare room. She lay on a small bed covered with a linen sheet. There were no windows, but a small glowing stalactite hung from the ceiling, lighting the entire room. A spider web pattern of gold covered the stalactite elegantly.

Liyah blinked. She propped herself up and groaned, "What…what did you call me?"

"All will be explained. Come now. There is much to see, but first, the queen."

Liyah stood. She realized that she was now wearing the same garment as the mysterious stranger. However, Liyah still wore her old heels and jewelry. A queen? Then it hit her. No doubt, she had obviously made it to Galeã. She didn't know when or how, but she knew she had arrived.

Her crossbow was gone. "Where—" she began.

"Come now," the woman interrupted.

Liyah followed silently. They left the room and entered a winding hallway. Liyah saw many more elaborately furnished rooms. Emerging from the hallway, Liyah found herself in a huge, domed room approximately the size of a small city. Liyah looked up to see a huge stalactite light looming over them. It was one-hundred times the size of the one in the first room.

They were walking along a plush red carpet with a trim outlined in gold. To their left and right were huge pillars and beyond that, balconies leading out into the fresh air. The whole building was crafted entirely out of a metal like gold.

Liyah turned her head forward. In front of them sat a large golden throne. Two warrior women stood on either side of it. They carried large spears, a bow, and a shield. They wore steel armor and full helmets with a plume that stuck out of the top, but as Liyah looked, she noticed that the plume was actually half of the warriors' hair. The other portion peered out from beneath the helmet. The women looked severe and disciplined. They stood on guard, still as statues. Two torches were mounted on either side of them.

It was obvious as to whom they were guarding. Sitting on the throne was a harsh-looking woman with an elegant golden crown upon her head. Golden jewelry with diamonds, emeralds, and rubies covered her body, and her long, black hair wafted down her shoulders. Her deep green eyes gazed wisely at Liyah. She wore golden armor inlaid with more jewels. No doubt, this was their queen. She reminded Liyah of someone, but she wasn't sure who.

"Speak," the woman barked.

This was not what she had expected to hear.

Liyah was taken aback. She stood open-mouthed for a moment, regained her composure, and said, "My name is Liyah of Faeciã., and I have come here in regards that I was offered a position here…and, that….I have nowhere else to go."

"We know who you are and of what accords you are here. You will begin your training immediately and be placed in the challenge on the next full moon," the queen said with authority. "You will receive your own personal trainer. She will help you prepare for some of the trials you will face. Jasira!"

The girl who had awakened Liyah immediately tensed and stood taller.

"You will be that trainer," the queen stated.

"Yes, my queen," Jasira replied.

"Welcome, Liyah Encarcerá, to Galeã. May luck follow you. You will need it."

****

"Come, Liyah, I will show you around. Then we will begin your training," Jasira stated, leading Liyah out of the great hall.

She was shown the remainder of the castle. There were many beautiful rooms, but most were off limits to people of Liyah's stature. Before leaving the palace, Jasira took Liyah to the armory and brought out a package wrapped in brown paper. She handed it to Liyah with a small smile. Surprisingly, Liyah's name was on it.

"Open it," Jasira smiled.

Inside the box were two blades that looked exactly like her old ones.

"Cross-blades!" Liyah exclaimed testing them. "How did you—"

"All will be explained."

Liyah beamed and when satisfied, placed them on her back.

Then, Jasira handed her a beautifully crafted bow. Made of strong oak, the bow curved at the ends elegantly. It had various designs etched into the wood, and the center bore the same symbol that had been on the guards' shields.

"What is this?" Liyah asked pointing directly to the symbol.

"The Galeãn crest. It shows you are a member, but technically, you aren't one yet. You must first take part in the challenge. That is all I shall say. Now, we will train."

She strapped a similar bow to her back and attached a long-sword to her right hip. Jasira was apparently left-handed. Afterward, Jasira led Liyah to the stable. "It is much faster upon horses," she stated.

Liyah felt a pang of sadness bite at her heart. Jasira sensed this and asked, "Liyah, what troubles you?"

"Nothing really. It's just when I was pushed into the river, my horse. I don't know what happened to her," Liyah replied in a melancholy voice.

Jasira smiled, "All is well. A warrior's horse can be her greatest companion. Do not be sad. Your horse is fine. She was taken in as well. All horses come along when they are special."

"Special?" Liyah asked.

Jasira did not reply, but whistled a high note. A dark brown horse cantered up to the gate. It had large, warm eyes and seemed to be the color of dark chocolate. "This is Cheria," Jasira smiled as she patted her horse. She let the creature out. "She belongs to me."

Instantly, Liyah knew what was so special about Cheria. Two graceful, feathered membranes protruded from either side of the steed's body.

Liyah's jaw dropped. "I thought they were just a legend," she exclaimed. "The mythical creature. She is a winged horse!"

"That she is. They are the ancient steeds of the Galiphem warriors. There was only one race greater than they, the Asgarnian horses of old, the Horses of Element. My friend, I give you *your* steed."

At that moment, Mystique emerged from within the darkness of the stable. It seemed to brighten as her horse emerged. Radiant light beams issued forth from her.

"Mystique!" Liyah exclaimed, running toward her. As she approached, Liyah realized that her horse, too, now had a pair of elegant wings.

"What happened?" Liyah asked.

"You were not aware, were you?" Jasira asked.

"Aware of what?" Liyah exclaimed, awestruck.

"Of what was yours. You, Liyah, own an Asgarnian horse of old, a legendary Horse of Element."

Liyah dropped her chin in awe as she patted Mystique.

"Climb on, Liyah. I must show you the kingdom."

Liyah hesitated and mounted cautiously. Jasira did the same, except more expertly. Liyah faltered around the wings.

Instantly, Liyah felt Mystique launch powerfully off the earth into the great expanse of sky. Liyah's eyes dilated, and she clung to the horse.

Wind whipped around Liyah's face, slashing her hair like a whip in the air behind her. All of the blood in her face left her, turning her deathly pale when she glanced down at the sights below. Mystique's wings beat powerfully against the currents of wind as she glided gracefully through the sky.

"At least one of us is calm," Liyah thought.

Jasira pulled in beside her and cried, "Liyah! You are too high. You must pull back."

"I would if I knew how!" Liyah snapped.

"Steer her like you always have. The only difference is when you want to go up or down, lean forward or back. It's quite simple," Jasira yelled over the wind.

"It's quite simple," Liyah mocked. She considered this and leaned forward, causing them to ease downward, lessening the wind current, and the air warmed. The pair of riders eased off and let the horses fly at their own pace.

"Down below is the castle of Queen Galetreã," Jasira informed. Liyah peered down and saw the huge golden palace glittering in all of its glory.

They traveled on to the east. Beneath the horses and riders, a small village lay. Many people hurried through the twists and turns in separate groups. Further east, a dark and sinister wood crept around a large lake.

"This is where warriors stay," Jasira stated. "The wood you see there is the Impenatiã Forest. It is a vile and desolate place. Never enter there unless informed by our queen. We must depart now. There is nothing much left to see, and we must begin our training." The girls headed due west toward the mountains.

****

"These are the Galeãn Mountains," Jasira explained.

After the girls had traveled across the island, they rested high in the peaks of the mountains.

"Why are we here?" Liyah asked.

"This is where we shall train. There are no distractions. Just the fight for precious life," Jasira replied as they dismounted.

"Life?" Liyah asked in shock.

Just then, a giant, white wolf the size of a bear with large fangs emerged from behind a boulder. Its eyes were blood red, and its claws clattered on the rocks as it stepped toward them, snarling.

"This is a saber-toothed firock. It has a little higher skill level, but I think you can handle it. You are to use your bow," Jasira instructed.

Liyah reached for a golden arrow and her bow.

She then took a protective stance as the white firock began to circle her. Liyah followed the circle as well, leveling the playing field.

"Picture what you want your arrow to become in your mind. Then, fire, and it will," Jasira stated.

Liyah drew her bow string back. Her arms grew tense as she took her aim. She released her arrow toward the firock with ease. As soon as the arrow began speeding through the air, it transformed to become sharper and caught fire.

The arrow struck the firock in the chest, and his fur caught fire. He did not howl or cry out in pain, but fell to the earth in a large heap.

Liyah turned to Jasira and smiled, "That was easy."

Jasira pointed back toward the creature with a smirk and grinned, "*Fire*-rock!"

Just then, Liyah felt a sharp pain run through her right arm. She glanced down and saw the firock, now black from flame, lick blood off his massive forepaw. It wasn't dead after all.

"Always mind your surroundings, and never turn your back on an enemy," Jasira laughed. She seemed to be enjoying herself. Liyah wondered what was wrong with her.

The firock finished cleaning his paw and stared at Liyah with his blank red eyes, hungry for more. All at once, he leapt off his hind legs, through the air, at his prey.

When it was just a moment from tearing into her flesh, Liyah released another arrow, but this time, the tip turned an acid green and struck the creature between the eyes.

The creature howled and fell once more to the ground as Liyah rolled out of harm's way. The firock lay writhing on the ground at Liyah's feet. It clawed and scratched at its head, then ceased movement altogether when the last breath of life left him.

"Poison. Very effective, Liyah. Well done!" Jasira clapped for her.

"Whatever. Thanks for nothing."

"You fought well, but you are here to improve. Before we move on, we should see to that wound. You did well in arrow choice, but you see, these arrows can become *anything*—daggers, swords, explosives. However, you must remember that your arrows can only become various things in a place of magic."

"I see," Liyah replied.

"Come. You have much more in store for you."

Chapter 15

"Remember the plan, Tyrese," Ryvan stated as he turned his horse. "Our best bet is to split up for now. But, stick to the plan!"

"I hope to see you again, my brother," Tyrese said.

"We will meet again. Now go!" Ryvan shouted, racing into the cover of the woods.

The Vortzans wasted no time plowing out of their tents for the fight. They were coming for Tyrese.

The warrior turned his horse toward the river and began to flee. The plan was to meet on the island of Geriã. Ryvan had said he would need to follow the river until details were revealed. He hoped the details would appear soon.

Tyrese ran for a short time, then turned back to see if the beasts were following. He was surprised to see that no one was pursuing him.

"That was easy," Tyrese mumbled. He slowed his horse to a canter, following the river and waiting for Ryvan.

Vatran trotted along the raging river, while Tyrese enjoyed the scenery and solitude. The sun was rising, and it illuminated the countryside with a red-orange glow. He was thoroughly enjoying himself, when the sound of approaching hooves filled the air.

Tyrese turned, and to his dismay, hundreds of Vortzans, were trailing him on horseback. The dark beasts with flaming eyes snorted as hot sulfurous breath surged from their nostrils, creating clouds of condensation in the air.

"Not again!" Tyrese cried. He urged Vatran on, and the beast lurched, kicking up earth where its feet had been a moment earlier.

****

The Vortzans had been following their fugitive for hours. Vatran was tiring and wouldn't be able to continue much longer. A strange sound reached Tyrese's ears as they ran on. A slight roaring became louder with each step.

Then a second before they were about to plunge over the cliff and down the waterfall, Tyrese pulled back hard on the reins and barely stopped the horse from tumbling down into the mist with the rocks.

Tyrese was trapped. Panicking, he could not find an escape route. The Vortzans surrounded him on all sides. There was nowhere to go, but down. A large Vortzan stepped out of the circle and said in English, "You are finished. You have two options. Come with us and die, or fall to your doom."

Tyrese spit and replied immediately, "I will kill myself before I hand myself over to demonic creatures of your kind."

Tyrese leaned far back on his horse, causing the beast to falter and both fell, separated into the depths below.

Melanie grasped her horse's reins, and the creature dragged her to the shore in order to escape the waters. Marentex pulled Melanie entirely out of the water and onto the bank.

Melanie coughed up water and gasped for air. She glanced up the bank to see two oddly dressed warrior women standing on the grassy slopes. One wore steel; the other wore silver armor. Helmets covered their heads and noses with a strip of metal running down the center. In their hands, they carried shields and ominous spears.

Melanie glanced at them, and her eyes grew wide. She stood and reached out for her horse to steady herself. When she looked at Marentex, she squealed and withdrew. Marentex had taken on her normal appearance, sprouting large feathered wings on either side of her back. She, too, was an ancient Horse of Element.

One of the warriors approached, saying, "It's the magic of this place. It brings out their true nature. Welcome to Galeã."

Melanie paused, shocked. She followed the warriors in a zombie-like stupor. The women escorted Melanie into a grandiose golden palace to see the queen. They told her the same thing they had told Liyah. However, instead of staying in the palace, Melanie was taken outside to begin her training immediately.

****

The warriors landed gracefully in the mountains. Melanie received the same tutorial that Liyah had. The warriors dismounted, allowing the horses to meander off, grazing.

"You haven't told me who you are yet," Melanie blurted.

Melanie and her trainer had been riding through the air without a word unless instructions were being given. Her companion raised the helmet off her head and shook her hair. She wore silver armor and carried a bow and long sword. Much of the armor was battle scarred. The she-warrior's light blond hair halted just above her shoulders. Her eyes were green that sparkled. She smiled sweetly, "Riela is my name. I will be your own personal trainer until you undergo the challenge."

The girls had stopped at the armory, and Melanie received her cross-blades. They were the only pieces of weaponry she carried.

"Now," Riela began, "in these mountains, you will face different enemies and destroy them on your own, while I watch and rank your performances, pointing out what you need to work on. We will work this course until you are ready to move on to harder material. Clear?"

"I suppose," Melanie stated, looking down at the blades in her hand. "But I'm a lover not a fighter."

"Good luck to you then. The old will die, and the new will grow."

Melanie heard the crunch of rocks behind her, and Riela grinned.

Ryvan shot through the woods, dodging trees as he quickly eluded the Vortzans. The demon creatures hated trees and wouldn't track him through the forest. They hated the life in the natural plants.

After running for awhile, Ryvan finally stopped. The Vortzans had probably followed Tyrese. He was easier to track because he was wounded. They could smell the life in him through his open wound.

Tyrese could handle it though. Ryvan continued on through the forest. Before he knew it, Ryvan had no idea where he was.

He was in a small, dark clearing surrounded tightly on all sides by large, ancient trees. Light filtered in past them, and Ryvan didn't know which way he had come from.

He muttered to himself under his breath.

****

As the sun reached its apex, Ryvan and Verexn stumbled out into a clearing near the Pricein.

"I can't believe it worked," Ryvan laughed.

The warrior still didn't know exactly where he was, but he knew to follow the flow of the river and watch for Tyrese. He glanced down to see that hundreds of hoof prints had churned the soft earth into a mess. However, Ryvan could make out that half were running downstream, and the others were coming back up. He jumped from his steed, dropped to the earth, and breathed, "Vortzans."

They must have chased Tyrese downstream, and something must have made them decide to come in this direction. Ryvan knew he had to see what had happened quickly. He raced off toward the cliff.

****

Ryvan rode up to the waterfall. He knew Tyrese had to be there somewhere. Ryvan dismounted to examine the tracks submerged in the rich earth more accurately. In one area, there was only one set of hoof prints. All of the Vortzan prints surrounded them, lingering dangerously close to the edge of the cliff.

Ryvan stepped closer. The prints appeared to have slid off the cliff backward. He knew what horse it had been, for the hoofprints were slightly smaller and less sharp than the others.

"No," Ryvan thought.

He peered over the edge of the cliff's jagged rocks down into the mist. As he was looking over, something seemed to shove him from behind.

He fell headfirst into the dark, tossing water below.

"Well done, Liyah," Jasira smiled when Liyah had destroyed another firock.

"Thanks," Liyah beamed, wiping the sweat from her brow.

"Let's get something to eat and bandage your wounds."

The pair of she-warriors climbed aboard their horses, and they soared up into the sky. They rode higher into the mountains to a small log cabin. After the she-warriors ate and cleaned up Liyah's wounds, they went back outdoors to continue Liyah's training. This time, they brought out the blades.

"You will be facing larger and more hazardous creatures in your training now, and we have moved on to the more dangerous area," Jasira stated. She climbed aboard her horse and took Mystique's reins. They lifted into the sky, just out of reach.

A rustle came from within the brush, and Liyah whipped around, poised for battle. A large black creature stepped out from the brush. The creature resembled a large, black bear except for one minor detail. It had an extra blank, yellow eye in the center of its forehead. The beast towered over Liyah.

"A zevra!" Jasira cried. She seemed surprised.

Liyah took a deep breath and let it out slowly, relaxing her mind and focusing. The zevra's center eye fixated on Liyah, and it began to charge.

"Here we go again," Liyah groaned.

"Uh, Liyah, if you need help, just say so!" Jasira cried from above. She seemed a little panicked.

"I can handle it."

The monster was three times Liyah's size. She couldn't block something like it. Instead, she rolled clear of the charging zevra's path.

The monster charged right past her. When it turned to face her, it reared upon its hind legs, swiping at Liyah with its gigantic forepaw.

The zevra's paw swept only centimeters from Liyah's face. However, in the swipe, it wrenched a cross-blade from Liyah, and she cried out in exasperation.

The zevra lashed out again. This time, Liyah sliced down deep into its paw with her left cross-blade. It howled in pain and anger, showing off all of its jagged and yellowed teeth. It was angry now, and it loomed over Liyah with malice. Somehow the creature managed to back Liyah against the steep mountainside.

The zevra approached slowly as its third eye gazed into Liyah's eyes. In one motion, the beast slammed its giant paw against Liyah's throat, pinning her to the rock wall.

"*Liyah!*" Jasira shrieked.

Liyah felt an immense pressure on her windpipe, cutting off her air supply. The zevra lowered its snarling face down to meet hers. Its menacing eyes stared into her two, and it pressed harder. Its rank breath encircled her. Liyah began to feel dizzy, and her world began to swim. She did not want to die like this. She had worked too hard and come too far.

Liyah pulled herself back into her body and cried out in one last attempt. She felt power and warmth leave her. Liyah watched a dazzling blue light explode from her and knock the zevra flat on its back. The beast roared out in pain, not knowing what hit it. Liyah wasn't sure she did either.

Suddenly, weakness overcame her, and she fell. The last thing she saw was Jasira standing over her saying with a large smile, "You're finished! No more training. *You are ready!*"

Then darkness.

Chapter 16

When the whirlpool spit Tyrese out on the island of Geriã, he fought to reach the shore. He was amazed that he was still alive and in one piece. The waterfall was one thing, but the whirlpool was too much. His arm stung where the demon had cut through him. The water had cleansed it, and it was raw once more. Tyrese glanced upward and saw a large castle, seemingly fashioned entirely of a golden metal. Tyrese slapped himself across the face to be sure he wasn't dreaming.

"Well, I'm definitely awake now."

At that moment, two warriors in steel armor approached the bewildered warrior, escorting Tyrese to the palace to meet with the king.

****

"Welcome to Geriã, Tyrese of Dreán," a voice boomed from a large man wearing a golden crown upon his head. He seemed powerful and appeared to demand respect and attention from everyone. His eyes were deep, ashen gray with golden flecks that seemed familiar somehow.

"You are strong. I have heard much of you and your companion, Ryvan. You will do well here," the king grinned.

Tyrese couldn't focus on anything but the king's appearance. He reminded him so much of someone.

As they talked, Tyrese was informed of training and the challenge that would take place on the next full moon. A trainer was brought out for him, and they departed from the palace to begin.

****

Tyrese and his new trainer rode on horseback to the mountain peak training course. Tyrese's horse had gone through the whirlpool as well and wound up on Geriã.

They traveled for a long time throughout the twisting and turning path while weaving in and out of trees and other various objects. Eventually, they reached the top of the mountain. It was much colder, and there was a single cabin that stood off to one side.

The trainer began going through a large saddlebag on his chestnut horse. Suddenly, he pulled out a pair of cross-blades.

"These look just like my old ones," Tyrese exclaimed.

"They are yours to keep," the trainer smiled.

"Thanks! Now, what did you say your name was?" Tyrese asked as he took the blades in his hands and admired them.

"I didn't," he replied tersely. "But, I will tell you. It's Draze."

Draze was a stocky warrior, a little shorter than Tyrese. He had brown wavy hair, and his eyes were mossy green. His smile was bright and cheerful.

Draze suddenly stared into the sky, and a deep frown crossed his face. Out of nowhere, Tyrese heard a noise from the direction Draze was facing. It sounded like a large bird, because the sound of beating wings filled the air.

Draze snapped his eyes down to meet Tyrese's. "Training begins now." Draze began to back away from Tyrese. Just as he was wondering what Draze was talking about, something large and fast sideswiped him.

Tyrese was knocked to the ground face-first. The large creature rose off of him and landed lightly on the ground. Tyrese pulled out his blades and rose to his feet to face his adversary.

The creature was pitch black. It had two pearly, white fangs protruding from high in its jaws, and it resembled a bat. However, this "bat" was about the size of a large dog, and it stood upright on two legs.

Quickly, the thing rose into the air and took a dive at Tyrese once more. Tyrese rolled to the side just in time. He dodged the bat, but he landed on something hard that jabbed into his side.

Tyrese scrambled back to his feet and glanced down to see what he landed on. On the ground at his feet lay a knife. The handle was what had caught Tyrese in the ribs. It wasn't just any knife, but it was his old one. Apparently, it stayed with him for the trip from Corresponding Point to Geriã.

The monster launched itself into the air and circled around them. It lunged again toward Tyrese, releasing a loud shriek and baring its fangs.

Tyrese stood his ground until the monster was just a moment from leaping upon him. Tyrese lashed out with his left blade and sliced through the beast's wing. It shrieked louder than before and backtracked in the air in a desperate attempt to get away. It flew with a slight waver as it dripped blood from the wounded wing. Eventually, it disappeared around the nearest mountain.

A moment later, from the other side of the mountain, it reappeared and dove again at Tyrese. Without thinking, Tyrese ripped the knife from his belt and threw the dagger. It plunged down into the beast's chest cavity. Upon impact, the monster fell, writhing on the ground.

Tyrese sheathed his weapon, and after catching his breath, he asked in exasperation, "What *was* that?"

"That was a surtran. They are just oversized bats with the arms and legs of a bear."

Tyrese sensed something and swung his weapon around violently, slicing the head of the approaching surtran clean off its body.

"I guess it wanted to finish the job," Draze stated. "Where did you learn *that* move?"

Tyrese faltered as he tried to spit out the words. Memories that pained him of Liyah fighting in the blades arena at Corresponding Point came flooding back.

"From a she-warrior."

"A she-warrior!" Draze exclaimed.

"Yeah, a friend of mine," he replied quickly.

Draze sensed the subject was closed, and they continued his training without bringing she-warriors up again.

Riela took to the air, bringing Melanie's horse along.

"Wait! What's going on?" Melanie cried.

"I suggest you draw your sword."

Melanie calmed down, attempting to figure out her situation. She cautiously took out her new cross-blades. Standing completely still, she felt something hot tickle the back of her neck. Her hair began to stand on end as she recognized it as breath.

Melanie trembled. She shut her eyes and drew a deep breath. Then, she spun around with her weapons raised. They collided with the oversized fangs of a large gray wolf-like creature.

"Meet the firock," Riela called in a bored voice.

The beast growled and bit down harder on her blades. Melanie didn't know what to do, and she stood frozen. And all at once, the firock swept a great claw down at Melanie's ankles, dropping her to the ground. When she fell, the firock released her blades which she barely managed to keep in her grasp.

The firock crouched down like a cat stalking its prey. Melanie was flat on her back and entirely exposed. When Melanie realized what it was doing, she braced herself. She didn't have time to scramble to her feet, or it would have been able to tear her to pieces. She lay motionless, waiting.

Suddenly, the firock leapt upon her. In the second before the giant creature crushed her, Melanie crossed her weapons vertically over her chest, catching the firock in the stomach with her feet. In one quick motion, Melanie flipped the firock off by using her feet. The monster squealed as it felt Melanie's cross-blades penetrate the soft flesh around its heart. The beast lay dying in the rocks of the mountains.

Melanie pulled herself to her feet and winced. She looked down at her ankle, seeing blood pouring from a wound.

The firock had sliced through her when it had knocked her to the ground.

"Well done, Melanie," Riela beamed.

****

They continued Melanie's training session until sunset. Riela thought Melanie was ready for the challenge by the end of the day. She had enjoyed watching Melanie destroy various creatures while she critiqued from a safe distance.

"So, will I face these same creatures during the challenge?" Melanie asked while the girls sat in the cabin eating bread and pheasant meat.

Riela looked around cautiously before replying, "I am not supposed to tell you anything concerning the challenge, but I think you should know," she began. "During the challenge, mind you I won't tell you anything else, you will face creatures much stronger and more horrifying than the ones in these mountains. However, I believe you will be able to handle it, because I have never seen anyone handle these creatures as easily as you."

"So, do I have a chance?" Melanie asked.

"Definitely," Riela smiled. "However, there are rumors of some new warrior here who handles the demons of the mountain as easily as you. She supposedly is something really special. However, she was almost killed by a high level creature that even I probably couldn't have killed."

"Oh."

"But, you are just as good."

Melanie settled in to get some rest for the night, oblivious to the fact that she would be placed in the challenge on the next night.

When Ryvan landed on the island, he found two warriors standing in front of him. One bent down and offered to help Ryvan to his feet.

"Thanks, man," Ryvan stated as he placed his hands on his head to steady his equilibrium and catch his breath. It appeared to be a bit past noon. The sun blazed high in the sky directly above, sending pure streams of sunlight down upon the island. It sent warmth back down into Ryvan's core. He shook his head and sent droplets of water cascading down toward the earth.

The warriors smiled and said, "Welcome to Geriã Island."

Ryvan looked up and saw the castle shining in the distance and raised an eyebrow.

The other warrior asked, "Is something wrong?"

Ryvan wiped the expression off his face and said, "No, everything is fine."

****

"Welcome to Geriã, Ryvan of Dreán!" the king exploded. "I have heard much about you."
"Thank you, sir," Ryvan replied.

"You probably don't know this, and I hate to be the one to tell you, for it is not in my nature, but you are too late to be part of the challenge. It shall take place tonight on both islands, Geriã and Galeã, and you have no training time. Without training, you cannot possibly be ready for the things you will face in the challenge tonight. Therefore, you cannot be part of the Warriors of Galeã—the Galeãns. I'm sorry, but you must go. If it was in my power to place you, I would, but alas, I cannot."

"Go? No! I mean, no, sir. I can take your challenge tonight without training," Ryvan stated.

"Are you willing?" the king asked. The surrounding guards gave each other mocking looks.

"I am confident in my abilities."

"You are aware," the king said, "that the likelihood of your death is very high without the proper training?"

Ryvan looked the king in his eyes and answered, "Yes, sir. I am aware. However, I must try. I have nowhere else to go."

The king sighed, "Very well. Then, guards, take him into the armory, and equip him for the challenge. Good luck, young warrior."

When they departed, Ryvan realized there was something oddly familiar about the king, yet he couldn't place it. As soon as the group reached the armory, Ryvan was given a new pair of cross-blades and a new dark oak bow, bearing the Galeān seal.

Ryvan tested the blades, and when satisfied, stretched his bow out. Quickly, he strapped it to his back. Arrows were given to him, and the warriors turned back to the main throne room of the palace.

The guards smiled as they reached another room that had a large lock on the door. One searched in his pocket for the key needed to unlock the large door. Ryvan kept a serious look on his face the whole time. He was still mourning his losses, and he knew he had to forget, or there would be serious consequences. He also knew he shouldn't have been associated with the she-warriors in the first place. This was exactly one of the things that he had wanted to avoid.

They unlocked the door and brought a torch down from the wall to light the room. Stacks of identical bronze armor lay in heaps all throughout the room.

"What are all of these for?" Ryvan asked.

"Warriors participating in the challenge," replied the guard carrying the torch.

The other guard rooted around in the heaps until he found what he was searching for, throwing the armor to Ryvan who caught it by reflex.

"Put these on," the guard said.

"What's wrong with the armor I'm wearing?"

The guards shot each other a look. But, the torch guard sighed and said, "We will explain."

Liyah awoke in the same room she had been in before with Jasira staring down at her. "Oh, good! You are awake again!" Jasira exclaimed.

"Haven't we done this before?" Liyah said, standing up. "I have got to stop doing that. Is it just me or have I been passing out a lot lately?"

Jasira just stared back at her with wide eyes.

Liyah frowned and was about to ask just what her problem was when Jasira cried out, "We are late, Liyah. It is already four!"

"Late for what?" Liyah asked. Instantly, Jasira grabbed Liyah by the arm and began to drag her along after her.

"I must explain and prepare you for the challenge."

"What's the rush? We have until the next full moon."

"The full moon is tonight!" Jasira squealed.

"Are you kidding?" Liyah exclaimed.

Liyah stopped suddenly, and that jolted Jasira backward. She jerked on Liyah again to make her move, and the pair rushed on down the corridors of the palace. Eventually, Jasira stopped dragging Liyah, and the pair ceased power-walking. Jasira fumbled around, trying to find the specific key that would unlock the massive oak door covered with intricate designs that they were standing in front of. Finally, she pulled out the correct key and stuffed it into the lock, gaining access to the interior of the room. The pair stomped inside. Liyah was purely puzzled by what she saw. There were piles of bronze armor stacked one on top of the other filling the entire room. Jasira held up an armor skirt and midriff chest plate.

Suddenly, Liyah caught on. "Oh, no!" a disgusted look crept into her face. "No way! You can't get me into one of those."

"But, Liyah! You must."

"Why?"

Jasira sighed. She was still holding up the armor. "Just put it on, and I will explain, but I can assure you that it is most necessary."

****

A few minutes later, Liyah was dressed in full bronze armor. "Explain." She wasn't in a good mood.

"Ok, here it goes. First of all, tonight you will take part in the challenge of placement." Liyah began to say something, but Jasira shushed her and continued. "This challenge will tell us if you belong with the Galiphems or not, and if so, then, it will tell us exactly *where* you belong by rank. It does this by armor."

Liyah's face regained the puzzled expression, but she kept quiet so Jasira could continue.

"The challenge takes place at night in the complete darkness with only the light of the full moon to guide you through the land. While you face the dangers that surround you, your armor will gradually change—or not change, depending on where you are meant to be placed. The armor reads deep inside your inner being and can determine exactly where you belong. The armor can go from bronze, iron, steel, silver, gold, and all the way to white gold. If you are not Galiphem material, then, your armor will rust, potentially to the point of falling off, adding to your humiliation of not making the cut. If it stays bronze, then, you are a warrior and nothing more. Iron armor will show the sign of being a palace guard. Steel equals a high ranking commanding officer. If you are granted silver armor, then, you shall become a trainer like me. Gold armor is only issued to those of the royal blood. Gold armor is rarely granted. The queen and her daughter are the only ones who currently have the golden armor."

"What about the white gold?" Liyah asked.

"Oh, yes," Jasira said absently as if she had forgotten it. "The white gold has never been gained. It is said to be the mark of the highest warrior and the greatest ruler to rest upon the earth. I've never even laid eyes upon white gold armor. I'm afraid I never will either," Jasira stated. Then she remembered that she was supposed to be explaining everything. "Oh, yeah! That covers the armor. Now, moving on. Your goal in this challenge is to reach the peak of the volcano, Mount Reolné, before sunrise. This task will not be easy. You will face many perils and puzzles.

One warrior is not enough to make it. That is why you are assigned a partner."

"No. I don't need a partner. I work alone," Liyah stated dryly. "There is only one she-warrior I would *ever* fight alongside, and she is dead." Her voice cracked at the end, and Liyah looked away.

Jasira grew quiet. Then, she said in a whisper, "I am sorry, but it is required."

****

Liyah went into the palace's throne room before the challenge. Many she-warriors decked out in iron armor along with Jasira escorted her down to the place where the challenge would begin. Jasira tapped Liyah on the shoulder and pointed off to her right. She whispered, "There's your partner."

Apparently, the other she-warrior was smothered in an iron clad wall of she-warriors like Liyah was. Liyah couldn't see her for the guards. They marched for quite some time, arriving at their destination at 11:45 p.m. The challenge was to begin at midnight. Fifteen minutes to go. In this time, Liyah would meet her partner whom she already disliked.

The clock ticked, and it became 11:50. Ten minutes to go. The guards instantly parted, and the girls were left facing each other with dark looks. They remained like that for a moment, and then, the other girl shrieked, running at Liyah. Liyah jumped at the sudden loudness, then, she, too, shrieked. The girls embraced each other, and the trainers met to discuss the event.

"Do you know what is happening?" Riela asked in a whisper.

"Not a clue," Jasira replied.

Everyone stared at the girls when they suddenly parted, and the strange girl said, "I never thought I would see you again, Liyah!"

"I didn't think I'd see you either, Melanie," Liyah replied.

Chapter 17

"Apparently, you two have already met," Riela smiled.

"Yeah, we go way back," Liyah smiled.

"So, I guess you won't mind fighting alongside one another," Jasira stated.

"Naw," Melanie grinned, "I think we'll manage."

Both girls were overflowing with enthusiasm. They were both more relaxed about the challenge now that they knew they could trust their partner.

"Ok, then," Riela murmured. She and Jasira both had confused expressions on their faces. Clearly, they had no inkling as to what was going on. They blew it off, and Riela continued, "Well, now that that's settled, we'll get back to business. You will have to reach the top of Mount Reolné, a large volcano on the edge of the Impenatiã Forest, near the sea, by dawn. You will face many dangers and must work together to prevail. As you fight, your armor will change to your ranking position. If you do not reach the peak of the volcano by sunrise, then you may be better suited as a member of the Galatrans. You will enter in a few moments, but once you enter, you may not come out until sunrise."

"Do you understand?" Jasira asked.

"Yes," Liyah and Melanie nodded.

"Alright, you will enter the gate in two minutes. Remember this place is different than any other you will find in the outside world. Strange things will occur. Expect the unexpected. Gather your thoughts," Riela stated.

Liyah took the moment to view her surroundings. They were all standing in front of a large black iron gate with intricate features lacing together. Beyond the gate was a thick wood with ancient trees that seemed to tower up above them in the very heavens themselves. The only light came from the moon and the torches the guard warriors carried. They stood stone-faced and still as statues. Riela and Jasira stood near the front with Liyah and Melanie directly in front of them.

"A word of advice, girls," Jasira grinned. "Stay away from the lights."

Before the girls could ask what she meant, the dark gates creaked open of their own accord, and Riela stated, "It is time."

Everyone grew silent as the two girls stepped through the open gate. As soon as they were through, the gates clanged shut behind them. The girls jumped, and they briefly glanced back to see the Galiphems mount their horses and fly off into the sky. Their trainers nodded, and then they were all gone.

The pair ventured off into the ominous forest. The challenge had begun, and Liyah drew a cross-blade, as did Melanie. The sounds of the night filled the air. An owl cried its query, and the crickets serenaded them. Rustles of small night creatures were heard occasionally, and the leaves tossed and kicked up in the breeze. The girls' eyes adjusted to the darkness enough to make out shapes and where they were headed. They walked through the forest and drew farther away from the gate.

When nothing leapt out of the darkness to devour them, Liyah began to talk. "It's great to see you again, Melanie, but, I've got to ask. How did you get away?"

"Well, it's a bit funny actually. To make a long story short, I wound up fighting three Vortzans, beating them, getting arrows shot at me, which by the way, one nicked my ear, then, falling down a large waterfall, and finally, being taken into a large whirlpool. Same old, same old. What about you?"

"I'm embarrassed to say, actually," Liyah stated.

"Why?"

"I didn't think I was so weak."

Before Melanie could say a word in response, the ground caved in beneath her feet. She shrieked and began to fall, but luckily, she grabbed onto the side of the earth before the ground swallowed her alive.

"Melanie!" Liyah looked down and saw Melanie looking up at her frantically. She clung to the wall of a deep hole about five feet wide. The closer Liyah looked, the more she thought she saw something. There was also a strange sound.

Liyah reached down for Melanie's hand, but Melanie slipped and began to fall down into the depths. Right before Melanie hit the bottom, Liyah managed to grab her hand.

Just then, Liyah knew what was in the bottom of the pit. They were snakes of some sort. Liyah pulled her up out of the pit, and they both collapsed a ways off from the edge. Liyah edged closer to it and peered down into the chasm. The creatures were definitely snakes. They appeared to be greenish with dark stripes and horns just above their slanted eyes. She had never seen snakes of that breed before.

"Maybe we should move on," Liyah muttered.

The girls picked themselves up and began to walk on.

Melanie dusted herself off and said, "Well, what were you saying?"

Liyah glanced at her friend and laughed, "That didn't even make you forget?" Melanie grinned, and Liyah continued, "Well, I wound up fighting the Mistress of the Darkness, and it seems that she had some problem with me. Something from the past. I was beaten badly. She destroyed my cross-blades and rendered me unconscious. I was furious with myself. I didn't realize I was so poorly trained. Then something pushed me into the river, and the rest is history."

"Wow, I wonder what she would want with you," Melanie wondered.

"I don't know, but I'm sure we'll both see her again soon."

"Oh, man."

"Yeah," Liyah said.

The girls were on guard once more. They cautiously made their way throughout the forest.

"I have so many questions for you," Melanie whispered.

"Like what?" Liyah asked.

"All sorts of stuff. For one, were you almost killed in your training session in the mountains?"

"Umm, yeah. How did you know that?" Liyah questioned.

"Riela told me."

"Well, the zevra was huge. Jasira told me that she didn't think I would wake up again," Liyah laughed.

"How did you kill it?"

"You are going to flip. I did. Some sort of magic came from me when I lost my temper. It burned the creature. I don't know exactly what it was. It was very creepy."

"That's really strange, Liyah. I wonder where that would have come from. It's odd," Melanie agreed. "Here's another one. When you got out of Corresponding Point, did you see our friends by any chance?"

Liyah didn't answer for a while. Eventually, she said, "No. There was nothing left."

Melanie began to speak again, but Liyah immediately quieted her companion. She leaned in to whisper in Melanie's ear, "I think we are being followed."

"What makes you think that?" Melanie whispered back.

Liyah stepped away and pointed her blade toward an area thick with shrubbery and brush. Melanie followed the blade with her eyes. Staring out from the underbrush was a set of red eyes. As Melanie looked around, she realized there were many more sets all around the girls.

Then, she said, "That's a pretty big clue."

Once they finished the training, Tyrese and Draze rushed back to the palace to prepare him for the challenge. Tyrese couldn't help but wonder what had happened to Ryvan. He was supposed to be here, too, but there had been no sign of him yet.

When they finally reached the castle, Tyrese was taken down a series of hallways to a locked room. Draze took a key from his belt and placed it in the lock. They entered the room, and Tyrese checked it out, while Draze rummaged around for something. Suddenly, Draze stood and handed Tyrese a set of bronze armor and explained what it was for. After this, Draze escorted Tyrese to an elaborate room with a large bed.

"You will stay here until the challenge begins. Food will be brought up for you soon. After you've eaten, I suggest you sleep. This will not be easy." With that, Draze turned and left Tyrese in the room alone to wait for his food.

****

11:45. Their time had come. The guards stepped away so the partners could meet one another. Ryvan grew tense. The moonlight shone down on everything as the clock ticked. The two boys saw one anther at the same moment and began laughing as they hugged one another in a brotherly fashion.

Tyrese smiled and said, "You ready for this?"

"Ready as I'll ever be," Ryvan replied.

Draze stood in front of them and explained what they were supposed to do. The same rules applied to them as the rules of the Galiphems. While the warriors waited for the time to enter, not a word more was spoken. Tension hung heavy in the air. Ryvan was anxious to start, while Tyrese was anxious to get it over with.

Suddenly, a clang and a screech of metal were heard. "The time is now. Good luck, boys. You may enter," Draze stated solemnly.

The boys entered the gate and began the challenge as the gate slammed shut behind them. The Galeâns departed, and the boys were left alone to take care of the problem at hand.

They slunk stealthily through the dark forest, and the solitude began to bother them. Something seemed wrong. There were no normal night noises. It seemed that everything was remaining quiet like they would in the instance when a predator was sighted. The boys were cautious, but they assumed it was merely them the creatures feared.

Ryvan broke the silence and said, "So, why did you slide off the cliff backward?"

Tyrese laughed, "Well, I—hey, how did you know I went over backward?"

"I tracked you."

"Oh, ok, stalker. Anyway, I had no other choice. It was either that, or let the Vortzans kill me."

"I see."

A sound came from their right side.

"What was that?" Tyrese asked in a whisper.

Ryvan put his finger up to his lips and drew his weapons. Tyrese followed his lead. They remained vigilant and watchful while they walked on.

Eventually, Ryvan hissed, "We are being followed. Don't make any loud—"

"What makes you think that?" Tyrese asked.

"Sh! Be quiet!"

Ryvan was slightly walking ahead, and Tyrese was watching everything but Ryvan. When Ryvan stopped, Tyrese ran headlong into him, hitting the bridge of his nose on Ryvan's crossbow.

"Ow!" he cried.

Ryvan whipped around. "I said be quiet!" he hissed.

"Sorry, I forgot."

While Tyrese said this, a gigantic hawk-like creature swooped down at Ryvan's turned back. Tyrese's eyes grew large, and he tackled Ryvan just before the large bird's talons wrapped around him.

They jumped up and held their breath, listening. When the large bird didn't come back, the warriors relaxed, and Ryvan breathed, "That was almost too easy."

Suddenly, the sound of wings filled the air. Ryvan turned to his friend, but he wasn't beside him any longer. In his place, a giant hawk sideswiped him, and he landed on the ground. The hawk continued flying. When Ryvan scrambled to his feet, he realized that Tyrese was standing off to the side with his weapons raised. There were at least a dozen hawks circling around him.

One hawk dove down at him, and he sliced through its wing. It let out a fierce cry. Ryvan hurried towards his friend, but was cut off by four of the large birds. He fought them off, and gained a brief moment of rest. Ryvan glanced in Tyrese's direction in time to see a hawk take him up in his talons from behind.

"Tyrese!" Ryvan cried.

But Ryvan was too late, and the large creatures circled around and flew off into the sky in a straight line, following the one carrying Tyrese.

Ryvan leapt to his feet and took off in a dead sprint after the hawks.

****

Dark shapes rushed past, while Ryvan raced through the darkness. His guides were merely hawks up in the sky. The moonlight cascaded down, illuminating the creatures just enough to show the form and shape. The great beasts glided through the dark night. Ryvan ran low to the ground, and his overhead view was soon blocked by the large trees.

"Not now!" Ryvan cried. Once more, he became enclosed in darkness. The warrior continued to run blindly through the menacing depths of the night forest, but Ryvan accelerated his speed. He knew he had to keep up with the hawks.

Out of nowhere, a tree positioned itself in Ryvan's path, and he ran headlong into it. Ryvan fell to the ground, shaking his head, and his nose began to bleed. When he regained his composure, he happened to lift his gaze to what lay ahead. Moonlight seeped through the trees in what seemed to be a large clearing.

Ryvan raced toward it, and when he stumbled out, he lifted his eyes up to the heavens to see the hawks circling around a large mountain. Up on the peak of the mountain, sat a large golden nest.

The mountain loomed above Ryvan, causing a sick feeling to contort the pit of his stomach. He knew Tyrese had to be in the mountains somewhere. Ryvan packed his weapons away securely, let out a sigh, and began his slow ascent of the mountain's craggy surface.

The eyes soon moved out of the brush as the creatures revealed themselves to the girls. Out of the bushes stepped a large black hairy leg twice the size of the girls' own.

"Wow! It looks like one of your legs," Melanie laughed dryly.

Liyah glared at her. "Look who's talking."

Before the girls could continue their pointless conversation, seven more of the black limbs protruded from the underbrush, quickly followed by a segmented body. Fangs seething saliva jutted out of the face where eight red eyes fixated on the girls.

"Is that all?" Melanie giggled. "This will be easy."

"Don't be so sure," Liyah blurted, for she noticed that many more of these creatures began appearing.

"Ok," Melanie stuttered. "We can still take them."

"It's not them that I'm worried about."

Melanie frowned. She glanced at Liyah to figure out what she was looking. To her horror, Liyah was staring above Melanie, and she felt something wet land on her right shoulder.

Melanie slowly lifted her eyes upward to see a gigantic spider about twenty times larger than the others towering above her. The wetness lingering on Melanie's shoulder was the monster's saliva.

"Oh, sick!" Melanie murmured as her whole body began to shake out of disgust. Melanie scampered over to Liyah's side, and the spider snapped its pincers in anger.

"Melanie, don't move," Liyah whispered. Her eyes were wide, and her weapons were drawn in front of her.

The spider-lings crept toward them as the mother lowered her head down to meet the girls' eyes. All eight of them fixated on Liyah and Melanie.

"Mel, on three, run. One. Two—" Liyah began.

The mother sent out a loud high pitched shriek which the spiderlings mimicked.

"Oh, forget it. Run!" Melanie cried.

The two girls turned and sprinted off in the opposite direction. They raced through the thick web of natural plants. The moon gave off little light, so, the girls didn't know what they were heading into. After they had run awhile Melanie asked, "Do you think they are still following us?"

A loud crash behind them confirmed it, and the girls sheathed their weapons, increasing their speed.

"What are we going to do?" Melanie yelled.

"We're already doing something. We're running!" Liyah shouted back.

"We can't outrun them forever, Liyah!" Melanie cried. "What do we do?"

"I'm working on it," Liyah replied.

Suddenly, the girls reached the edge of the trees. They instantly noticed that the light grew more intense. A large grassy slope blocked the girls' vision. They sprinted up the hill anyway, and when they reached the top, the pair skidded to an abrupt halt. They were standing on the edge of a large ravine that seemed to go down forever.

Liyah took a step back. Melanie was having a hard time grasping her balance. She was leaning at an awkward angle, and moving her arms in a circular pattern. Just as she was about to tip over into the ravine, Liyah grabbed the leather X of her cross-blade straps, and jerked her backward.

They grinned, and then, another loud crash of breaking wood shook the forest behind them. The girls instantly began running along the abyss. Ahead of them, a large rotting log created a makeshift bridge to the other side.

Liyah began to cross it when Melanie grabbed her arm and asked, "Are you really going to do this?"

Liyah looked back and saw the smaller spiders gaining ground. "It's our only option."

The girls began to walk carefully across the shoddy bridge. It was slow, but they were making it across. When they reached the halfway mark, Melanie felt something sharp cut into her left ankle. She cried out, causing Liyah to spin around and almost lose her balance.

Hanging onto Melanie's ankle was one of the smaller spiderlings. It had gotten ahead of its brothers and sisters. Melanie ripped out her right cross-blade and slashed the spiderling across the face, and it howled and fell off the log into the precipice. The two girls rushed on across the bridge. When they reached the other side, Liyah stopped and drew her bow. The spiderlings began to cross the bridge.

"Liyah, that won't work," Melanie shouted. "There's too many!"

Liyah began shooting arrows at the monsters, ignoring Melanie. One after the other fell down into the abyss. Eventually, the largest of all began to cross. Liyah knew no mere arrow would hold her off. However, she drew her bowstring back once more and took aim. Immediately before releasing, she shut her eyes.

The arrow landed on the log directly in front of the beast. Melanie gasped, "You missed! How could you miss?"

Liyah sheathed her bow, took Melanie's jaw in her right hand, and made her watch the arrow. Melanie watched as the golden arrow incinerated, and the log caught fire. The log began to crackle, and the spider was not phased at all. She kept walking across the fire.

All at once, the log crunched and fell down into the darkness of the precipice, dragging the mother monster with it. Melanie beamed and flopped to the ground. She took one look at her ankle and winced. The spider's fangs were still there.

Liyah bent down to examine the wound. "Those need to come out now."

"Then do it."

Liyah tucked her hair behind her ears and grabbed onto the fangs. She jerked them out, and Melanie drew in a deep breath. Her ankle immediately began to bleed.

"Oh, great," Liyah breathed.

They heard something along the edge of the forest.

"What was that?" Melanie whispered.

"I'm not sure, but let's go see."

Liyah pulled Melanie to her feet, and the girls went off toward the forest. Melanie was limping badly, and she grasped

Liyah's arm for support. When they ventured into the trees, they heard another sound. It was almost like a deep growl from somewhere below them.

Liyah and Melanie looked at each other, and then looked downward. Below was a deep pit resembling the one Melanie almost fell into at the beginning of the challenge. Instead of snakes, there was a large, black, snarling panther. When it spotted the girls, it seemed to relax somewhat.

"We can't just leave it down there," Liyah mused.

"It could tear us to shreds," Melanie squealed.

"I don't think it will."

Melanie rolled her eyes and walked off. Liyah spotted a large, fallen tree to her left. She walked to it and began to slide it across the slick grass toward the pit. Melanie reluctantly joined her, and they managed to push it in. Instantly, the panther climbed up to meet them. Its eyes flared with an emotion they could not place.

The panther opened its mouth, and instead of tearing them to shreds, the creature said, "I thank you a thousand times. I am eternally grateful."

The girls stared in awe. It bowed, and Liyah said, "No problem?"

"Yet, it was. Now, because of you, I am free again. I will spare you," it said.

In one instance, the panther gazed up at them and seemed to be overcome by shock. It bowed yet again and said, "It is an honor to be indebted to the pair of you." It looked up again and continued, "You know nothing of who you are, do you?"

The girls shook their heads, and the panther said, "You will know in due time. It is not my place. In the meantime, you are far off track. Allow me to show you the way."

It slowly turned and began slinking off into the darkness. Its silky fur glistened in the moonlight. The girls sprinted after it.

When Ryvan reached the top of the mountain, he noticed all the hawks, except for one, circled the entire mountain obliviously. The other hawk stood positioned beside a large nest. It was an extravagant creature that appeared too noble to be attacking the good guys. Its tawny feathers seemed to be coated in a shiny gloss.

The hawk stood, watching out for anything that might take its prey from it. That was exactly what Ryvan was about to do. Its eyes were sharp, and it was focused intently on its mission. However, the darkness still made things hard to see, but Ryvan could make out Tyrese's silhouette in the giant nest. It seemed that he was the only thing there.

Tyrese then stood and began to sneak away from the nest, but when he was about to make it out, the hawk turned and raced back to the nest. Tyrese began to run, but the hawk lifted up into the air, snatched the leather X on Tyrese's back up in its beak, and flew back to the nest, dropping him in the dead center. They had done no physical harm to Tyrese. It seemed the hawks were merely holding him captive, almost like they were trying to prevent him from reaching his destination on time.

Ryvan watched as the hawk returned to its guarding position. He couldn't think of anything he could do to help his companion. Ryvan didn't want to kill the hawk, but it seemed to be his only option. Ryvan unhooked his bow and stepped into the open in the hawk's field of vision. Tyrese could see Ryvan's armor shine in the light, and he knew that was what had captured the beast's attention.

The hawk screeched, and Ryvan watched as the hawk stretched out its gigantic wings to warn Ryvan to get away. It was attempting to intimidate him away from the nest. This attempt was futile because Ryvan was not moved.

The hawk screeched again, louder this time. When Ryvan did not move, it rose into the air with one sweep of its mighty wings, allowing Ryvan one more chance to run, but when he didn't, the hawk bore down on Ryvan like a golden bullet.

Ryvan drew his bowstring back. He really didn't want to kill it. The last thing he thought before he released the arrow was that he wished he had a large net to trap the noble bird in. The arrow cut through the air like a knife, but instead of penetrating the hawk's heart, the arrow had morphed into a giant net which entangled the hawk, immobilizing it in mid-air. Before the hawk knew what had hit it, it fell to the ground with a dull thud. It thrashed about in the net, becoming even more desperately tangled.

Both of the warriors were dumbfounded. They had no idea what had occurred. Tyrese stood open-mouthed, while the hawk thrashed about. Ryvan replaced his weapon and motioned for Tyrese to follow just before he turned to leave.

Tyrese jumped out of the oversized nest and ran to catch up with Ryvan. The trapped creature realized that its prey was escaping and raised its voice to a screech in alarm. At once, all the circling hawks directed their attention to their struggling friend.

Tyrese ran to the edge of the cliff, but he couldn't see Ryvan. He looked around until he heard Ryvan hiss, "Ty! Down here."

Tyrese looked down the steep cliff and saw Ryvan making his way down quickly. Tyrese took a deep breath and began to do the same. When he stepped over the edge, he sent a few loose rocks clattering down below him. A moment later he heard Ryvan's angry hiss.

"My bad," Tyrese began.

"Sh!"

They continued climbing down until Ryvan called up, "There is solid ground directly beneath you. Hurry and get down here. The hawks are coming."

"Oh, ok," Tyrese replied, and then, he let go. What he didn't know was that there was a good six feet until he would reach the solid ground. Ryvan, who wasn't watching, got an unexpected surprise when Tyrese landed on him in a heap. Both warriors wound up on the ground in a confused stupor.

Ryvan jumped to his feet, extended a hand, and whispered, "What the heck is your problem?"

"Uh," Tyrese took the outstretched hand and continued, "You said the ground was directly below me!"

"I didn't mean for you to let go. You were supposed to climb down."

Just then, they heard the sound of monstrous wings once again. They took off running, but the sound only grew louder as the hawks gained ground. There was no place to hide, so their only choice was to continue sprinting down the mountainside rapidly.

Suddenly, Ryvan felt the pain of large talons lift him off the ground. He looked down and saw the ground ripping past beneath his feet. Then he noticed Tyrese was being lifted by another bird, also.

These birds were really cramping the young warriors' style, and they were growing weary of the birds' efforts. The creatures were beginning to waste too much of their time. It was almost like they *wanted* the guys to fail.

Ryvan lost his temper and ripped out a knife. When Tyrese looked his way, Ryvan made sure he understood what to do. Tyrese took out his weapons, also. They flicked the knives open, and Tyrese looked down at the passing earth and saw more trees. Then, Ryvan gave the signal, and they both sliced across the large bird's talons.

The hawks screeched and instantly let go of the struggling warriors. The boys fell into the space below, while the pained hawks cradled their wounds in the sky above. It took the warriors a moment to realize what was happening, and when they finally came to their senses, it was too late. The warriors crashed down into the trees.

****

Tyrese landed face down on the ground, while debris littered down all around him. He shook his head and lifted his body into a kneeling position. He spit and was slightly surprised to see blood.

"Ryvan!" Tyrese shouted.

The only reply he received was another screech from above as the hawks searched for their lost prey.

"Ryvan!" Tyrese hissed. This time the reply was a human groan.

"What?" Ryvan whispered back. Then Ryvan picked himself up out of the underbrush. Ryvan rubbed the back of his head and frowned off the pain of the fall.

Tyrese stood, meeting Ryvan's eyes. The canopy above was much thicker than what had been overhead before. Vines hung down all around them. Assorted plants grew in every direction. A hot scent from the flowers' perfume tickled their nostrils. The only light making things visible came from the two spaces where the warriors had fallen through.

Just then, they heard another loud screech. The boys stared up through the large gaping hole in the canopy. What they saw sent them into a dead sprint. All of the hawks were lining up and shooting straight up into the sky above. Shortly after, the leader pulled into a dive, heading straight for the hole. The others followed.

Tyrese lost sight of Ryvan as the darkness swallowed him. Suddenly, Tyrese felt something seize him around the shoulders and jerk his body to the right in midstride. When he landed, he realized Ryvan had pulled him underneath a rock ledge, concealing them from the eyes of their predators. The boys watched the hawks pour down through the opening in the trees, flying past them without detecting the warriors.

The instant they knew the hawks were gone the warriors stepped out from under the rock ledge. They realized the ground beneath their feet was soggy and wet. Moss hung from the trees around them. The colors still appeared murky, but they knew the water was an acrid greenish-brown. However, the volcano could be seen in the background.

"That was a close one," Tyrese panted. He began to step out into the marsh, but Ryvan restrained him.

Tyrese turned to face him. Ryvan responded by whispering, "Don't step out just yet."

"Why?" Tyrese asked.
"Something dark stirs the water."

Chapter 18

The two girls walked briskly through the forest on either side of the panther as if they were its bodyguards. As they walked, they began a conversation with the intriguing creature.

"So, how did you get stuck in that pit?" Melanie asked.

Liyah stared ahead intently. The panther replied, "I was hunting, but I was caught unaware and stepped directly into its fake covering. The pit was too steep for me to jump out of, and I couldn't climb the crumbling walls."

"Begging your pardon," Melanie mused, "but what exactly *are* you?"

This made the creature laugh. "Me? The real question is what are *you*? However, that is not my place. I am a mere Galeãn panther. My name is Tychel. I rank as the leader of our pack. We dwell in this forest to prevent unworthy warriors from surviving the challenge, but I owe you two; therefore, as I said, I shall spare you."

"You mean, you kill warriors?" Melanie muttered.

"Not the good ones. The ones that are merely trying to harness the Galiphem powers are the ones that should worry about my pack. I usually allow an escape route of some sort for the others."

Melanie relaxed a little. They walked on in silence until Liyah asked, "Why are you so honored to accompany us, Tychel? We are just she-warriors."

"It is not my place."

"How many times have you said that?" Melanie asked.

"I believe three," Tychel answered.

"How many times are you going to?" Liyah questioned.

"As many times as needed."

Liyah laughed. Melanie stared ahead and noticed the scenery began to change. Moss hung from branches of the overhead trees, and everything seemed to grow dull. Even the ground began to grow damp and sodden. The girls' high heels began to sink into the earth, making it even more challenging to walk.

Melanie continued walking, and the darkness enclosed around her. Then, she realized that Tychel and Liyah were no longer beside her. She stopped walking and looked around, but she couldn't see anything. Melanie took another step forward that she regretted. Her high heel sunk completely into what seemed to be water. She couldn't feel the bottom, and her foot kept going down. She lost her balance and began to fall forward.

Just as she began to fall, she felt a strong hand grab the back plate on her armor and jerk her backward. She fell back into Liyah who kept Melanie on her feet, while Tychel sat back on his haunches and watched. "This water is very deep. This is as far as I will lead you. You must figure it out on your own from here. Do not drown," Tychel stated. "I bid you farewell." He turned and vanished into the covering of the forest. Liyah and Melanie were left facing the deep water of the marsh.

"How are we going to get across this?" Melanie asked after a while.

"Why do you ask me? Why is it always my job?" Liyah spat.

"Because, you always have the ideas, and I help by standing there looking cute."

Liyah sighed, "Whatever. Why do I even bother?"

"Because you love me."

"Right. About that."

The girls stared on trying to think of something. Melanie broke the silence again. "We've got to do something. We're losing time."

Liyah frowned and walked toward the water. She reached down and felt the surface. She drew so close that her amulet skimmed the surface of the water. Light illuminated their surroundings.

Liyah stood up, frowning. Immediately, the light faded and died. Liyah looked up at Melanie from there. The light of the amulet lit up her features making her appear even more powerful. "Come here."

Melanie stepped up to Liyah.

"Touch your necklace to the water like I did."

Melanie bent down and did as directed. As before, light issued forth, but this beam was red. Melanie jumped back. Liyah tilted her head to one side. She began to step out onto the water, but Melanie jerked her backward.

"What are you doing?" Melanie cried.

"Trying something."

Liyah stepped out again, but when her foot touched the surface, blue roses and their vines began to weave themselves underneath her feet. Liyah said, "It's not quite stable enough to hold my weight. Step."

Melanie's eyes grew large. "If it won't support your weight, then what makes you think it will hold both of us?"

"Just do it!"

Melanie took Liyah's outstretched hand and cautiously stepped out. As soon as her foot rested on the vines, red roses bloomed out of the mass Liyah created, and more vines began to weave in and out. Liyah took her other foot from the bank and stood on the vines. Even more vines and blue roses seethed out over the surface, forming a pathway meant for a queen. Melanie joined her friend, and both watched the aftereffect of the red roses and strengthening vines. The girls smiled and began walking down the path over the water's surface. It felt as stable as solid ground, and the murky water around them shimmered in the moonlight.

From farther ahead, Melanie noticed the landscape had changed yet again. Towering over the land was the large volcano, Mt. Reolné. She told Liyah to look up. When she lifted her eyes from the path, she tripped and almost fell into the water. As soon as Liyah regained her senses, something caught her eye. At first, she thought it was a trick of the light, but then, she looked closer.

Melanie waited as Liyah watched. She couldn't help but wonder what her friend was thinking. "What are you—" Melanie began.

Liyah slapped a hand over Melanie's mouth to silence her. With the other hand, she raised a finger up to her lips, and she pointed out over the water. Melanie frowned at being silenced like that. Then, she followed Liyah's gesturing, and her gaze quickly changed from angry frustration to horror.

Off in the distance, light flashed. The light appeared to be brief blazes of fire. The fire came from the mouths of some disfigured creatures that couldn't be distinguished from the distance and darkness.

"Continue walking. They might not see us," Liyah whispered, removing her hand from the shuddering Melanie's mouth. The girls crept along the rose path for a time in the darkness undetected. Soon, they were close enough that they could see the creatures more easily.

The beasts measured up to be about six feet in length. They were halfway submerged in the murky water with only the tops of their bodies showing. Smoke rose from their nostrils. Their eyes were fiery hollow-looking spheres with a single sliver running down through the center. Two ivory horns protruded from their crowns, while spikes of the same material lined up in a queue down their backs. The skin was a light green that appeared to have been burned repeatedly.

"What are those?" Melanie whispered.

"Creatures of the dark," Liyah replied and drew her blade.

They walked on in silence until they were directly in the lair of the beasts. Amazingly, they still seemed to be undetected. Suddenly, Liyah felt Melanie grasp onto her shoulder. She sensed Melanie's fear, and Liyah turned quickly to see one of the larger creatures rushing toward them through the water, smoke billowing from the monster's snout. Liyah's eyes got bigger, and she put away her sword.

"What are you doing?" Melanie asked.

Liyah didn't reply, but she drew her bow, preparing to fire. She stood at the ready and shot a single arrow down the creature's throat when it opened its mouth to barbeque them. The creature lurched sideways as the arrow struck its target. A gurgling noise came from the beast's throat, and then, Liyah strapped her bow back on and hissed, "Run. NOW!"

Melanie was shocked, but when Liyah started running, she instinctively followed. She had no idea why she was running, but she quickly found out when she and Liyah were knocked flat on the thorny path. The sound of an explosion reverberated all around them and shook their bodies. Melanie's ears began to ring.

"What did you just do?" Melanie cried, stumbling to her feet again.

Liyah stood and dusted herself off. "The Galiphem arrow can take on the form of anything the archer wishes. In this case, an arrow with a pack of gunpowder on the end, plus one fire lizard, equals two things. One: you and I getting knocked flat. And two: barbequed fire lizard. Can you say buh-bye?"

Liyah put her mouth to an open wound on her arm and took care of the blood. Then she turned down the path.

"Oh," Melanie murmured.

"What is that?" Tyrese whispered.

"I'm not sure," Ryvan hissed.

Up ahead, the water seemed to shake. Then, from the depths of the lake, bubbles rose to the surface angrily. The number of bubbles increased. Air met air.

"What?" Tyrese began.

An enormous dark green and cream colored snake-like creature with dark green fins hanging from its sides shot straight up from the water into the air above. Tyrese and Ryvan were dumbstruck and stood open-mouthed and staring, while the creature curved in the air and dove back down into the water. It paid them no mind, just began slithering through the water at high speed in a quick rhythmical pattern.

Directly after the creature submerged, a second beast performed the exact same stunt as the first. This creature greatly resembled the other, but there were a couple differences. It possessed a dark purple slash across its forehead, and it was much darker in color. This beast began following the other, seemingly chasing the first.

"What the heck is that?" Tyrese murmured.

"They look like sea serpents."

Apparently the serpent heard the warriors, and the first beast turned toward them, speeding through the parting waters in their direction. The other pursued it.

"Whoah! Not cool!" Tyrese cried.

"Back up," Ryvan instructed. "It doesn't look like it could reach us on land. No legs. Just fins."

The boys began backing up, and by the time the serpent had reached the shore, they were far enough that it could not reach them, but it leered out of the water and stretched out to them to its full length. The serpent ended up stopping about a foot from their faces. Each of his eyes met up with the warriors. There was a look in them that seemed to make the boys feel sorry for it. But, its head was about the size of a human body. The serpent opened its mouth and begged, "Help me, please! I will help you cross!"

The guys were confused, and they just stared at it. When they did not reply, the serpent turned and looked over its back. They all realized that the dark creature was directly behind the other, and the light serpent hurriedly turned, diving back down into the dark water. The dark serpent slammed onto the bank and momentarily was stunned. Then it slipped down into the water after its prey. All was still.

"Where have I seen that mark on the dark serpent before?" Ryvan asked.

"The Vortzans at Corresponding Point had them on their throats," Tyrese replied.

"Then, that means that the dark serpent is working for the Dark One," Ryvan contemplated.

"What does that mean?" Tyrese asked.

"It means that we must kill it."

"Oh."

The two serpents shot up out of the water and began fighting on the surface. The warriors noticed that the dark serpent was much larger than the light one, but the small serpent was putting up a good fight. However, it was obvious that he didn't have a chance. The little one delivered a severe blow to the larger one's neck. While it was recovering, the light one swam off once again, trying to escape.

When the dark one realized his prey was gone, he began the pursuit once again. The little serpent swam past the warriors once more, and this time, when the dark one followed, Ryvan leapt on its back and grabbed a hold of his fins under the neck. The serpent attempted to shake off the attacker, but only made it dizzy. The beast rose up straight into the air and roared. Its jagged teeth glistened in the light.

In one motion, Ryvan let go of the creature's fins, ripped out his bow, and shot an arrow down into the serpent's forehead. It cried out in pain, and just as Ryvan replaced the bow and dove down into the water, it began lashing its head violently. Ryvan disappeared in the dark water. His armor was weighing him down, and he couldn't reach the surface. So he slowly began sinking down into a watery grave.

Tyrese watched from shore while the small serpent dove down below. A moment later, he resurfaced with Ryvan on its back. By then, the dark serpent had regained its senses and went in for the kill. Ryvan couldn't do anything because he couldn't see the dark creature. The light serpent had its back turned to its attacker without realizing it. The only one that noticed what was about to happen was Tyrese, and he stood far back on the shore. Then he had an idea and decided to run with it.

Tyrese ripped out a knife and threw it sharply forward. It sliced through the air directly toward Ryvan. He ducked, and the knife blade caught the serpent in the back of its opened mouth. It reared back and opened its mouth even farther. The sound of pain as the knife struck alerted Ryvan as the beast closed its eyes. Ryvan took advantage of the moment and drew his bow again. He fired another arrow into the serpent's open mouth. This time, the beast stopped moving and let out an earsplitting wail. Then the dying beast slowly began to sink down into the water.

The green serpent slithered to the shore with Ryvan. Tyrese ran to the edge of the bank and jumped on the creature's back.

"Thank you, both. I am eternally grateful!"

"I would say it was no problem, but I almost drowned," Ryvan laughed.

The serpent calmly slithered through the dark water.

"We will reach the other side momentarily," the serpent stated.

"Uh, I was just wondering why that beast was chasing you," Tyrese wondered.

"That is a very good question. It was after you two," came the dreary reply.

"Why us?" Ryvan queried.

"You are enemies of the Dark One; therefore, this creature was sent to get rid of me, so it could kill you."

"I knew it!" Tyrese exclaimed. "But, why would it try to kill you?"

"In a challenge, you would normally have fought me, and if you won, I would take you across. If the monster had succeeded in killing me, it would have fought you and lost purposefully. Then, halfway across, it would have eaten you while you were unaware."

"Oh," the boys murmured.

"However, I imagine the fact that you helped me is reason enough to help you," the serpent chortled. "We are nearing land."

A moment later, they reached dry land, and the serpent rose up out of the water and stretched out across the shore. The boys jumped off, and the serpent slithered backward into the water. The only part of it that stayed above water was its head. The serpent stared straight into the eyes of the young warriors and said, "I bid you farewell, young ones. Be wary, and watch out for one another. All will be well."

With that, the serpent slid back into the murky depths. The warriors nodded seriously and turned. They walked straight into a thorn wall. "Ouch!" Tyrese cried as the thorns dug into his arms and face.

They backed away and examined the wall. It towered above them by ten feet and stretched all along the coast as well. There was no way around it.

"How do you want to do this?" Ryvan asked.

The girls stepped onto dry land at the same time, so neither one would fall into the depths of the water. Instantly, the rose pathway disappeared, and the girls turned into a large wall of green bushy plants standing in their way. They noticed it stood high above their heads. They tried to pull back, but they were stuck. Their necklaces restrained them.

Quickly and efficiently, they unhooked themselves from the wall. When they were out, more red and blue roses instantly appeared, blossoming over the hedges.

"What's with these roses?" Liyah asked.

"Don't know, but I sure am glad they are here," Melanie smiled.

The girls glanced over to their left and noticed a large opening was formed into the hedge. They walked over and peered in.

"A maze," Melanie murmured.

"Oh, boy," Liyah exclaimed in sarcasm.

The girls entered, and the roses grew out of the hedge on either side of them as they walked through. After they had walked a while, Liyah tensed.

"I don't like this," she said. "Something could be waiting for us around any one of these corners."

"Liyah, you are so paranoid," Melanie began. She began walking ahead of Liyah. Red roses preceded the blue ones. "You have always been that way. You need to learn to loosen up. Kick back and yipe!"

Liyah snapped her head forward to see Melanie struggling to walk. Her feet appeared to be stuck.

"Mel, are you shrinking?"

"No! More like sinking."

Melanie was standing in quicksand.

"Ok! Don't move. I've always heard that you sink slower if you don't move," Liyah explained.

Melanie stopped moving and instantly went from being up to her stomach in quicksand to being up to her head.

"What happened to not moving?" Melanie cried.

"Hmm, I don't think this is normal quicksand."

"Liyah, sweetie," Melanie smiled angelically. "GET ME OUT, NOW!"

"Oh! Right!" Liyah snapped into action. "Grab my hand."

Melanie pulled an arm up out of the sandy mass. Liyah grabbed ahold of the outstretched hand and pulled her nearer. Melanie was up to her nose and sinking fast.

"On three, ok? One."

"HURRY, PLEASE!"

"Two," Liyah began.

"Why do you have to always count to three? JUST DO IT!"

Liyah gave a strong tug on Melanie's hand. Melanie moved up a bit, and Liyah grabbed her around the shoulders, hoisting her up and out of the sand trap. Both girls collapsed on the ground. Both Melanie and Liyah's arms and torso were coated in sand.

"That was a close one," Liyah laughed.

Melanie glared at her. The pair stood, and Liyah smiled.

"What are you so happy about? I almost died!"

"I'm paranoid?" Liyah's voice dripped sarcasm.

"You're loving this, aren't you?"

"Oh, yes."

"This wall isn't going to give way," Tyrese panted.

The boys had been slicing through the thorn wall for several minutes. They had at least cut through four feet, and they seemed to be getting nowhere.

"Just keep cutting, we'll make it through."

The boys continued hacking through until the final thorns fell away, and the boys were faced with an open pathway with towering thorn hedges on either side.

"Yippee, a maze," Tyrese muttered.

****

The boys had been walking through the thorny maze for quite awhile and had come across nothing. They had made several wrong turns and had to backtrack repeatedly. Now they stopped to rest for a minute and regain their bearings.

Tyrese's armor began to sparkle in the light, and it caught Ryvan's interest. He watched intently as Tyrese asked him, "What are you looking at?"

"Your armor," Ryvan mused.

"What about it?"

"It seems to be a different type of metal now."

"Really? What color is it?" Tyrese questioned.

"It looks kind of like silver."

"I can't tell what yours is, though," Tyrese stated.

"Oh well, it's dark. It's probably still bronze," Ryvan laughed.

Just then, they ran into another dead end. The boys stopped laughing and grew serious again.

"Great. I think we are lost," Tyrese sighed.

"Oh, yeah."

"So what do you think we should do?"

"We have one choice."

"What's that?"

"Backtrack, walk some more, and hopefully, we won't run into any more dead ends."

"Or more of the Dark One's minions," Tyrese chimed.

"Shoot, I'd rather see another one of them than another dead end. That way we would at least be faced with something different."

"Whatever, let's just get moving, or we'll never make it out by sunrise," Tyrese sighed.

"Good point."

Tyrese slung his blade over his shoulder, and the boys started to retrace their footsteps.

Chapter 19

"We've been walking for hours!" Melanie complained.

"It's been fifteen minutes, Mel," Liyah laughed.

"Well, it feels like it's been much longer."

"I have to agree. It is taking up time, and it is so boring."

"What do you mean by boring? The fact that we haven't been on the verge of death isn't enough to satisfy you?"

"Exactly."

"Why do I even try?" Melanie murmured under her breath. Liyah didn't hear her.

"I think we are about halfway. These roses really help. If we didn't have them, we would be lost," the elder she-warrior stated.

"Yeah, no joke!"

Just then, the girls turned another corner and were greeted by the bones and armor of many humans. The fallen warriors lay on the ground still in their full armor with shields and weapons still raised. Moss and dust gathered on the bones, clinging to the long unused surface of the warriors' inner skeleton.

The girls made a face of disgust, and Liyah drew out her other cross-blade. Melanie followed her lead. Quietly, they stepped in between the long-since dead warriors' corpses. It was deathly quiet. All went well for a time, until Melanie accidentally kicked a bone and it clattered into another skeleton, making the sound reverberate through the whole maze. Liyah glared at her companion and braced herself for something to come attack them. Nothing came. What did come was the sound of Melanie's voice.

"Well, if that didn't bring out the beast that did this, then nothing will."

Liyah replied, "I hope not."

They continued walking through the maze until Liyah peered around a corner and said, "I guess we were farther than I thought."

"What makes you say that?" Melanie asked.

"Mt. Reolné is right through there."

"Well, what are we waiting for? Let's go!" Melanie exclaimed.

Melanie tried to walk past her and around the corner, but Liyah lashed her blade out and stopped it directly in front of Melanie, making her stop short.

"You might not want to do that *just* yet," Liyah whispered.

"Why not?"

Liyah motioned for her to peer around the corner. Melanie did this and realized what Liyah meant. The volcano was there, but there was also a guard at the exit of the maze.

The guard seemed to be massive and oddly covered in fur. They could only make out the form of the guard and its weapons, but they couldn't tell what it actually was. Melanie leaned back and saw Liyah preparing for battle. All was quiet, except for the birds cawing now in the darkened trees. It sounded like the mourning call of the ravens.

Suddenly, a deep growling voice called out to them, "Come out! I know you are there!"

"He's found us. Come on," Liyah sighed.

The warriors stepped out into the main segment of the path directly within the monster's line of vision.

"Come closer," it called out. "You might as well come see what you are up against."

The girls stepped forward to see that the guard was actually a minotaur. Over seven feet tall, with the head of a bull and the body of a man, the minotaur stood about two feet above the girls, and he looked down at them with a malicious grin. His hair was a dark brown and covered his entire body. Two horns protruded from its massive skull. It wore an iron chest plate and carried a spear that glistened wickedly in the light cast down on it.

"I have to admit," the creature began, "you have done well to get this far, but it is as far as you will go."

"Not by our standards," Melanie retorted.

"You also have heart. That can be a strength and a weakness. It depends on where it lies. Be careful that you know the difference," the minotaur informed.

"Yeah, thanks for that. How do we get past you?" Melanie asked.

"You don't. However, if you want to try, then you would have to defeat me in combat."

"Well, then," Melanie began, "bring it on."

Liyah stopped and glared at Melanie. "You sure do have a different attitude."

"Yeah, I kind of like it. What do you think?" Melanie stated.

"Yeah, I do—" Liyah began.

The minotaur interrupted, "Can we just get started so I can defeat you?"

"We can get started," Melanie began.

"But you won't be defeating us," Liyah finished, looking insulted at having been so rudely interrupted.

The minotaur raised his spear and charged the girls. They dove out of the way in the nick of time. The monster twirled his spear and charged again. The girls knew that the monster was too large, and that if they stayed where they were and confronted him, they would end up warrior women on a stick. So they dove out of its way once more.

The monster turned to face them and allowed them to regain their composure before attacking again. As soon as the girls were on their feet, he charged again. The only difference this time was when he passed, Liyah and Melanie both whipped their legs around to trip the charging guard.

When he hit the ground, the girls paused to give each other a surprised look, and Liyah said, "Nice!"

"Back at you!"

The minotaur scrambled to its feet and stared head on at the girls. They knew it would be an up close battle from this point on. Liyah drew up to a defensive stance, while Melanie tightened the grasp on her weapons. The minotaur again twirled its spear and then pulled it back and brought down a powerful blow from the wooden handle. He was aiming for Liyah.

Liyah caught the spear in an X of her blades making two gashes in the wood. She tried to wrench the spear from its hands, but the minotaur only lifted her off the ground and shook her off, throwing her into the maze wall. Melanie watched her companion being tossed through the air like a rag doll. She noticed that Liyah was fine, and she was getting to her feet.

Meanwhile, the minotaur whipped the spear underneath Melanie's feet, and she fell on her back. The minotaur then raised his spear to deliver another blow, and it landed with a dull thud on the earth where Melanie's head had just been. She had rolled to the side just in time. However, the minotaur kept delivering blows to the earth as Melanie rolled, trying to avoid them, for she did not have time to rise to her feet. Melanie rolled away, but collided with the minotaur's hoof. He had her trapped to where she couldn't roll away from him. He lifted the spear back to skewer her alive. Suddenly, Melanie saw an arm wrap around the minotaur's massive neck. It was Liyah, and she held a blade to the minotaur's throat.

"Let us pass, and I will spare you," Liyah proposed.

"Not a chance!" the minotaur cried as he lifted her arm up and grabbed the girl around her waist. He then threw her into the side wall yet again, only there was much more force behind this throw.

This gave Melanie the opportunity to get to her feet, but the minotaur quickly turned back to her and brought his spear down at her head yet again. Melanie caught the spear in an X like Liyah had, and somehow managed to land in the same spot, making the gashes sink in deeper. Then an idea sparked alive in her mind.

There was only one problem; Melanie's cross-blades were stuck. She held onto them tightly while the minotaur tried to shake her off. Suddenly, they gave way, and Melanie flew through the air and struck against the hedge.

Melanie slid down the wall and landed on something. It then groaned. Melanie rolled off of the object and glanced in its direction. The object turned out to be Liyah. She was lying on the ground with her head resting on the hedge. Her forehead was gashed open and bleeding. The blood began to run down her face and neck. Her eyes were closed.

"Liyah! Wake up!" Melanie called to her distant friend. Liyah didn't stir.

The minotaur began approaching them slowly and menacingly. It was very confident that it had won. Melanie began to shake Liyah. "Liyah! Wake up! Please, wake up! Don't you leave me again! Please, don't leave me!"

Still, Liyah didn't move, and the minotaur was getting closer. Melanie didn't know what to do. She couldn't defeat the minotaur alone. Liyah's breathing grew shallow and slow.

"Did your friend take the fall for you?" the minotaur called. It walked ever closer.

Melanie didn't answer.

"You do know, she went out protecting you."

"She's not dead," Melanie cried through gritted teeth and tears.

"Yet. She will die in a matter of minutes. Let me guess. Her breathing is slow and shallow? It won't be long."

"She won't die."

"Such a waste, too! She could have been great."

"She *won't* die!"

"Suit yourself. Live in ignorance."

Melanie's anger flared, and she rose to her feet. She crossed over to the minotaur. Her weapons were raised.

"You think you can defeat me alone?" the minotaur laughed.

Melanie said not a word, just began a barrage of attacks against the monster. He blocked every one. This is what Melanie wanted. Each time he blocked a blow with his spear, Melanie's cross-blades cut deeper into it.

Suddenly, the minotaur delivered a blow down again, which Melanie blocked with a cross-blade X as before, but this time, he was overpowering her, and she knew it. In one instant, Melanie felt her strength billow up within her like a hot spring. She forced this bottled up power into slicing through the spear and knocking the monster flat. While he was stunned, she crossed her swords above his neck.

"You are done," she hissed. Her hair hung around her face and blew about in the breeze, causing her to take on an unearthly role.

"All is fair. I have lost. You may pass."

****

A while later, Melanie crossed through the gate with Liyah strewn over her back.

"Be sure to watch out for the dweller of the volcano!" the minotaur called through the gate. "If I could not defeat you, she will!"

Melanie began her long trek up the volcano. She knew it would be a race against time now, because her journey would be twice as arduous now that she carried her companion up the side of a volcano. Light was already growing in the sky.

Suddenly, Melanie saw the landscape change. The path became ash and soot mixed with volcanic rock. A dark sulfurous smell filled the air. It grew extremely hot. She was nearing the top of the volcano.

"We've been walking for forever," Tyrese whined.

"Yeah, we have, but we are back to where we started."

"Is that a good thing?"

Ryvan gave him a vacant look, and he kept walking. Finally, he turned around a corner and stated, "I think we found the volcano."

"Sweet! Let's go."

The warriors stepped out into the clearing. In front of them, a large iron gate like the one at the entrance of the challenge area stood, hovering above the maze walls. The boys ventured over to the gate and looked up. They pulled on the iron bars, but it didn't give way. Their shadows were cast through the gate and landed on the volcanic pathway just out of their reach.

Suddenly, another shadow joined theirs. It was much larger, and it placed one of its large hands on each of the boys' shoulders. They tried to turn, but they were hoisted up off the ground. Instantly, they were face to face with a giant minotaur.

It roared, "How dare you infidels encroach upon my gate without that right!"

It thrust them both back into the thorny wall of the maze. They felt the thorns sink deep into their flesh. While they were stunned, the minotaur began walking up to the spot where they rested. It raised a large iron spear and was about to finish them off.

Suddenly, the moonlight intensified, and the minotaur's face went from enraged disgust to a look of pure terror. He instantly dropped back from the boys and fell to his knees. The boys were confused, and Tyrese took a step towards the creature. He cowered away and cried, "Have mercy upon me! Spare me! I beg of thee!"

"Huh?" Tyrese asked.

"My liege, I did not know. I am sorry. I apologize a thousand times over!"

Tyrese shrugged and looked back to Ryvan. "He talks funny."

Ryvan ignored the comment and rose to his feet, thereby joining his companion.

"Calm yourself," Ryvan stated. "Tell us, what is it you fear?"

The minotaur stared at him with confusion and disbelief. "I did not know what you were! I was only doing my duty! I did not mean to threaten two high authorities as you!"

"Rise, and tell us of what you speak," Ryvan commanded.

Tyrese looked bewildered. "*You* talk funny!"

"As you wish," the minotaur stated as he rose up on his hooves. "However, I am not worthy."

"Why do you speak this?" Ryvan asked.

"You know not?"

The boys shook their heads.

The minotaur continued, "It is not my place. You will find out soon enough. I shall let you pass for sparing me."

The guard rose and shoved his spear into the dark metal lock, and the gate squealed open. The boys thanked him and stepped through the metal gate onto the thick volcanic ash-laden path to the top. When they were beginning to move up the volcano, the minotaur called back, "A word of caution to you! Beware the mistresses of the mountain. They shall not fear you as they should. They care not."

"Thank you for that. We shall, uh, take heed unto your words!" Tyrese called back awkwardly.

"Good luck, young warriors!" the minotaur cried. Then, he muttered under his breath, "You shall need it in the near future. The time is at hand." With that, he shook his shaggy head and returned to his guard position.

****

The warriors climbed high up the volcano through thick ash and large chunks of volcanic rock that had obviously rained down upon the slopes in decades past. So far, they had made it halfway up the rocky face without coming across any problems.

The higher they climbed, things began changing rapidly. At first, there had been lush grass appearing in thick patches, but now, replacing it was dark ash and rocks. There were many rocks strewn about the ashen slopes. Small rocks tumbled in all directions as they climbed. The temperature gradually increased and quickly, the boys became dry from their swim in the lake. The air smelled like the sulfurous breath of a demon, which made the young warriors' eyes water. Then, as quickly as the landscape had changed before, the elements around them began changing yet again.

In place of the pools of occasional lava, water was now visible. It wasn't like hot spring water either. It was clear and crystalline. The air continued to smell of sulfur; however, another scent began to combine with the noxious smell. The smell was somehow sweet like the distinct aroma of flowers.

"How can you describe this?" Tyrese asked.

"Ominous."

Soon, small pools of the calm water surrounded them on all sides. Tyrese stepped toward a pool of water in a trance-like state. He sank to one knee and gazed deep into the pool's depths which stretched on for an eternity.

Tyrese saw his own reflection staring back from the surface of the sparkling clear-blue water. Then, the water began to stir. At first, Tyrese thought he had dropped a pebble into the pool, causing the rippling effect, but then, something changed his mind. The water began circling gently in a calming manner. Tyrese took a step back from the pool as a figure began rising from the depths.

The figure grew until its feet were flat upon the surface of the water. It was the same crystal blue color as the water itself, but it seemed to have a solid surface to it. The warriors realized it was in the form of a beautiful woman with long hair and smooth features wearing jewelry and gypsy clothing. The figure began beckoning to Tyrese to come to her. He hesitated. When he did, the woman continued. And then, she began to sing. Her song went right to his heart. Tyrese had never heard such a beautiful, sad, melodious song, yet it had no form. He began to come to her when he heard Ryvan call out, "Don't listen to her!"

Tyrese snapped out of it and tried to back away, but the creature suddenly changed its form. It was still a woman, but in place of her beautiful pearl teeth, fangs protruded from her gums as she bared her venomous teeth. Her eyes turned blood red, and her nails went sharp. She lost all her beauty.

It was too late for Tyrese to get back, and the creature knew it. She instantly reached out and grabbed Tyrese by the neck. The beast began pulling him down into a watery grave. Tyrese sank his heels into the earth, but it gave way, for it had lost its illusion and turned back into ash. The surroundings went back to their natural shapes, and the creature turned to lava.

Just as Tyrese was about to go under, a sword flashed, and instantly, the creature released him. It shrank back and cried out in a deep anguished voice of pain. Ryvan stood between Tyrese and the creature. It said, "You who have prevailed yet so far, now seek something far stronger in power. You may defeat *us*, but there will be a price."

Ryvan said, "At what cost?"

"*We* do not reside in these mountains. *We* come from afar to defeat you!"

"Why? What are we, but mere men unto you?" Tyrese asked.

"*We* care not! *We* were sent! *We* care not!" Just as she said this, the monster swept its arms out again to meet Ryvan, but he slashed through the lava, making the beast cringe back and cry out again. A wave of heat rustled his hair.

"Who sent you?" Ryvan asked with authority.

"The great Navaira! The Mistress of Darkness! She sent *us* forth!"

"You shall let us pass," Tyrese stated.

"Never will *we* fall!"

"Why do you continue to say 'we' and 'us'?" Tyrese questioned.

At that point, the creature split in two. Then, each one split into two more, and again until there were eight of the creatures standing before the warriors.

"*We* shall fulfill *our* duty for the mighty Navaira!" they all cried in unison. Out of the lava, a weapon formed to each one's hand. "*We* shall defeat you! *We* know of who you are! *We* care not! *We* care not!"

"What are you?" Ryvan demanded.

"*Demons of darkness! Fulfillers of fire! We are sirens!*"

All eight sirens brandished their weapons and formed a tight circle around the warriors. The boys drew their cross-blades and began preparing for a fight. The fire burned, creating a ghastly glow against the sky.

"You shall *not* defeat *us*, oh, warriors of old! *We* shall not fall!"

While these words poured from the lead siren's mouth, Ryvan and Tyrese each slashed through two sirens, causing them to sink back down into the lava pit in a furious pained cry of defeat.

"*We* shall just rise again!"

Tyrese took out two more, while Ryvan finished off another.

The lead siren only remained. She seemed distraught at the sight of no rising sirens. "What are those blades? No mere *blade* can banish *us* to the abyss! No mere *blade can banish us! What of your blades?*"

The boys didn't think about it before. They honestly didn't know what the siren spoke of.

"It matters not!" the siren cried as she regained her composure. "The mighty ones shall fall!"

Ryvan then did an odd thing. He sheathed his weapons. His companion and adversary both stared at him in disbelief.

"Foolish one! What art thou doing?"

He ignored her and began walking past the large lava pool toward the peak of the volcano. She glided through the lava after him silently.

"Come and face me like a real warrior!" she cried.

Ryvan ignored her again and continued walking. He had his back turned to her. The siren realized this and took the advantage. She began to bring down a fiery blow to destroy the young warrior. Only a split second before the blade struck down, Tyrese leapt out of nowhere and caught the siren off guard. Quickly, he delivered the single powerful blow that sent the siren tumbling down into the lava again.

"Nice," Ryvan smiled.

Tyrese sheathed his white-hot blade and laughed, "That was almost too easy!"

"All talk."

"Nothing to back it up."

They moved on.

Melanie paused after moving farther up the volcano's slope. Her legs ached from the combination of the weight of her companion and the volcano's sloping side. Large boulders began to litter the landscape. Then Melanie noticed a strange sight. About twenty boulders were piled off to the side of the mountain, forming a sort of cave.

She stopped and stared into the small cavern for a moment while she tried to catch her breath. Nothing but darkness peered back at her. All was deathly still. Nothing moved or made a sound. Something about that cave was very peculiar, but she didn't know what. For some reason, she couldn't shift her gaze from the depths of the cavern. Suddenly, something stared back at her.

Melanie blinked and made sure she was seeing things correctly. When she looked again, the eyes were still there. They were small slanted slits of light coming from the darkness. It was real. Melanie moved back an inch or two trying to decide whether to fight or not. Gently, Melanie placed Liyah on the ground and drew her cross-blades without looking away.

The eyes blinked and then began to move out of the cave. Before the creature stepped out into the moonlight, it called out to Melanie, "Young one, do not fear, I mean you no harm."

The voice was slick and cold with darkness to it. It also had a lazy slur. Melanie did not sheath her weapons, but only took up a defensive stance.

"As you wish, but as I've said," the creature stepped out, or rather, *glided* out, "I mean you no harm."

Melanie stared at the thing floating above the ground in front of her. It was like a person—only you could see right through it to some extent. It was very pale and wore a black tattered dress. Its long, ratted, black hair floated in an unseen breeze. A pair of fangs protruded from her pale blue lips. Those cold, slanted eyes bore deep into Melanie, freezing her where she was. Melanie then knew what she was facing—a demon banshee.

"Close your mouth, child," it hissed. "Sheath your weapons."

"How can I be sure I can trust you? You are a demon."

"If I wanted to harm you, I would have done it by now."

"How can I be sure?" Melanie repeated.

The banshee sighed, then opened her mouth and let out an earsplitting wail that slashed through the silence like a knife. Melanie instantly dropped her weapons and covered her ears, but she could not escape the banshee's wail. She fell to her knees, shaking her head.

Suddenly, the wailing stopped, and the banshee cackled, "That could have been a thousand times worse! If I had wanted, you would have fallen down dead before you even knew what hit you. So, again, I say, sheath your weapons."

Melanie did as directed and asked, "Why do you mean me no harm?"

"I know the power of which you carry, even though you do not. I know of your past."

"So? What does that mean?"

"If I were to seriously go up against you, I would fail. I am wise enough to know that. Demons cannot prevail against the light," she hissed with malice.

Melanie did not reply, for Liyah moaned and was gradually rising to her feet. She instantly spotted the banshee and ripped out her blades.

"Must I do it again? I'm what woke her in the first place," the banshee droned.

Melanie told Liyah, "Put them away. We will be fine."

Liyah seemed hesitant but did as directed. Then, the banshee said, "It pains one to look upon you. Continue your journey up the volcano. You will find what you desire there. Now, LEAVE MY PRESENCE!"

The girls clapped their hands to their ears and began to run up the mountainous volcano.

****

As the girls drew closer to the mouth of the volcano, the rocks and boulders started to form a rocky face that the girls had to climb over. Some parts were quite steep. The girls reached the top of the rise and looked up. The mouth seemed to be just above one other rise. Liyah began to climb. Melanie watched as Liyah made her way up almost spider-like. It took her awhile to get to the top, but she then vanished over the rise.

Melanie took a deep breath and began climbing up the steep rock. She finally gained some confidence and relaxed a bit, but just as she was about to reach the top, she lost her footing and began to fall down on the rocks below. She closed her eyes and felt a hand grab onto hers, and when she opened her eyes again, she realized that she was face to face with Liyah who said, "I come in pretty handy when I'm not unconscious, do I not?"

"Stop talking funny and pull me up," Melanie laughed.

Liyah hoisted Melanie up over the rock with ease, and they turned to continue. When they did this, they were hit by a blast of heat from a bursting bubble in a pit a few yards in front of them.

They had reached the top.

"I think the top is just over these next couple of rises," Tyrese called back to Ryvan, who was making his way up directly behind Tyrese. The boys made it over the first rock wall and started on the second. The smell of sulfur was more pungent than before. It was almost sickening.

Ryvan moved in alongside Tyrese, and they rose over the steep cliff side at the same time. What they saw surprised them. A large creature with the head of an eagle and the body of a lion greeted the boys. A pair of wings protruded from his back. Its large talons dug into the earth, while his lion tail swished back and forth.

It surprised both boys when the griffin spoke. It cawed, "Welcome, young travelers." It sat back on its haunches and began preening its feathers.

The boys hoisted themselves over and noticed skeletons were strewn here and there. Also, directly behind the griffin, a cast iron gate stood, blocking the way to the top.

"To get through there, you must get through me," it smiled nonchalantly.

The boys drew their blades, ready for the fight, but the griffin only laughed and said, "I shall not fight you. You must answer one of my riddles. If you answer correctly, you shall pass. If not, you will join the others."

The boys laughed. Tyrese blurted, "You can't be serious."

The griffin stopped preening and replied indignantly, "Of course I am!"

It swept its talons one inch from his face and continued, "Would you like to hear the riddle, or shall I finish you off now?"

"We'll go with the riddle," Tyrese croaked.

The griffin moved back into his sitting position and began happily, "Very well, then. Here it goes. Listen carefully. You may take as long as you need, but you only have one try."

"Ok," Tyrese sighed.

"Are you ready?"

"Yes," the boys replied.

"I make man both strong and weak. I am the thing that people most often seek. I give hope to the desperate. I save the lost. I am the one that led our Savior to the cross. I can be found in courage, and in sacrifice, because I am always more than willing to pay the price. And when the sun goes down, and in the darkest night, you know I am there with you by your side. What am I?"

The boys were quiet and thought carefully. The griffin was thoroughly enjoying himself and lay catlike on its stomach with its front paws crossed.

The boys thought continuously. After some time, Ryvan smiled slyly and said, "Tyrese, answer these questions."

"Ok," Tyrese began.

"What do we fight for?"

"Those we care about."

"What led our Savior to the cross?"

Tyrese frowned, but he did not answer.

"What brings us courage? What do we sacrifice for?"

"Wait." Tyrese was catching on.

"What makes us willing to keep on fighting?"

Tyrese smiled at his companion.

"So what's the answer?"

"Love," Tyrese smirked.

The griffin grew angry. In a flurry of rustling fur and ruffled feathers, the griffin took off into the sky with a loud screech.

When he finally landed, he angrily demanded, "How did you know my riddle?"

Ryvan frowned, "I have heard it before somewhere. It was so familiar to me. May I ask what it was from?"

The griffin snapped its beak and paced back and forth. A couple of feathers fell to the ground. "It is from an ancient Asgarnian book. The passage it comes from is called Ψrivent. Are you familiar with it?"

An image of Liyah's leather bound book flashed in his mind. "It is possible."

"A deal is a deal," the creature stated angrily. "You many pass."

The top was within their reach. It seemed things merely grew easier. The griffin moved aside, snatching up an old skull and crunching it angrily in its beak instead of attacking the warrior. The creatures respected the warriors' power.

Chapter 20

The girls stared down into the pool of lava just as the sun began to peer over the mountains of Galeã, illuminating the features of the island. Suddenly, the sound of wings was heard above the boiling lava. The girls looked up into the sky and saw Jasira and Riela descending from the sky on their mounts. Alongside them, their own horses lighted delicately on the ashen surface.

"You girls pass," Riela stated.

"Quickly mount your horses, and we will go to the palace," Jasira beamed.

The young warriors mounted happily, and all four rode off into the sky. The girls were relieved that they were finished, and they suddenly realized that they were exhausted.

****

The morning sunrise tinted the island all different shades of pink, orange, and yellow. A slight breeze blew through the girls' hair while they rode through the sky. Suddenly, the palace came into view. The sun caught on the golden surface, causing it to reflect back with an even more radiant light.

When the four lighted down on the green grass directly outside the palace, Riela said, "I am very impressed with both of you. You have shown that you truly are pure in heart."

Jasira interrupted, "You will be fine additions to the Galiphems. That is, if you wish to stay."

The girls were dumbfounded. "Why wouldn't we stay?" Melanie asked.

Riela and Jasira looked at each other and shrugged.

Jasira said, "You have proven your worth, but *we* personally think you don't belong here."

"What?" Liyah burst. "You just said we would make fine additions—blah blah blah! What's the deal?"

Riela replied, "We feel that you belong somewhere else."

"Like where?" Melanie countered.

"I cannot say, for I do not know," Jasira stated.

"You're not making sense," Liyah declared.

"Come, let us get you something to eat," Riela blurted.

Even though that suggestion sounded wonderful to the girls, they didn't want to drop the discussion. The four began walking toward the palace when Liyah said, "Why are you saying these things?"

"You do not know?" Riela and Jasira said in unison.

"No! I don't know anything!" Melanie cried desperately.

Everyone paused to give her an awkward glance, then Riela spoke, "We did not know you hadn't realized."

Jasira laughed, "Look down at your armor, oh, great ones!"

The girls did as directed and lowered their heads. There, shimmering in the sunlight, causing white light to spread all around, white gold armor stood in place of the original bronze.

"And I thought I'd never see it," Jasira mused.

The boys stood at the top of the volcano staring down into the lava pit. Suddenly, the sound of beating wings was recognizable over the bubbling lava. Both warriors looked up in time to see the talons of two gigantic hawks wrap around them. Only this time, the hawks dropped them onto the backs of two other hawks.

The creatures swept through the sky in formation. They began heading out of the forest at an impressive speed. Soon, the hawks began heading in the direction of the palace. Ryvan and Tyrese relaxed and let the creatures take them to safety.

****

"Welcome back, young warriors!" the king welcomed them as soon as the hawks landed on the ground. All the warriors from the island stood outside the palace to greet them. A loud cheer rose up from the multitude.

The king waited until they had quieted down before he said, "You boys have done a wonderful job. I am very pleased to announce that you have passed, and you do not belong here."

Another cheer rose from the crowd of spectators.

"Wait a minute!" Ryvan exclaimed.

"Care to run that by me again?" Tyrese asked.

The king laughed and said, "Sure! You don't belong here."

"What do you mean?" Ryvan demanded. "We passed with flying colors!"

"Yes, and that is enough for you to belong here, but there is one minor detail," the king continued.

"What's that?" Tyrese queried.

"Apparently, you have not seen, yet."

The crowd began to laugh as the king bellowed, "Look down at your armor, oh mighty warriors from afar."

The boys peered down to see the same thing the girls had—white gold armor.

"Do you understand now?" the king questioned.

The boys stood open-mouthed and stared at each other.

"Are you ready for a break?" a young warrior asked from the side.

The boys nodded.

"Follow me. We will get you something to eat and a place to rest."

"Before you boys drift into unconsciousness, there is something I must tell you," the king called.

They stopped and allowed the king to tell them, "There has been word received that there are two others that have gained the armor of white gold. You must meet with them. It is essential. Tell my wife hello. She is the queen. You will depart first thing tomorrow morning for Galeã."

As the girls walked toward their room, Riela and Jasira continued speaking.

"There has been word received that there have been two other warriors to achieve white gold armor. However, these warriors are on the warrior island of Geriã. They will be coming here to have a conference with you. It is very essential that you meet them," Jasira stated.

"Geriã?" Liyah asked. "Isn't that where the guys train?"

"Right," Riela confirmed.

"Amusing," Melanie murmured.

The four paused outside a door, and Jasira smiled, "This is where you will stay tonight and tomorrow night."

"The princess of Galeã is waiting inside. She wishes to speak with you," Riela said.

The girls looked surprised as Jasira grinned, "I think you will realize it is worth your while."

The trainers departed, leaving Liyah and Melanie to open the door and meet the princess alone. The girls stepped into the room and opened their mouths in awe. The room was huge and extravagant. A fire roared in a large hearth at one end of the room, and a silver rug lay on the wooden floor in front of it. There were two large canopy beds for the girls to sleep on, one was silver, and the other was gold. Also, there were many comfortable looking chairs gathered around a large table. Wooden furniture gathered around here and there finishing off the look of the room. Everything was silver and gold.

"Wow," Melanie murmured.

"It's too princessy for my taste," Liyah scoffed.

"There's nothing wrong with that," a voice called from a golden armchair.

Both girls turned to greet the Galeãn princess. Standing in front of them was none other than Vera. She was fine except for one single gash on her left shoulder. She looked much better than Liyah, who still had blood running down her face.

Melanie and Liyah rushed over and gave Vera a hug, while Melanie cried, "We thought you were dead!"

"I thought you were, too. When the Vortzans attacked, I stayed and tried to fight, but they were too powerful. One delivered the blow to my shoulder, and I decided I would not be able to defeat them, so I decided to come back here."

"Back?" Liyah asked.

"Yes, this is my home. The queen is my mother. I am a princess," Vera laughed.

"Are you kidding?" Melanie blurted.

"Nope, but that is not important. What's important is that you two have achieved something that no one else has achieved in the entire history of Shroeketia. Therefore, we are deciding what to do. I can't tell you much yet because we have to wait for the other two warriors," Vera began.

Liyah interrupted, "What of our other companions? Have you received any word from them?"

"None of what I have heard, I'm afraid."

The girls grew quiet, and then Melanie asked, "And your brother?"

"Well, he is fine. He is coming up with the two golden warriors."

"Glad to hear it," Liyah grinned.

"Well, I must leave you now. I know you must be tired. I know I was when I took the challenge. I will be in touch in the next few days," Vera stated as she stood up and made her way to the door. "Good luck."

And then, she was gone.

The girls stood for awhile, and Melanie said, "I don't know about you, but I want to eat."

Just as she said this, someone knocked on the door. "Room service," called Jasira's voice from the other side of the door. She walked in with a large tray full of steaming hot breakfast foods. As soon as she sat it down, the girls leapt upon it. Food had never tasted that good. It warmed them inside and out. Jasira left them alone, and the girls started talking.

"What do you think those other warriors are going to be like?" Melanie asked around a mouthful of food.

"I don't know. It's hard to say," Liyah replied.

"I'm curious to see if they are as good as us," Melanie smiled slyly.

Liyah laughed, "I don't know about you, but I'm not going to let some guys show me up. I don't care if they achieved white gold armor."

"Count me in," Melanie grinned.

The girls finished off their breakfast in silence. Once all the food was polished off, the girls yawned and stretched. A wave of exhaustion covered them.

"Man, you look terrible," Melanie mused.

"Yeah, thanks. You're a real beauty yourself."

Melanie laughed. "So do you want the silver bed or the—" she began.

Liyah interrupted, "Ain't no way I'm sleeping in a gold bed."

With that, Liyah jumped on the silver bed and kicked off her heels. Melanie lumbered over to the golden bed and did the same. When the girls felt comfortable, they settled in for a long sleep.

After the boys rested and ate, Draze went to meet up with them. He spoke of the journey they would take in order to meet the other golden warriors. As soon as they had gathered all their supplies, Draze descended the palace steps to bid the boys farewell. When the warriors found out Draze would not be accompanying them, Tyrese blurted, "How else are we going to find our way?"

Draze replied, "You will have another guide."

"Who? And can he be trusted?" Ryvan questioned.

"It is none other than the prince himself," Draze answered.

"Great, all we need is some royal-blooded prince to watch after," Ryvan mumbled.

"Oh, I'm not all that inept," a voice called from the castle entrance. The boys turned around to see a warrior leaning against the castle with his arms crossed over his chest and a defiant smile on his face. Immediately the boys beamed from ear to ear and rushed up to their friend.

Shace grinned back at them and asked, "Are you guys ready to get going?"

****

"Welcome to Galeã," a young she-warrior welcomed the trio at the entrance of the palace.

"Thank you, Jasira," Shace stated. "Where is my sister?"

"She is upstairs with your mother," Jasira replied.

"Good, I will go to them. Please show these two to their room," Shace said.

"Yes, your highness," Jasira replied obediently as she bowed. Shace bid them farewell and departed. Then Jasira said, "Well, we shouldn't stand out here in the night air. Come, I will show you to your room."

It was late when they reached the island. Both boys were exhausted and wanted nothing more than to sleep. Jasira led them down many corridors to an elaborate room. The only difference from the girls' room was that the colors were royal blue and forest green.

Ryvan dove into the royal blue bed and prepared to sleep. Tyrese did the same, leaping on the green one. When they turned out the lights, Tyrese mused, "I wonder what these golden warriors will be like."

"I don't know. But, I refuse to let a she-warrior show me up," Ryvan laughed.

Tyrese joined in, and then they began to drift into sleep. Just before Ryvan shifted into another realm, Liyah's image filled his mind. His heart stalled, and he couldn't believe she was gone.

****

The next morning at around seven, the boys were sleeping soundly and peacefully. Tyrese lay flat on his stomach horizontally across the bed so that his legs were hanging off the side. Ryvan lay on his back to where his head was at the opposite end of the bed where his feet should have been. It was a peaceful morning, and the birds were singing outside the massive windows. Everything was calm and relaxing, that is, until the door to their room burst open, and a voice called, "Good morning, boys! Time to wake up!"

This startled the boys so much that Tyrese fell off onto the floor, and Ryvan sat straight up in bed, tangled in the sheets. Then they recognized what had awakened them. In their doorway stood a she-warrior in silver armor. She had wavy brown hair and harsh green eyes. She wore a huge smile on her lips, and she seemed ready to laugh.

"You boys need to get ready because the breakfast meeting is about to start. The girls are already downstairs waiting. Shace will be here momentarily to show you the way to the conference room."

They stared blankly at her until she stopped laughing and cried, "Well, let's go!"

She closed the door and left the boys to get ready for the conference. It didn't take them long. They put their armor back on and gathered their weapons. Ryvan was ready earlier and sat back down on his bed as a thought came to his mind. It was his birthday.

A few minutes later, a knock on the door told them that Shace was ready to take them downstairs. The three boys entered down into the main part of the castle. Suddenly, Shace stopped and stated, "You will just go around this corner, and you will be there. I cannot join you, for I am not expected at this gathering. Good luck. Don't be too surprised."

Then he left them alone to attend their meeting. The boys walked around the corner into a large room with stone walls and maroon and gold décor. A large rectangular table stood in the center of the room on a maroon rug with gold designs running all along the edge. Chairs were placed all around the table. The woman who awakened them stood at the front of the table, and two blond she-warriors in white gold armor sat on either side of her.

The boys did a double-take as the she-warriors turned to face them. One smiled broadly, while the other showed a reserved, yet knowing smile. No mistake—these girls were none other than Liyah and Melanie.

Melanie jumped up and hugged them both. Liyah stood slowly and gave Tyrese a hug and then Ryvan. When she hugged him, she whispered, "Happy birthday, Ryvan."

"Thanks," he whispered back, smiling more warmly than he intended, wondering how she had known.

"Please have a seat;" the silver she-warrior smiled kindly. "Glad to see that you two boys are awake."

"Yeah," Tyrese said slowly, glaring at her.

"Well, now that we are all here, we shall begin," she stated seriously. "To begin with, I am Rihannai. I am the one who recruited the girls to be Galiphems. My brother recruited you two boys. We are both from the ancient land of Asgarnia.

Chapter 21

Everyone stared at Rihannai. The room itself seemed to change as a serious air overtook them. Rihannai continued, "I was a general in the king's army, so I spent most of my free time in the palace. I got to know everyone very well.

"The king and his wife were very kind to me. They treated me as if I was one of their own little ones. I even felt like I was somewhat of an older sister to the king's daughters. I spent a lot of time with them, and became their playmate. I even became acquainted with their bodyguards. Their names were Anya and Arête.

"Everything was fine until one solemn day. Someone stole the king's youngest daughter directly from under our noses. There was no sign that anyone had been there. The young one just seemed to vanish into nothingness. The entire kingdom was devastated, and they all looked for her everywhere. But, sadly, she was nowhere to be found.

"Eventually, they finally gave up their pointless search as war threatened the kingdom. With only one daughter remaining, the king made sure that she was heavily guarded at all times. She had her own personal guardians and a small set of warriors to watch over her wherever she went.

"Everything began to look up for quite some time. However, on a quiet day the young princess and her guards went missing. No one ever found out for sure what happened to them, but it was suspected that the Mistress of Darkness had something to do with it, just like before with the younger daughter. So the king waged war on her kingdom in response to her actions against him.

"I was recruited and battled alongside the king himself. But, in the end, we lost violently, and our kingdom fell to her dark hand. The king fell, as did Asgarnia. The land that held it all together in peace had fallen. The world began to crumble. Everything began to fall to the Dark Mistress. Shroeketia is the final land. If it falls, then, the Dark One will rule over this pathetic remainder of a world."

There, she stopped, and Melanie asked, "I'm sorry, but what does this have to do with us?"

"You, young she-warriors, could be the lost princesses of Asgarnia."

Melanie stared blankly at Rihannai. The boys stared at the girls, and Liyah started laughing loudly and very unladylike. Everyone turned to stare at her.

Between fits of laughter, Liyah asked, "Do I look like a princess to you?"

"No. Does Vera?" Rihannai asked.

This made Liyah stop laughing, but she started talking again. "What makes you think we are the princesses?"

"Because you carry all of the signs."

"Like what?"

"For one, every royal blood Asgarnian is born with a tattoo under their skin. The princesses were no exception. The younger had a shooting star, said to symbolize her good fortune and lighthearted nature." Rihannai moved to Melanie and lifted her arm indicating the tattoo. "The other a moon on fire to symbolize her fiery serenity and mystical nature." And she did the same to Liyah who jerked away.

"So what?" Liyah asked. "Anyone could have these."

"Have you seen anyone?"

"Well, no," Liyah muttered.

"And yours are birthmarks."

"Anything else?" Liyah was not convinced.

"You carried Asgarnian cross-blades."

Liyah didn't have a comment for this. Melanie was convinced. So were the boys.

"Also, you own horses of element that were given to the girls upon their birth to be their companions until they found their true steeds."

"If so," Liyah began. She was almost beaten. "Why is it that we cannot remember any of this?"

"That, I cannot tell you. But it is another clue pointing to the two of you. The Dark One must have cast the spell to keep you from reaching your destiny. Or, someone may have cast it in the thoughts of protecting you," Rihannai stated.

"That's all fine and good, but why did the Dark One want the princesses in the first place?" Liyah questioned.

Rihannai glanced at her and said, "It is said there was a certain magic flowing through the girls' veins. The Dark One wanted to harness this particular power, for there was none like it in the world. Therefore, she resorted to kidnapping."

Rihannai seemed to read Liyah's mind because she began answering the question Liyah was ready to ask next. "That would, of course, explain how all dark creatures seem to know who you are. In fact, those creatures probably know much more than we do."

Liyah wouldn't believe that she was a princess, and Melanie was close to going over the edge into blind belief. Liyah was just waiting for her to yell, "Sign me up for a crown!"

"If the Dark One took us, then, how did we escape?" Liyah countered.

"We don't know. Something saved you."

"So, what does this have to do with us?" Ryvan asked.

Everyone had been ignoring the boys up to this point. Finally, Rihannai answered, "We are not sure, but we do know that you both have just as much to do with this as the two girls."

"How?" Ryvan asked.

"You carry similar signs. You may contain royal blood, and you definitely hold the power that these girls do. You are Asgarnians as well."

"So, what's going to happen to us?" Tyrese wondered.

"That, I *can* tell you. You four will depart from here first thing in the morning. Vera and Shace shall accompany you. You will go into the Kingdom of the Elves. We assume that they can tell you much more than we ever could. Also, they could train you better."

"Elves?" Melanie murmured.

"Yes. The Elves are knowing and gifted creatures. They can help. But, before you leave, there will be a banquet in your honor tonight, celebrating your victory and the rise of four new leaders of the resistance."

"Great," Liyah thought to herself. "That's just what we need."

When the meeting ended, Rihannai told all of them that they could do whatever they wanted for the rest of the day. Then the silver she-warrior left the four to talk. Everyone was excited to see one another again, but they were fairly quiet because of the information they had just received.

Tyrese sat quietly, watching everyone. Liyah sat slumped down in her chair. She wasn't talking. Ryvan wasn't either. He sat stiffly in his chair, and Melanie seemed like she wanted to talk but didn't. It went on like this for quite a while. Then, Melanie stood up and said, "I'm going to go check this place out. Anyone want to join me?"

Tyrese stood up. "I'll go."

With that, the pair left Ryvan and Liyah in the meeting room.

"Haven't we done this before?" Tyrese joked.

"Not us," Melanie laughed sarcastically. "Must have been someone else that you are thinking of."

"So what are you going to do for the rest of the day?"

"I was thinking of touring the kingdom on horseback," she replied. "Care to join me?"

Tyrese's face brightened, and he replied, "Sure."

The two walked out of the palace toward the stables.

****

Liyah stood. Ryvan watched her as she said, "I'm going to go shoot. You want to come?"

Ryvan sat there for a while then said, "Sure, why not?"

The two walked down the hall silently. Ryvan knew Liyah was miffed, and that she didn't want to be a princess. It didn't fit her, but it would explain a lot.

"So, where is the archery course?" Ryvan asked.

"Jasira told me there was one out behind the castle."

They both stepped out into the light and winced at the brightness. They slowly made their way around the palace to the training course. Ryvan decided that if Liyah wanted to speak, then, he would let her do the talking. He didn't want to upset her anymore than she already was. He would just let her vent.

As soon as they reached the course, Liyah ripped out her bow and began target practice. She drew her bowstring tight, making the muscles in her arms flex to their limit. The arrows flew with such force, that they struck more deeply than usual in the target—dead center.

After some time, she seemed to loosen up a bit. She turned to Ryvan and asked, "Are you going to shoot with me, or are you just going to stand there and watch?"

"I'm content just watching for now," Ryvan commented as he leaned against a nearby tree with his arms folded behind his head.

"Ok, that's good. I'm almost done."

About thirty minutes later, she finally re-strapped her bow to her back.

Ryvan was sitting in the grass, and so, he rose up to his feet. "What happened to almost done?"

Liyah smiled, "Sorry. I got a little carried away, but I do feel better."

"That's good," Ryvan laughed. "Now, come with me."

Liyah looked at him blankly. "Where are we going?"

Ryvan smiled, "Just come on." He turned and began walking away. Liyah stared after him, then took off running to catch up.

****

"Are you sure Liyah won't mind me riding her horse?" Tyrese laughed awkwardly as he tried to mount the winged horse. "Maybe we should walk instead."

"It's fine and way fun! Besides, it's just like riding a regular horse."

"This isn't exactly what I thought you meant when you said we were going on horseback."

Melanie just laughed and launched upward into the sky. Tyrese mounted awkwardly and followed Melanie's lead. She shouted out the instructions, and the pair soared through the sky. Honestly, Tyrese didn't think Liyah would be too happy that he was riding her horse, but Melanie told him to leave it up to her.

They tore through the sky at a high speed. They did this for around forty-five minutes, then they started heading back toward the palace. They were almost there when Tyrese looked down and saw a large waterfall with a deep, inviting pool beneath it. He called out to Melanie who looked down and cried, "Let's go check it out!"

The pair dropped down from the sky and lighted elegantly next to the pool. Well, Melanie did. Mystique landed awkwardly and reared back, making Tyrese fall backward into the water. She then flew off into the sky. Tyrese breached the surface and spit out a mouthful of water. "Do you think we should catch her?"

"No," Melanie laughed. "She will head back to the palace herself to go find Liyah."

"Well, now that I'm wet, I might as well swim. You care to join me?"

Melanie dismounted and strode over to a large boulder. She took off her high heels and dove down deep into the water. Tyrese watched for her to come up, but she never did. He started to worry when something grabbed him from behind and pushed him underneath the water's surface.

When he resurfaced, he was face to face with a laughing Melanie. He splashed her and laughed, "Not cool!"

****

A little while later, Liyah found herself walking up a rocky cliff. They were following a river and the farther they walked, the louder the sound of a waterfall grew. Ryvan occasionally took the lead, and Liyah hurried to catch up to him. Soon, they found themselves at the top of a waterfall overlooking a large beautiful pool and something else. Liyah's horse stood off to the side, grazing.

"What?" Liyah began. "I wonder how she got here."

"Maybe she flew," Ryvan laughed.

"You're funny," Liyah shot sarcastically. "This really is strange."

"Yeah, it's probably not that big of a deal."

"It better not be."

They moved to the edge of the cliff and looked down.

"It's beautiful," Liyah commented. She really meant it, too.

"Yeah, it is." Ryvan turned and faced her. They looked at each other for a moment, when Liyah's expression changed. A sly smile crept across her face, and a spark caught in her eyes.

"Why are you looking at me like that?" Ryvan asked. He took one cautious step back from her.

She followed. "No reason. In fact, I don't even know what you are talking about."

Just then, Liyah began to circle around him. Then, out of nowhere, she pushed him over the side of the cliff down into the beautiful, sparkling pool below with a playful laugh. Ryvan created a huge splash when he landed. Melanie and Tyrese heard it and stopped their water fight to see what had landed only a few feet away from them.

Ryvan drifted to the surface and then casually swam toward the two. They looked at him for a while. Then they burst out laughing. Ryvan joined them and said, "She's in a better mood now."

"Good. What happened?" Melanie mused.

"She pushed me off a cliff," came Ryvan's calm reply.

Melanie looked up, then, frowned, "Where is she?"

Ryvan pointed up and laughed, "Three. Two. One."

Liyah came charging over the edge of the cliff into a beautiful swan dive. She cut into the water like a knife, barely creating a splash. They all began laughing as they started a new water fight, she-warriors against the warriors.

When the water fight ended, Liyah looked up into the sky to check the position of the sun. Then, she stated, "It's nearing time for the banquet. If we want to look presentable, we had better leave and go get ready now."

Tyrese glanced to the bank where Mystique now stood. "You can take your horse if you want. It will be faster."

Liyah raised an eyebrow at him, "Thanks."

The girls pulled themselves up to the bank, strapped on their high heels, and rose into the air with a quick good-bye, leaving the boys alone to walk back to the palace.

****

A few hours later, Rihannai came and knocked on the girls' door.

"Come in," Liyah called while she put her earrings in.

Rihannai entered and beamed at the girls. "You two look great!"

The girls' armor had been shined up, and they had their hair and make-up redone. They were almost ready to go to the banquet in their honor. The girls only lacked their weaponry.

When Melanie began putting hers on, Rihannai stated, "You won't need those."

Melanie and Liyah both looked at her stupidly. Rihannai crossed over and took all of their weapons. They even took Liyah's knives.

"Why do you do this?" Liyah asked angrily.

"You will find out soon enough, Liyah Encarcerá," Rihannai replied as she began inching toward the door. "The feast is being held in the grand throne room. Please, hurry and come down."

With that, Rihannai was gone. Melanie glanced at Liyah and saw that she was absolutely fuming. Melanie thought to herself, "If she doesn't get some knives or something soon, things could get ugly."

Liyah interrupted Melanie's thinking, and asked in a voice more calm than she looked capable of using, "Shall we go downstairs?"

She ripped the door open and began walking down to the throne room. Melanie was surprised the door hadn't come off its hinges.

****

The girls walked into the throne room and were instantly greeted by applause. Galiphems, Galeãns, Galatrans, and Gryafans were all standing together in the giant room. They were all turned to face the girls.

This caught the she-warriors off guard, and they jumped at the sight of so many warriors. The room looked beautiful, decorated for the occasion. There were more torches lined up all around the room, and streamers hung from all directions in colors of silver and gold. Tables littered the entry way except for one single large area serving as a dance floor. Music played over the buzz of people. At the front of the room, the queen herself sat on her elegant throne. Standing next to her were Vera and Shace. They caught the girls' eyes, and they waved. Soon, they awkwardly began making their way toward them through the mass of people. The girls waved awkwardly, recognizing the applause. This caused the applause to dull down to a low hum. At this point, the noise wasn't so deafening, and Vera and Shace had made their way over.

Shace hadn't seen the girls until now, so, they greeted each other and as they started talking, another roar of applause started up. The four turned to see Ryvan and Tyrese walk into the throne room. They seemed as surprised as the girls had been, and they, too, waved awkwardly. When the noise quieted, Shace called them over. They greeted one another and before they started talking, another voice called out their names.

Liyah turned around and was greeted with a hug. She looked down and saw Shanillé wrapped around her waist, holding her in a bear hug. Liyah decided to hug her back now that she knew who it was. They let each other go, and Shanillé instantly hugged all the others. Ryvan and Tyrese were fairly shocked when she hugged them. Tyrese hugged her back with one arm, while Ryvan patted her on the back lightly. Liyah and Melanie laughed. Just when Shanillé released everyone, Alana, Christina, Maiyah, Miacah, and Siscilia rushed out of the crowd to greet them. Shortly following them out of the crowd came more familiar faces. Bryen and Creshvan stepped up with the rest. They all had a great reunion while music and laughter continued to fill the air.

"So, what happened to you guys?" Liyah asked.

"We were all together when Corresponding Point began to burn," Shanillé stated.

"We watched and tried to fight the monsters, but we knew it was too late, and we couldn't do anything about it," Alana continued.

"So," Bryen added, "we fled to the warrior islands because we had all been accepted as well."

Just then, Liyah noticed what color of armor everyone was wearing. Tyrese, Ryvan, Melanie, and Liyah were all obviously wearing white gold. Vera and Shace wore gold. Shanillé, Alana, and Bryen wore silver. Creshvan, Siscilia, and Christina wore steel while Maiyah and Maicah wore iron.

"What happened to you?" Maicah asked.

The four recited their stories once again. Everyone seemed surprised. They stood in their circle, talking everything over. They went on until the music died, and a voice called out over the other voices.

"Thank you all for coming tonight!" The voice belonged to Queen Galetreã. "We shall eat momentarily, but first, would our four golden warriors please come to the platform?"

Liyah, Melanie, Ryvan, and Tyrese all began walking toward the platform where the queen stood. Everyone began clapping again. When they stood next to the queen, she continued, "These four warriors have demonstrated skills and bravery beyond that of which we could even compare. For this reason, they will depart for the Kingdom of the Elves tomorrow to further their training."

Another roar rose from the multitude. The queen silenced them and continued, "Before these four made it here, they were faced with the creatures of darkness and at a time, the Dark One herself. In these moments in time, their weapons were destroyed. Since they have attained white gold armor, we have brought out something very special for them. Rihannai, Jasira, Riela, and Draze, please bring out the items."

The four trainers appeared from the entryway at the same time. Each one carried some sort of long box covered with a maroon cloak. Jasira and Rihannai carried beautiful oak crossbows on their backs like the ones Liyah and Ryvan had used in the challenge, only these were so much more magnificent.

A murmur moved through the crowd as they made their way toward the four warriors. When they reached the platform, they all took places in front of the golden warriors. Draze stood in front of Tyrese, and Riela stood in front of Melanie. Rihannai was positioned in front to Ryvan. So, Jasira stood by Liyah. Slowly, the four trainers began to take the cloaks from the boxes' surfaces. When the cloaks were cleared away, they revealed glass boxes with beautiful curving cross-blades inside.

"These are none other than the legendary Asgarnian cross-blades," the queen smiled while the warriors examined the beautiful weaponry. "Once it was said that four royal golden warriors would appear from the land of Asgarnia to claim their destined blades. The blades would yield to none other but the true four. These are those blades, and you four, are those warriors. I bestow these unto you."

The four reached for the blades, lifting them out of the boxes with care. They all tested the elegant blades, then sheathed them respectfully. Draze and Riela backed out slowly while bowing. Rihannai and Jasira knelt and unstrapped their crossbows, offering them up to Liyah and Ryvan.

The queen continued, "These are some of our finest crossbows. We wish you to use these until you can acquire those of the Elves."

Liyah and Ryvan recognized the honor of the weapons and accepted them humbly, bowing. Rihannai and Jasira each hugged Liyah and Ryvan as they stood. So quickly that most people missed it, Rihannai gently kissed the side of Ryvan's cheek, and the warrior turned a shade of red. Liyah glowered and turned red as well. They strapped the bows to their backs, and then accepted large bundles of arrows. They were all set. All Liyah and Ryvan needed were their knives, but they knew they wouldn't gain them here. It was probably best that Liyah had none on her person with the way she was eyeing Rihannai.

"We know you are capable of using these weapons to their full capability. Please wield them with strength. Now, let us feast!" the queen laughed.

Everyone applauded once more while they moved to their seats. The queen placed her hand on Liyah's shoulder and said, "You shall sit with me."

The four followed the queen and her offspring to a table near the front of the room. The queen sat at the head of the table with Vera, Liyah, and Melanie on one side and Shace, Ryvan, and Tyrese on the other.

****

After an elegant banquet was served, music began booming out again. Warriors and she-warriors began moving onto the dance floor. Waitresses began clearing the tables very quietly. The golden warriors sat around the table with three-fourths of the royal family. Soon, the other fourth came into view. A large man that resembled Shace ambled up to the table and asked the queen to dance. It was obvious that he was the king. As soon as the queen left, Tyrese and Melanie stood up to dance. Liyah laughed. It was so typical. Eventually, Vera and Shace found dance partners and left Liyah and Ryvan sitting at the table alone. Melanie could tell they weren't talking yet.

"I wonder if we are going to get in trouble for this," Melanie wondered while they were dancing to a slow song.

"I don't know for sure, but I would probably have to say, yeah," Tyrese laughed.

"I thought so."

At that moment, the song ended, and a fast one came on.

"Any minute now," Tyrese smiled.

Melanie looked over just in time to see Liyah start talking.

"Wow," Melanie began. "Liyah just smiled."

"What's so 'wow' about that?"

"She's been even more solemn than usual lately. Also, she has seemed irritable toward Ryvan since the ceremony began."

"I see," Tyrese stated.

Just then, the fast song was replaced by a slow one. The light then grew dim. Tyrese and Melanie danced again. Melanie watched Ryvan and Liyah stand.

"We are *so* good," Melanie whispered to Tyrese.

He moved to where he could see them and said, "It's about time!"

Melanie shifted her gaze. Things were good again for the time being.

****

"Have fun?" Melanie asked. The girls were upstairs in their own comforting room once again. Liyah and Melanie sat on their beds facing one another.

"I suppose. And yourself?"

"I enjoyed the party," Melanie smiled.

"Party?" Liyah smirked.

"Hey! What about you? You *cannot* talk."

Liyah flopped down on her back and sighed, "Whatever. You and Tyrese are going to get some sick payback someday. Mark my words."

"Oh, really?" Melanie raised an eyebrow to that.

"All is fair in love and war." Liyah flipped off the light.

"Yeah, especially—" *SMACK!* "Ow!" Melanie cried.

Apparently, Liyah 'accidentally' tossed her high heel across the room, and it just so happened to land on Melanie's forehead.

"It's too early," Melanie yawned.

"Who you tellin'?" Liyah muttered.

"What are you guys talking about? It's the best time of the day!" Tyrese laughed fairly sleepily himself.

Ryvan walked up to the girls. Melanie seemed to be ready to go to sleep any second. Liyah looked like she was asleep on her feet. It didn't even look like she had seen him. Ryvan shoved Liyah on the shoulder and down she went—flat on her backside. Everyone laughed at her. She glared at him and scrambled to her feet, ignoring his outstretched hand of apology.

The reason everyone was so tired was the fact that it was around four in the morning. The group consisted of Liyah, Melanie, Ryvan, Tyrese, Shace, Vera, Rihannai, Shanillé, Alana, Bryen, and Creshvan. Once again, they were all in their old leather/metal armor. They all stood outside of the palace, preparing for their journey to the Kingdom of the Elves to further develop their training. Shanillé, Alana, Shace, Vera, Bryen, and Creshvan all were accompanying the four golden warriors, for Rihannai said, "There is safety in numbers."

Now, even before the sun peeked over the horizon, the young warriors and she-warriors were prepared at last. Jasira and Riela meandered out of the palace and up to the golden warriors.

"Always expect the unexpected," Riela smiled. "Best of luck."

Rihannai stepped forward. "It has been interesting. I hope to see you all again one day. But, until then, here is what you must do. Follow the path until you reach the whirlpool where you entered. Go down into the pool. When you reach the mainland, go straight through the towns and see what remains. When you have done this, Shanillé, Alana, Vera, Shace, Bryen, and Creshvan must return to this island to report to us. You four shall continue and find the Elven Realm. You must leave the mountains and venture through the Zaira Forest. There, the Elves shall be. Good luck."

"Thank you," Liyah replied. "Thank you for all you have done. Good-bye, Rihannai." Liyah placed a hand on her shoulder as did Rihannai, and they stared into each other's eyes for a moment, letting a certain understanding pass between them. This could be their final encounter.

****

The sun hadn't even breached the tip of the sky by the time the troupe reached the water's edge. They had crossed through the whirlpool and reached the mainland. The guys watched as the girls rung out their long hair. Liyah flipped hers back and got Melanie even wetter. She shot Liyah a nasty look, and the group mounted their horses.

They were ready to head out. Everyone started out except for Liyah and Ryvan. Ryvan had waited with Liyah while she readjusted the saddle on her now wingless horse. Ryvan was fuming. Liyah bent down to wash her hands off in the water. Ryvan then muttered, "I can't believe they took our knives."

Liyah glanced up at him, sighed, and stood up. She walked over to her horse and placed her left hand on the creature. She then bent down and pulled a knife out of a strap on her upper leg just covered by her skirt.

"Here," she said calmly as she tossed the knife to Ryvan and clambered on her horse. "Keep it."

"Where did—"

"And I thought more of you than that," Liyah teased. She nudged her horse to start after the others.

Ryvan rode in alongside her. "So, you kept one of your original knives?"

"Nope."

"Then?"

"I kept two of them."

"Are you serious?" Ryvan laughed.

"Yup, sure did."

"And you didn't get caught?"

"Caught?" Liyah scoffed. "And I thought you knew me better than that! I'm disappointed in you," she laughed and kicked her horse into high gear.

Ryvan laughed and shook his head, pocketed the knife, and rode off after the she-warrior. Not one of them knew what they were headed for. If they had, they might have turned around and gone back in the other direction.

"How could they have *all* gotten away?" Navaira boomed, making her dark palace shake. She was verbally attacking her army of Vortzans. They cringed back every time she opened her mouth like a flaming sword that would strike them all down. "Couldn't you have just gotten one of them? They are merely warriors and she-warriors!"

One large Vortzan stepped forward. He was one of her new commanding officers. "I'm sorry, your highness," he gurgled, "but it was not our fault."

"Not your fault? Not *your* fault?!" Navaira cried. Again, the Vortzans cowered back. "Then, whose fault is it? Are you implying it is *my* fault?"

She began to draw her sword when the Vortzan called, "No, not at all, my liege! In all respects, I was merely saying that they have shown powers far greater than that of any mere warrior or she-warrior. There was no way we could comprehend. There was nothing we could do against them."

Suddenly, an eerie calm crept over the Dark Mistress. She sheathed her sword and sat back down on her black throne. The Vortzans relaxed. "Very well. What's done, is done. We will make up for it in the time to come. There is no way the little she-warriors will defeat me. I have gone through far too much. Move out the ranks and carry on with the plans. Prepare to send out the qairas."

The lead Vortzan bowed and left. Then Navaira called him back. "Oh, one more thing," she beamed when he reached her throne. She stood, and in one swift motion, ripped out her sword, and the freshly slain Vortzan hit the floor moments after she resheathed her blade. "Do not defy me."

****

Part IV
Rising Darkness

Gashes and wounds purge impurities,
and defeat cleanses the warriors' spirit.
—ðhumtan 8:33

Chapter 22

"Liyah, only danger waits ahead for you. Turn back now, and all will be well for the time."

The voice came from a beautiful woman with dark black hair and green eyes. She was dressed in an elegant blue dress that a queen might wear. Liyah had never seen her before in all her life.

"However, it is your choice. You can go back and be what you are, or move on and become what you were destined to be. But trouble beyond your nightmares lurks ahead of you. It lies in wait of you like an assassin poised to kill. The path of sorrow, tragedy, and pain lies ahead. I knew I must warn you. Good luck, Liyah."

Liyah woke with a start. Tyrese was propped up against a tree, sleeping while Ryvan crouched down by the river, getting water. Everyone but Melanie gathered in a circle. Melanie stood over Liyah. She offered a helping hand to her friend. Liyah took it and rose.

"Liyah, I just had a weird dream," Melanie stated. She seemed fairly shaken.

"Me, too," Liyah said. "What was yours?"

"A strange woman was telling me—"

"That we should turn back to stay safe?" Liyah finished for her.

"Yeah! How did you know?"

"I had the same dream."

"Creepy!" Melanie mused. "What should we do?"

"We should tell everyone. Wake up Tyrese, and I'll go get Ryvan."

****

"So, you're telling us that just because you had a dream, you want us to turn back?" Vera asked skeptically.

"No, I'm saying that this was an odd dream, and I think we should take it into our perspective. I've never had a dream like this," Liyah stated.

"Yeah, and we can't just invent the same person. She was vaguely familiar, but I don't remember ever actually seeing her before," Melanie countered.

"Well, what do you propose we do?" Vera exploded. "*You* always seem to have all the correct answers, Liyah. Why don't *you* tell us what *you* want *us* to do for *you* today?"

Creshvan leaned over to Bryen and whispered, "Oh, boy. Catfight."

Liyah stepped up face to face with Vera like she was ready to start something. Vera accepted the challenge and drew herself up to her full height. Just before things went too far, Tyrese pushed in between the two, separating them.

Vera dove for Liyah, but Tyrese caught her, and Shace raced up to help restrain his angry sister. Liyah made a move toward her, but Ryvan and Melanie grabbed her by the shoulders to stop anything from taking a dark turn. Liyah almost overpowered them, so, Ryvan wrapped his arms around her waist and clinched them together in a firm restraint.

Tyrese began talking in a calm, yet demanding voice, "You guys, we are on the *same* team here. We *have* to work together. It is our only hope. We are the world's hope. United we shall stand, yet divided, we shall surely fall."

Everyone stared at him.

"Yes, I know. It's me. You know I'm right though. Work with me here, people!"

They all agreed and grew quiet. Liyah looked at Ryvan. He knew exactly what the look meant. She didn't want to say anything for the fear of starting something else. So, he said it himself, "Ok, guys, what do you think?"

Everyone grew quiet.

"Let's move on, then," Ryvan stated.

They all moved to their horses and mounted. They began heading in the direction of the desolate town that was once Corresponding Point.

The travelers passed through town after town. Everywhere they went, the results were the same. Every town was burned to the ground. There were no people or animals anywhere in sight. When they had passed through Ayaye, Alana had been devastated. She had loved her town and her people. But nothing was left.

Beura had been even worse. A sick feeling hung in the air. Everyone was silent. The same sick feeling began to creep into Liyah and Melanie's thoughts after they passed through Beura. They knew what they would find in Faeciã. A disturbing silence settled over the land. Everything seemed darker. The light of hope had left the Osheyk Mountains. The landscape was dark and desolate. The beautiful region had been burned, and all the water had dried up. Navaira's dark power had evidently infected the entire land, and it looked like the darkness had prevailed over the light.

They reached Faeciã to find the same thing as in the other towns. The troupe ventured through the charred remains of the small village. Suddenly, Melanie dropped off her horse. She stared blankly ahead with a pained look on her face. She stopped and fell to her knees in a pile of burned debris that appeared to have once been a hut.

"Melanie?" Tyrese began. She didn't answer. "Mel," he said again, but Ryvan restrained him. "What's she doing?" he asked Liyah.

Liyah didn't say anything. She let loose a long sigh and breathed, "Oh, no."

Liyah got down from her horse and approached Melanie, leaving the others behind. She placed a hand on her friend's shoulder and bent down next to her. Apparently, she said something, but the others could not hear what. Then, they understood what troubled Melanie. This had been their home, the place they ate, slept, and lived out their lives.

Eventually, Liyah stood, extending her hand to the kneeling Melanie. Melanie looked up at Liyah. Sorrow clouded her face, but she caught Liyah's hand in hers, and Liyah pulled her up to her feet. Together, they walked back toward their horses.

****

After taking a good look through Dreán and Faeciã, the group decided to turn back. They made it back halfway to Beura before everyone started feeling the endless hours of constant horseback riding. Darkness had set in shortly after they left Dreán. It had crept upon them like a blanket, making it harder to breathe. Even the horses began sweating and grew weak.

"I think we should at least let our horses rest," Ryvan stated.

"I agree," Melanie said.

The travelers dropped off their horses to set up camp. Their bodies ached from the long journey, and as soon as they had eaten and doused the fire, the exhausted warriors fell into a deep sleep before their heads even hit the ground.

"Melanie, it is time we leave," Liyah stated seriously.

Melanie rubbed her eyes and rose halfway up onto her elbows. "But, the sun's not even up yet," she yawned.

"That's what you think," Liyah had a very serious edge in her voice. "See for yourself."

Liyah pulled back the tent flap to reveal a dark sky with a deep purple and blood red sun rising in the east.

"What's going on?" Melanie asked suddenly wide awake.

Liyah dropped the flap and sighed, "We are living in dark days now. Navaira is winning, and the darkness is rising."

Then Liyah walked out of the tent to prepare her horse. Melanie hurriedly got dressed and followed. The others were preparing their horses as well. Melanie reached her horse to see that it was already loaded and stood waiting. Liyah was tying supplies to her own horse now. Melanie knew Liyah had done it for her. When things bothered Liyah, this was the type of thing she did.

"Thanks!" Melanie called over to Liyah.

Liyah looked up and smiled.

****

"Welcome back to Ayaye," Alana muttered when they reached the old borders of Ayaye. "It seems like its worse than it was before."

"That's the darkness," Liyah stated.

"It's enclosing," Ryvan finished.

The troupe slowly picked their way through the wreckage. After some time, they reached the center where the party had been held. Suddenly, Shanillé asked, "Does it seem to be, umm, getting darker to anyone else?"

Everyone stopped. It *was* getting darker. A frown crept over Ryvan's face, which spread to Liyah's.

"Wha—" Melanie began. Vera clapped a hand over her mouth.

"Shh," Vera hissed. "Listen."

The others heard it, too. They drew their weapons, bracing themselves for an attack. The noise grew louder. It sounded like wings pulsating while they ripped through the air.

Suddenly, Tyrese's eyes grew large and he cried, "Liyah! Watch out!"

Liyah turned and dove off her horse just as a dark creature flew over her, barely missing its target.

"What *was* that?" Bryen cried.

Nobody answered. It was quiet. The sound of wings faded. All was calm until Melanie screamed. The black dragon-like creature had circled around and pulled Melanie right from the back of her horse. Melanie squirmed in the monster's talons.

Liyah ripped out her bow, and an arrow sliced through the air suddenly accompanied by another arrow. The arrows landed in the dragon's throat, creating an X. It screamed out in pain and quickly dropped Melanie before it plunged to the earth, landing in a heap. Melanie fell straight down through the air with a scream. Right before she hit solid ground, something stopped her downward motion. Melanie came out of her shock to see Tyrese holding her up off the ground.

Liyah was more curious about the second arrow. She looked over to Ryvan. He was placing his bow back in its original position. It had been him. Liyah looked to him with surprise. He merely mocked her expression and laughed. Then, a screech pierced the dark air, and a dozen more dragons appeared out of the darkness. They swooped down upon their unsuspecting prey in a pattern of attack.

Another scream reached the ears of the warriors. It wasn't a scream of terror, but more like a scream of frustration and rage. This time the scream belonged to Liyah. She was now in the air. While everyone with bows shot at the dragon, Melanie was jerked off the ground by another. While the two dragons flew through the air, the other encircled the grounded warriors, preventing them from aiding the air-borne she-warriors.

They tried everything they could think of to help the two girls. Liyah kicked and thrashed about wickedly. Suddenly, the glint of a knife could be seen in her hand. She reached up and cut through the dragon's leg. Black dragon's blood showered over her, but she was dropped from its talons only to be caught by another dragon. Melanie couldn't shake her captor. The arrows couldn't find their target so Melanie just kept shrinking into a little dot in the distance.

Liyah kept slashing dragons that caught her until one dragon brought its head down to meet Liyah eye to eye. Its fiery red eyes stared into her brown ones. Suddenly, the dragon clutched her hand in its massive jaws and bit down with impressive force. Liyah cried out in pain, and the knife fell from her hand. The dragon flew on. She then flipped up her legs and kicked the dragon in the face. It squealed in response. Then, it let her go immediately. Another dragon swooped in to catch her. Liyah's arm bled freely while the dragons carried the two girls off into the rising darkness.

They were gone. There was nothing else that could be done. The dragons were completely out of sight now and seemed to be heading west. The group ventured over to the fallen dragon. The beast they thought was dead was actually in its last stages of life. The crossing arrows both Liyah and Ryvan had shot protruded from its neck. It took deep long breaths as it lay on its side. It didn't have long to live.

The dragon was pitch black and had fiery red eyes. Its talons were the size of the warriors' cross-blades and looked as if they could slice through anything. The creature's wings deeply resembled black leather. Sharp black talons protruded from the tips of the wings. Its body was snakelike and covered in scales. There were sharp spikes running all the way from its forehead to the tip of its tail. Two sharp horns came directly up from its temples.

Just then, the creature breathed its last breath and departed from its body. As soon as this occurred, the dragon began to change in shape. It grew smaller, while the features grew more rounded. When the beast had totally reformed, what was left shocked the warriors. The dead monster still lay before them, but it was not of the same form that they had seen only moments before. In its place was one of the vortzan horses. Apparently they were bewitched by dark magic.

****

"You know what you must do," Ryvan stated.

"Yes, we know," Shace replied.

"Much luck to you all. We shall meet again," Tyrese said.

The others nodded, and they turned back toward the ocean. They had decided that it was for the best to have Ryvan and Tyrese track the dragons while the others returned to Galeâ to retrieve help. Ryvan and Tyrese watched their friends shrink off into the distance. Then, something caught Tyrese's attention. It was a slight spark of metal.

Tyrese ventured over to the spot to find Liyah's bloodstained knife. Blood of both Liyah and the shape shifter coated the blade and hilt. Tyrese picked it up and handed it over to Ryvan. "When we find her, she'll want this back."

Ryvan smiled.

"You ready for this?" Tyrese asked.

Ryvan sighed. "I'm always ready for a challenge."

"Well, let's go then."

"Right with you."

Just then, the boys heard a moan.

"What was that?" Tyrese wondered.

The sound came again. This time, they caught the direction from which the sound came. Ryvan steered his horse over to a pile of burned rubble. It moved as he approached, and Tyrese followed his partner. The pair dismounted and drew their blades. They each bent down and grabbed a side of a large chunk of charred debris. At the same time, the warriors ripped the debris from atop the source of the moaning and stood in a ready position. Lying under the rubble, covered in soot, and looking half gone, the Ayayian bodyguard looked up to them. The boys were so surprised that they just stared.

The bodyguard coughed and managed to wheeze, "Have no worries. They will be fine."

"What?" Tyrese asked.

"They will…be fine. I know them. I was…a palace guard for them in…Asgarnia. The princesses…can take care of themselves." He coughed and groaned again.

"We need to get you some help," Ryvan stated. He bent down to help him up, but the bodyguard wrapped a strong hand around his forearm, stopping him.

"No, it's too late. Do what you have to do. Do not worry about me. Help them. You shall find them alive. But hurry. They may not be able to fight her for too long if you delay."

Chapter 23

Liyah and Melanie raced through the air in the talons of the remaining eleven dragons. The wind whipped their hair into knots and burned their faces. They had given up fighting long ago. They had grown far too weak to do any serious damage to their captors. Melanie looked terrified, but she was trying to remain calm. Liyah looked mostly angry, and that terrified Melanie even more. There was no telling what Liyah would do in her rage. Liyah's arm continued to bleed. This made her even more upset. However, she had lost so much blood that her energy was beginning to fail her.

"Where are they taking us?" Melanie called over to her friend.

Liyah looked at her sympathetically and then looked forward again. She didn't answer her friend but pointed forward with her good arm. Melanie didn't want to look, but she knew she had to face her fate. So she slowly turned her gaze back toward their primary direction. What she saw made her sick.

Blackened mountains towered up all around them. There was no sign of life, and the mountains appeared to be volcanic. The most peculiar sight was that of the center-most mountain. It seemed to be a palace. In fact, it was the Dark One's twisted castle that had been created from a hollowed out volcano. A moat of lava encircled it. A dark black cloud of ash circled above. Directly outside, legions of Vortzans and many other dark creatures gathered below. When the shadows of the dragon creatures passed over them, they all looked up, and some even pointed. A great eruption of victory went up in the crowd of demons.

Suddenly, the dragons started diving. They were headed straight for the bridge to the palace. The closer they got, the more could be seen. The dragons dropped the two she-warriors, slamming them into the shoddy bridge over the lava moat. Liyah rolled over onto her stomach, refusing to groan in pain. When she opened her eyes, she saw a pair of feet in front of her face.

"Oh, great," she murmured.

Liyah pulled back to where Melanie sat. She pulled her friend to her feet and together, they stood, facing the new lead Vortzan and his many guards.

"Hello, girls," the Vortzan spit. "Take them."

The guards attacked the she-warriors.

****

The floor rushed up to meet the she-warriors' faces. The cold cement under a plush purple carpet bit into them, busting their lips. The Vortzans stood on either side of the girls, making sure they had no means of escape. They were in a dimly lit room on a purple carpet leading up to a gray cement platform. On the platform sat a throne with the Mistress of Darkness, Navaira, sitting comfortably upon it. She didn't have her hood on this time. She wore a white garment, and her hair was pulled back into a tight ponytail and curled loosely. Her lilac eyes pierced the she-warriors' hearts. The witch lounged horizontally in her throne.

"Welcome to my home. I hope you are enjoying the sights," the witch smiled.

"What's your damage?" Liyah asked.

Navaira smiled again. "Why, whatever do you mean, Liyah?"

"What did we ever do to you?" Melanie asked.

Navaira's smile vanished. "What have *you* ever done to *me*? Are you serious? You have to be kidding me."

Liyah and Melanie exchanged glances then said, "Uhh, yeah."

"I cannot believe that you can't possibly know. Of course, you must be lying."

"We have done nothing," Melanie spat. "So you can just come off it."

"Although, if you want a reason to fight me, then that can be arranged," Liyah threatened. Her eyes were the fiery red color again, and she took a menacing step toward Navaira but was quickly restrained by Vortzan guards.

Navaira turned a shade of red that almost matched her hair. "Guards, take Melanie's weapons. Leave Liyah's. There are other plans for her."

The guards took the blades, throwing Melanie to the ground. She stood up again, her kneecaps bloodied and raw.

"What? You want to fight me again so you can lose?" Liyah mouthed back.

"Silence!" Navaira cried. "Take the small one away!"

"Hey!" Melanie exclaimed. "I'm not small!"

A Vortzan guard stepped forward, turned Melanie, picked her up, and carried her under his arm like a football. Liyah was restrained by the other vortzan as she dove at the vortzan guard carrying Melanie out of the room. Melanie thrashed and struggled, but it was of no use, and just before she was gone, the two girls' eyes locked. Melanie was pleading for help, and Liyah's stomach turned. When Melanie was no longer within hearing distance, Navaira cackled, "Don't worry about her, Liyah. I have something far worse in store for you."

And so, Liyah was left to confront the Demon of the darkness. The thoughts of the impending future made her sick to her stomach. Liyah did not want to think about what was going to happen to her as she stared at the door Melanie had disappeared through.

The two boys raced on through the great desert. They had burst directly out of the thick foliage of Zaira Forest only a moment before. They had caught the demon horses' trails. The creatures were flying due west with the victims. As the boys raced on, thick clouds of dust began to fly up from the explosive power issuing from their horses' hooves.

The horse-dragon creatures were, however, much faster than the boys and were steadily taking a greater lead. But the boys were persistent and didn't give up. Then, hours later they saw the black mountains looming up against a deep blue sky. The sun was falling down to the horizon. Darkness rose.

****

Ryvan and Tyrese stopped their horses. The dark dragon creatures flew up all around Navaira's castle like vigilant watchdogs. They took in the sight along with the eerie feeling that accompanied it. "How are we going to get into that?" Tyrese asked.

Ryvan dropped off his horse. "On foot, and we'll break in."

"How will we get past that army?"

"I'm not saying we will."

The boys ducked behind boulders to avoid being seen by the monsters. Finally, they drew close enough to the front entrance that they noticed a mass of Vortzan guards.

"Maybe we should try to find another way in," Tyrese trailed.

"No."

"What? Are you stupid?"

"We enter here," Ryvan stated in a monotonous voice. He then stood and began walking toward the gate. Nothing offered any protection from the dragons. The Vortzans spotted him and drew their swords.

"I guess he is," Tyrese launched himself out of the underbrush and raced forward to help his friend

Ryvan walked on without being influenced by the Vortzans. They drew closer. Tyrese took out his weapons as well, and the Vortzans leered toward them. Their teeth were barred, and their mouths foamed. Something bad was about to happen. You could smell it in the air.

The boys drew closer still. The vortzans were on the brink of an attack when Ryvan suddenly raised his hands and drew his swords. However, he didn't hold them in his regular defensive position. Instead, he set them blade over blade directly in front of his body. Tyrese tensed. Just as the Vortzans leapt at them to attack, Ryvan snapped his blades apart, and golden rays of light swept in an ark in front of the boys. The Vortzans all fell to the ground in mid-stride. Ryvan sheathed his weapons, and Tyrese finally regained control of his jaw and laughed.

Ryvan smirked, "They didn't even know what hit them." He walked in through the entrance the Vortzans had been guarding so carefully.

Tyrese laughed, "*I* don't even know what hit them." Then he ran to catch up with his companion. "How did you even know that would work?"

"I didn't."

Tyrese's jaw dropped again, and he stopped walking completely. Ryvan continued on, leaving Tyrese staring openmouthed after him.

****

The palace was even more horrid on the inside than out. Torches full of enchanted purple fire were mounted along the dark musty hallways leading through the castle. The same deep purple of the fire lay on the plush carpet on the stony ground. The eerie feeling steadily increased. Ryvan and Tyrese slowly made their way down the corridor not knowing where they were heading. Amazingly, they hadn't run into anyone or any*thing*. Just then, the shadow of a being was cast upon the curve of the wall directly in front of the boys. The flickering flames made the shadow dance upon the wall, looking all the more menacing.

The heavy iron bars slammed shut directly after a pair of large Vortzans threw Melanie into the cell like a rag doll. Darkness closed around her, and the only sliver of light came through the openings between the bars. Melanie's eyes adjusted to the darkness, and things became clearer. She sat on a dank, stone floor with moss growing in the crevices and corners. Chains hung from the walls. Melanie sank back against the wall and relaxed for a moment. The Vortzans had stolen every last one of her weapons. It looked like there was no way to get out.

Melanie was worried about Liyah. The Dark Mistress had something nasty in store for them both, but Melanie knew she didn't have any time to waste worrying about it. She had to get out and help her best friend/sister. Melanie stood and walked forward to the bars that kept her in the cell. Cautiously, she put her hands around the bars and immediately felt a powerful shockwave pulse through her body. Purple light shot from the bars, and Melanie was thrown back against the stone wall once again.

"Well, that's definitely not an option," she coughed.

Suddenly, Melanie could see a dim, red light shining about the room. She carefully glanced around, looking for the source. Finally, she looked down and realized that the amulet around her neck was the light source. Melanie reached up to feel the amulet and felt a surge of warm power course through her veins, giving her more confidence and bravery to continue on. She removed her hand, and the light grew brighter. A warm sensation coursed over her arm. Melanie realized her tattoo was glowing red as well. Melanie stood up with a new determined feeling. Suddenly an idea formed in her mind. Melanie calmed herself and clasped her hands together. The red light then moved to her hands. It looked almost as if she was holding a ball of fire. Slowly, she began pulling her hands apart. She began to feel a strong resistance, but she fought it. As she drew her hands further apart, the metal bars began to twist and turn, creating a large opening that Melanie could easily fit through. Finally, Melanie made her hands fists and pulled them completely apart with a quick jerking motion. Suddenly, she snapped her link, and the light faded in an instant. Melanie stepped out of the jail cell, dusting herself off. When she looked up, she noticed two Vortzan guards staring at her with pure fear in their faces.

"What?" Melanie asked.

The Vortzans threw down their weapons and ran.

Melanie turned cocky and yelled, "Yeah, you better run."

She paused, then murmured, "Whoah. I'm starting to sound like Liyah."

****

Melanie quickly gathered up her weapons. She had found out where the Vortzans had stashed them and snuck in to steal them back. She stepped out into a dark corridor and began walking cautiously down the hall. She had no idea where it would lead to, but for some reason, she was drawn to it. Suddenly, a large rat scurried across Melanie's path, causing her to jump backward into a large suit of black armor. It clattered to the ground with an earth-shattering explosion of sound echoing through the corridors. As soon as the noise quieted, a new sound filled Melanie's ears. Immediately, she took off running, for the noise she heard came from the rattling armor of about a dozen Vortzans sprinting to find out what the trouble was.

Melanie raced down the corridor without paying much attention to where she was running. As she was flying around a curve, she turned to see how close the Vortzans were. While her head was turned the other direction, Melanie slammed into something solid. The something reached out to steady her and kept her from falling. Melanie looked up to see Ryvan staring down at her. He looked at her awkwardly. Then he grabbed her by the shoulders and moved her out of his path directly into Tyrese's. A large grin spread across Tyrese's face, and he cried, "Melanie! What happened? Are you ok?"

Melanie gasped for air and turned to look over her shoulder again. She turned back with fear in her eyes. "No time! We've got to go! Vortzans are coming!"

The boys frowned and turned to run the other way, but they were cut off by even more Vortzan guards. There was no way of escape. There was no hope. The Vortzans overtook them.

Instead of fighting the fugitives, the Vortzans bound them. Ryvan and Tyrese were escorted down the corridor by a large group of Vortzans. A single Vortzan looked at Melanie, bent down, and slung her up over his shoulder like a sack of potatoes. They walked down a series of corridors until they ended up in a large gray and purple room. On one end, a large portrait of Navaira was mounted on the wall. A deep purple carpet led up to the throne. Two heavy barred doors stood on either side of the room. The three warriors were in Navaira's throne room where she sat on her throne, filing her nails and looking amused.

"Welcome back to my throne room, Melanie Encarcerá," she smiled.

"Thanks," Melanie spat. She was still slung over the Vortzan's shoulder. "For the record, I'm not bowing. I just can't stand to face you because this hunk of rotten meat won't let me down."

The boys smirked, and the Vortzans shoved them.

"I expected you would not feel the need to bow to the like of my power as of now, but the time is drawing near when you shall cower away at the very mention of my name."

"That'll be the day I die."

"Bite your tongue, infidel!" Navaira cried. The Vortzan dropped Melanie to her feet, and she faced the witch. "You have the tongue of your foolish sister! And look where that got her!"

"What have you done with Liyah?" Ryvan cried.

"You shall know soon enough," Navaira beamed. "I think you will find your situation quite frightful."

"What have you done?" Melanie yelled.

Navaira ignored her and spoke to a Vortzan who was taking away all of the weapons.

"Leave those. They will need them. They might keep them alive long enough to see their companion."

The Vortzan threw the weapons down at the warriors' feet.

"Cut the restraints."

The Vortzans did as commanded, then shuffled out of the room. The three warriors were left alone with the Dark Mistress. She sat on her throne, staring at them smugly. The air was full of hatred and disgust. Suddenly, Navaira broke the silence by saying, "You might want those weapons. You will need them." She yelled, "Bring it out!"

Two Vortzans ran into the room and hurriedly made their way toward one of the heavy doors at the side of the room. The guards pulled the door open with a massive amount of their strength. Nothing but darkness could be seen in the tunnel. Then the ground shook with footsteps, the Vortzans ran, Navaira cackled loudly, and the three warriors gazed at their adversary, knowing this would be a tough battle.

Chapter 24

Out of the dark tunnel, a monstrous-looking creature stepped. It stood like a man and was covered in dark black armor. The creature was a good foot taller than its adversaries. It carried a blade about half the height and width of the warriors. One blow from that blade would end it then and there. The warriors could hear its rasped breathing through its dark helmet.

"This shall be very amusing," Navaira beamed.

The three warriors drew their weapons.

"Not so fast!" Navaira called. "Only one of you can fight my creation at a time. Two will sit and wait. When one of you falls, the other shall step up to the challenge."

"No way! This thing will annihilate us!" Tyrese cried.

Navaira ignored him and continued, "I will let you choose who goes first; however, I already know which one of you is most likely to step up to this challenge. I can guarantee that you will find your companion if you win this challenge."

"We won't do this!" Melanie stated. "We'll have no part in your sadistic games."

"Very well, then. Darkellâ!" Navaira cried.

Purple light issued forth from Navaira's palm directly into Melanie. Melanie cried out in pain as she was electrocuted and thrown back into the wall farthest from the group. Her eyes clouded over, and after several minutes, Melanie rose to her feet slowly. Her vision was blurred, and her head felt like it had been ripped open.

Navaira called to her, "I have only but to change one letter in that same word, and you would perish. I advise you to, as you put it, play my sadistic games."

Just then, four Vortzan guards raced into the room.

"Choose your first player."

The three warriors exchanged glances. They had to do this for Liyah. Melanie began to step forward, but Ryvan placed a hand on her shoulder and whispered, "I'll go."

Melanie started to say something, but the look in Ryvan's eyes stopped her. She instantly understood and nodded her admittance. Ryvan stepped forward and drew his cross-blades. The large creature breathed deeply and waited for Navaira to give it the command to attack. The four guards rushed Melanie and Tyrese, restraining them to the far wall with heavy chains.

"It is only fair to warn you, you do not know what trouble you face. The pain will be great. You should fight your hardest," Navaira smiled.

"I don't need your advice," Ryvan spat. Malice dripped from every word he spoke.

"Very well," Navaira smirked. She then gave the creature its command and it leapt into battle mode.

Ryvan couldn't block the blows from the massive sword, so he had to dodge every swing. At times, he had to roll out of harm's way. Every now and then, Ryvan could get a shot at the creature, but it did no good. The armor was stronger than it should have been. It must have been enforced with a dark spell. Melanie and Tyrese cheered him on from the wall where they were chained. Navaira sat coolly in her chair, shouting out catcalls every now and then. Ryvan rolled out of the way just as a blade crashed down on the ground. The blade hit stone with a nasty clang. He was running out of energy, while the creature seemed only to get stronger.

"If you keep fighting like that, then you will never be able to help that despicable creature you call a golden she-warrior," Navaira scoffed.

She hadn't bothered Ryvan much, up until this point. Now, she struck a raw nerve. Anger licked like a flame inside of him. A spark of something stirred in him.

Navaira caught the anger and continued on, "Why care for a beast that is not capable of caring? She is dark on the inside. Ice and darkness fill her heart. Sure she is worth it?"

Ryvan grew even angrier when she said this. He began fighting with even more fury than before. Tyrese and Melanie knew what was about to happen and kept from saying anything for fear of Navaira hearing. Navaira didn't notice them and said, "You know, she is a lot like me."

That got Ryvan. He ducked a horizontal swing of the massive blade, and before the creature knew what Ryvan was doing, a golden current of energy shot down Ryvan's cross-blades. He swung the weapons horizontally into the creature's torso. The creature flew back into the stony wall and caused bits of rock and dust to fall from the ceiling. The creature didn't move. The impact had been far too great. Ryvan glared up at Navaira who was smiling. Ryvan was breathing hard from the fight he had endured. He had defeated Navaira's creation without a scratch. The pain she had said he would feel did not come. He had won. Ryvan glanced at Tyrese and Melanie to see that they had an odd look on their faces. He looked back at Navaira who said in mock surprise, "Look what you have done." She was pointing at the creature, covering her mouth.

Ryvan turned in the monster's direction. It still didn't move, but its armor began to fall off. Piece by piece, the armor shuddered, then, clattered to the floor. Soon, the helmet fell off, revealing the face of the creature. Its face was pale and soft. Its eyes were closed, and its long blonde hair was damp with sweat from being smashed under the hot helmet for so long. She looked so peaceful.

Ryvan ran over and dropped to the ground beside Liyah. His weapon clattered to the floor. She did not move or make any recognition that Ryvan knelt beside her. Ryvan reached out to her, but before he could touch her, her eyes shot open. Before Ryvan could react, Liyah made a large sweeping motion with her blade, catching Ryvan on the side. He backed away in shock. His hand covered his waist.

Liyah rose. She threw away the dark sword and took out her cross-blades. Her side was pouring blood from the wound Ryvan had created. She lifted her blades and began another series of attacks. Her blood began to soak the stony floor. Ryvan didn't fight back. He continued to step back out of her range. Liyah wouldn't let up. The pain from her wound had to be killing her, but she obviously ignored it. Ryvan, however, was feeling his wound.

"Liyah?" Ryvan whispered.

Navaira laughed, "She can't hear you, Ryvan. You see, this is the pain I said you would feel. Liyah is under a spell to make her fight anyone I command her to. She will tear you to pieces, for you will not fight back. She won't stop until her job is complete. I will then awaken her and show her what she has done. The pain alone will be enough to destroy her. Weakling."

Liyah swung at Ryvan, and he ducked, causing the blade to slam into the nearby wall. The battle continued. Ryvan was in shock and continued to back away from the enraged she-warrior. Liyah continued her barrage of attacks with even more fury, cutting violently through the air and barely missed taking Ryvan's head off.

Ryvan kept backing away in shock. "Liyah," Ryvan murmured.

Liyah ignored him. She merely continued trying to kill him. Navaira yawned. "If you won't fight back, then this is a waste of my time. I have other affairs to attend to. I bid you, farewell. I will not be seeing you again."

With that, a streak of purple light filled the room, and then Navaira was gone. The only ones in the room were the four warriors, and they had one main raging problem to face. While Ryvan and Liyah fought, Melanie whispered to Tyrese, "How is she even staying on her feet? That wound is far too deep."

"I think it's part of the spell. She is much stronger than she would normally be." Then Tyrese called out to Ryvan, "Hey! Snap out of it! If you can get us free, then we can help!"

Ryvan shook off his shock for the time being. He dodged a swing from Liyah and took off running toward the pair. He hacked away at the chains, but they would not give way. While he attempted this, Melanie suddenly squealed, "Look out!"

Ryvan turned around in time to duck down from another deadly blow. The shot missed Ryvan, but it was so powerful that when it struck the wall, Tyrese and Melanie's restraints shattered. The pair shook them off, and Tyrese stated, "We can help now." They drew their blades as well.

Ryvan replied between dodging, "No, I have to do this on my own."

The two warriors glanced at him.

"You need to go after Navaira and find out what she is up to. Trust me! I can handle this. And the world has better use of two warriors alive than four dead ones."

They hesitated. Liyah swung once again, barely missing Melanie.

"Go!" Ryvan called. "I'll handle it!"

They reluctantly turned and ran out, leaving Ryvan to do what he had to.

"I hope I have the strength," Ryvan murmured.

Another sickening, metallic ring filled the air. More debris fell from the ceiling, showering over both Ryvan and Liyah. Liyah didn't even seem to realize the damage she was doing both to herself and the structure of the palace. Ryvan assumed that if she kept this up much longer, neither one of them would win the battle. There was such anger seething through Liyah. Every slice through the air between them fueled her hatred. The longer they fought, the more exhausted Ryvan grew. The more exhausted Ryvan grew, the more power Liyah gained.

Suddenly, Liyah spun a blade above her head and slashed out at Ryvan in a violent motion. The attack caught Ryvan off guard, and she cut him across his stomach again, but this time, Ryvan leapt back just enough so that it didn't do any serious damage. Nevertheless, Ryvan had the air knocked out of him, and he couldn't help doubling over to catch a gasp of oxygen. It only took half a second for Ryvan to realize his error, because in that instant, the side of Liyah's foot caught Ryvan on the left side of his face. Before Ryvan could do more than stagger away, barely holding his footing, Liyah followed her attack by delivering a crushing kick to Ryvan's stomach with such force that he was thrown back against the wall. Ryvan fell to the ground in a heap and saw Liyah standing only steps away, staring down at him in his weakness. Her arms were out, and her blades sparkled in the torch light. Ryvan could see light traces of blood on the ends—*his blood.*

Her wet hair crept down over her eyes, making her look even more unlike herself than ever. A dark look covered her face, leaving a haunted expression in her eyes. In that instant, Ryvan came to a conclusion. There was nothing he could do. He couldn't win. She was backed by too much dark power. Suddenly, Liyah straightened up to her full height and began walking toward Ryvan with a victorious stride. She never shifted her dark gaze from him. Ryvan knew what was about to happen, and there was nothing he could do about it. Finally, he resorted to the very last thing he could think of. He was desperate enough to try anything. He spoke to her.

"Liyah," he began, "I know you gotta be in there. Deep down I know it's you. Liyah, can you hear me? Listen to me! Please, Liyah."

Liyah stopped, and her expression softened. She blinked a few times, and the darkness in her eyes disappeared. She looked up at him and vaguely murmured in an exhausted voice, "Ryvan?"

Ryvan gathered his energy and stood. He kept his distance, watching. They merely stared at one another for a moment, then, thunder exploded, shaking the palace, and the lighting flickered. Instantly, darkness filled Liyah again, and a sickening voice cackled from her, "Oh, Ryvan, give it up. This has just begun."

Just as Ryvan recognized Navaira's voice, Liyah lunged at him to start another round of fighting. Navaira had complete control.

Tyrese and Melanie sprinted out of the massive throne room with a sinking feeling in their stomachs. Leaving Ryvan was hard, but they knew they had to try and stop Navaira. All they could do was put their faith in him. They knew the possibility of seeing Ryvan or Liyah again was low. They knew Ryvan would stop at nothing to defeat Liyah and keep her from Navaira, even if that meant taking him along with her. At the time being, however, they had to focus on the task at hand. The pair sprinted along the same dark corridors. Suddenly, they came to an open area in the palace where three different hallways branched off into darkness. The warriors were at a loss.

"Great. Which way are we supposed to go?" Tyrese asked.

Melanie glanced at him and then took a step toward the hallway nearest to her. A deep look of concentration crossed her face.

"What are you doing?" Tyrese asked.

Melanie held up her hand to quiet him, then stepped to the mouth of the next corridor. Her look of concentration deepened.

"Melanie? What *are* you doing?" Tyrese asked again.

She didn't acknowledge him.

"Melanie!" Tyrese was getting irritated.

Suddenly, Melanie stooped down and picked something up.

"Are you going to tell me or not—" Tyrese began, but was cut off by a small rock that Melanie threw at him to shut him up.

"Sh," she hissed.

She stepped up to the mouth of the final hallway and then, smiled smugly, "This way."

"At the risk of being hit again, how did you know which way to go?"

"If you would shut up for a minute, you would know."

The pair of warriors began walking down the dark expanse. The further they ventured, the more a faint noise became clear to them—*voices*. Soon, they were close enough to hear what was being said. Navaira was the one speaking. She spoke loudly as if she had to shout to be heard even though it was deathly silent. The warriors peered around the corner of rock and realized that they were standing in the very back of a large balcony overlooking a massive expanse. That expanse was packed with vile, putrid Vortzans hanging on Navaira's every word as though she was a goddess speaking to them. There were *thousands* of them. Their rotting stench soon began burning inside of Tyrese and Melanie's nostrils. Quickly and quietly, they moved out of sight where they could watch and listen without being noticed.

"The ranks will move out and proceed as planned. We will not let this faze us!" Navaira exploded. "We've taken the mountain pass, ridding ourselves of any potential threats. The four golden ones are destroyed by one another. Soon, both the Elves and dragons will join with man and bow to our power!"

A roar went up from the crowd, making Melanie's stomach churn. Thoughts were rolling through the warriors' minds. They understood only bits and pieces of what Navaira said.

"Our allies will be arriving within the next few hours. We will be unstoppable! The four tribes have gathered! The Gryafans, Galeãns, Galatrans, and Galiphems are all on Galeã preparing. They will be taken easily. Without the golden ones to protect them, we will triumph over all. Soon, we will conquer all of Shroeketia and finally unlock the mystery of Asgarnia!"

Another roar went up. The vortzans raised their swords high and cheered. Navaira smiled ruthlessly down upon them with the warmth of a battle won. She knew she had the power to conquer all of Shroeketia, and there was nothing that could stop her. Tyrese and Melanie understood then and there, nothing could be done to prevent this. If attacked, the Galiphems would fall to the dark powers. There was no hope left. Darkness began enclosing around them. They were too late.

Chapter 25

Ryvan blocked another attack at the last possible moment. Another second and Liyah would have skewered him through the stomach. Navaira no longer spoke through Liyah. She had proven her point and left him in silence to think about what he needed to do. There was no way he could beat her, and they both knew it. By now, Ryvan was tiring no matter how he fought it. Small cuts were appearing all over him now from barely escaping Liyah's deadly attacks every few seconds. Liyah fought more violently as the battle continued. Now, she showed no mercy whatsoever. Ryvan couldn't even get a shot in. All he could do was block all the attacks that came his way, and he began slacking out of pure exhaustion.

Ryvan suddenly got a bad feeling that something was about to happen. And that's when Liyah used all power in her and took a shot at Ryvan. He blocked it, but it had so much energy that it was transferred to him, knocking him back into the wall. Ryvan spit blood on the floor. The force of the impact knocked air out of him, and he was in too much pain to move. His body locked up. All he could do was watch as the possessed she-warrior strode up in an ominous manner.

Time began to slow as Ryvan noticed small, insignificant things. He watched as beads of her sweat began to drop to the floor, glistening in the light of the torches that cast the ghostly, flickering shadows on the wall. Ryvan's blood pooled on the floor. Liyah stopped walking only a few feet away from Ryvan. Her eyes were completely dark and clouded. Her body jerked lightly, and a deadly smile appeared on the corners of her mouth. Ryvan had seen this smile before. It was the evil smile of the Dark Mistress.

Her demonic voice filled the room. "Well done, Ryvan," she teased. "You've lasted much longer than I assumed you would."

She paused, waiting for something.

"That's fine. You do not have to speak if you feel you do not have the need to," she continued. "I'm just curious, how do you feel to know that you are about to be finished off by a she-warrior that you have risked your *life* for several times?"

Ryvan looked up at her, and a flash of memory returned to him. No complete memory came, but only fragments. Rain. Lightning. A foreign word.

The memory deserted him.

"After all these years, I have another chance, and you will *not* stand in my way this time. However, you don't remember either. I'm not surprised. It's been a long time coming. You know you don't have anywhere to turn. You don't have the strength to defeat her. If you attempt magic, you will destroy yourself. If you don't use magic, she will destroy you piece by piece."

She waited again.

"What? Still you do not speak? I know your rage is about to cause you to explode. Fine with me, but I will leave you now. I would say it's been nice knowing you, but it hasn't been."

Liyah pulsed again as Navaira departed. She began coming toward him again with her sword held high. A determined look crossed her face. Ryvan had only one option. He had to reach Liyah somehow.

"Liyah," he began. "I know you are in there."

No reply.

"Come on, Liyah. I *know* you are there!"

Nothing.

"I *know* it. Come on, Liyah. It's me! You know me! Come *on*. You *have* to remember!"

Liyah kept walking, trying to decide where to strike.

"It's me, *Ryvan*. Can't you remember? I know you *are* there, and you *can* hear me, and you *do* know me."

Liyah was prepared to strike. A hateful look was in her eyes and issued from her. Ryvan knew he only had a few seconds. It wasn't working, and more urgency crept into his voice.

"I'm the guy that followed you across the river. I'm the one you fought at the Corresponding Point Games. I'm the one that you poured a bottle of water over. I'm the one that you pushed off a cliff. I danced with you!"

She was positioned for the attack.

"Liyah! You *have* to remember! Snap out of it! You have to care because *I do! I care about you, Liyah!*"

She froze. Nothing happened. She only stood, with weapons raised, ready for the attack, but she was frozen still as a statue. A war was going on inside of her mind while she stood immobilized and not even breathing.

Darkness. Black. Cold. Trapped. *Darkness.*

Liyah wasn't in control of anything. Her body was dying, and she was barely even alive. Only her subconscious remained, the purest form of her. It was almost like being chained. She wasn't herself. She felt contained and broken. She was shattered. She knew she had lost it all, and while she physically fought Ryvan, subconsciously, she lay shaking on the floor of her mind, surrounded by chains, darkness, and fear. She watched helplessly through her eyes as Navaira controlled her every move like a puppet on a string. Ryvan was failing, and Liyah would be forced to watch from her fetal position as Navaira used her body to finish him off. All she could do was rock back and forth in a form of attempted comfort, covered in chains.

Liyah had lost all her power, bravery, authority, ability, and above all, she had lost her *fire*. Darkness filled her, smothered her; the icy chill of defeat drowned her. Through it all, she lost her will to fight. And there was no one to save her from her own mind. Liyah felt Navaira's presence vaguely, and everything clouded over, but she still heard what poison poured from the Dark Mistress through her own lips. She taunted Ryvan. All three knew it was over. Navaira had beaten them. She would have her fun forcing Liyah to destroy Ryvan. Then, she would snap Liyah back into full authority and allow her to destroy herself for what Liyah knew she had done. For now, however, Liyah could care less about anyone or anything. She *couldn't* care about their fate. Navaira departed, and things cleared a bit. Liyah saw Ryvan—his eyes held defeat, sorrow, and pain.

Then he did something that threw Liyah. He started talking directly to *her*. He was trying to get her to recognize him through and through. She tried to listen, but the spell forced her to shrug it off. It forced her to ignore his pleas and go back to wallowing in her own self-pity and defeat. Everything was cloudy. She couldn't form comprehensive thoughts. Then he tried harder. The spell tried to close her ears, but she couldn't help listening. She lifted her head to listen, but then couldn't hear. There was such urgency in his voice. What was he even talking about? He hit deeper. He reminded her of their memories. Each reminder punched her in the stomach until she could hardly breathe.

He moved in for the kill. "I care about you, Liyah!"

Liyah sparked back to life as his words made sense to her. She tried to rise to her feet. Instantly, she felt Navaira's presence. Liyah stood and felt like a ton of bricks had landed on her. She was forced back down. Navaira stood above her. "Not this time."

Liyah got angry. The haze was breaking. She was tired of being controlled. She harnessed that rage and stood again. "It starts again."

"It ends."

"No."

"You shall fall."

"No."

Navaira dove at Liyah, and they fought for control, causing Liyah's body to freeze.

Ryvan gathered his energy and stood. Liyah still didn't move or breathe. Her eyes were glazed over black. She stood with her weapons raised. Suddenly, a power began to reverberate within her. Ryvan backed away. Something was about to happen. Liyah began to shake, and a shriek of pain poured from her mouth. At the moment she cried out, an explosion of dark power pulsated forth from her body. It hit Ryvan with a force that knocked him off his feet. It extinguished the torches, and above all else, it made the palace quake, and larger chunks of debris rained down upon them.

The force took Liyah down as well. She mustered her strength and picked herself up just enough so she could balance on one knee. However, the she-warrior swayed unsteadily from side to side. She almost toppled over several times. Her head was down, and her weapons were on the opposites sides of the room. An unseen wind stirred Liyah's hair. She stared at the ground, finally steadying herself.

Ryvan whispered, "Liyah?"

Liyah's head snapped up. Her eyes were still black-clouded. There was no recognition there. Ryvan shook inside and out. His blood froze. Suddenly, Liyah closed her eyes and breathed deeply. When she exhaled, she opened her eyes again, and a single black tear streamed down her face. The tear rolled down her cheek and off her chin, plummeting to the floor where it landed with a hiss.

Liyah smiled and stood. Her legs betrayed her, and she began to fall to the floor. Ryvan rushed forward to catch her. It was obvious that Liyah was weak. Ryvan knew just from holding her up. He held her close, smoothing her hair. "Did you mean what you said?" she whispered.

Suddenly, a large chunk of debris fell again, barely missing them. The palace lurched again, and repeatedly, pieces of the structure began raining down. "When you forced out Navaira, your power emission must have damaged the palace structure to a higher extent. We'll have to talk about this later. We have to get out of here!" Ryvan exclaimed. "Don't worry; I'll help you."

****

The palace went down. Tyrese and Melanie watched from a distance, for there was nothing they could do. Their stomachs lurched, and Melanie whimpered, "Do, do you think—"

She didn't have to finish. Tyrese understood.

"I...don't know."

Melanie broke down and sobbed. Tyrese embraced her and let her cry with her face buried in his shoulder. Tyrese watched as a cloud of dust drifted around where the palace used to stand. Suddenly, Melanie whispered, "What do we do now?"

"We continue on," Tyrese replied. "We will find the Elves as planned. If they survived, they will do the same." He paused. "If they didn't, they would want us to continue on without them."

Melanie looked at him.

"It'll be ok."

****

Liyah and Ryvan sat on the opposite sides of a fire. The pair camped out in the desert. Their plan was to head toward the Realm of the Elves. They were sure that would be where Tyrese and Melanie would go.

They hadn't talked much about what had happened. It strained them to even think about it. Both were injured from their fight. And they carried physical and emotional exhaustion. A time was coming when they would speak more of it, but not now. Ryvan was lost in thought. The surroundings were dark and still. Peacefulness filled the night air. Ryvan randomly looked to Liyah. He smiled to himself. Liyah lay on the desert sand. She was engulfed by a deep heavy sleep.

"That's exactly what she needs," Ryvan whispered.

He glanced at her. The firelight glistened off her face and made her emit a surreal beauty. Slowly, Ryvan rose and extinguished the flame, so they would not be tracked. He walked over to the sleeping she-warrior and looked down at her. He dared not touch her for fear of waking her from her desperately needed sleep. He resolved to stand watch through the night. Before he turned away, he smiled and whispered, "I meant every word."

****